MER-LOVERS

ILLUSTRATED COLLECTORS EDITION

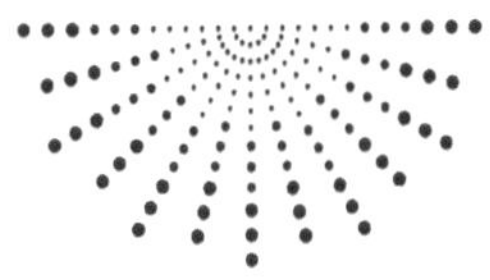

TAMSIN LEY

Illustrated by

RAVYN HUMPHREYS

Illustrated by

TAMSIN LEY

A Production of
Twin Leaf Press

the
Merman's
Kiss

BRIANNA DROPPED THE pregnancy test into the bathroom trash and joined Eric in bed. He had his laptop across his knees, studying one of his corporate financial projection reports.

"Negative," she said, fighting the crack in her voice. The sheets felt frigid against her skin.

Without looking away from the screen, he reached over and patted her shoulder. "We'll try again next month."

After a stillborn baby girl almost two years ago, they'd followed the doctor's advice to wait a year before trying again. Now another year had passed without a ray of hope. What if she'd lost her only chance to be a mother? A tear leaked from the corner of her eye, soaking into the pillow. "Maybe we should stop trying."

"If that's what you want." He scrolled the mouse.

Brianna's chest ached. "Eric?"

"Mmm?" He tapped his finger against the mouse pad.

"Eric." Her voice did crack this time. At least he looked away from the computer. His eyes reminded her of the fish in the tank at his office, round and dark and emotionless. She swallowed her tears and slid her head forward to rest her cheek on his arm. "Make love to me."

His forearm bunched as he pulled it from beneath her. Her chest lightened for a single heartbeat, then his arm settled back down around the top of her pillow. He patted between her shoulder blades and returned his gaze to the computer. "It's late. We'll try again next cycle."

⋘⋙

THE SALTY BREEZE blowing across the pier tasted of tears. Behind her, a few scattered people went about their off-season business along the boardwalk. Ahead, only empty, colorless gray sky and water.

Brianna stepped off the pier.

The heavy fishing weights cinched around her waist did their job, pulling her toward the bottom quickly enough to make her ears pop.

She'd heard drowning wasn't a bad way to go, but the salty water stung her eyes and nose. And the water was cold. Really cold. As the light above faded to a murky blue, she watched the final pockets of air billow upward from her blouse. Who knew the bottom was this far down? A school of fish blocked the meager light a moment, and then they were gone.

Her chest burned with need, but she was afraid to take a breath. Was she sure she wanted to do this? She and Eric had been married three years before she'd realized he was such a cold fish and would never change. Even the stillbirth of little

Pauline hadn't seemed to touch him. But he also wasn't the only fish in the sea. Would divorce be so bad? Just before he'd died, her father had made her swear never to divorce her husband. Her mother's abandonment had torn out a part of his soul. So she'd promised.

But he was gone now. This was her life.

Or her death.

This is stupid! She snatched at the rope belt weighing heavy against her hips. The entire thing was full of knots where she'd attached the five-pound weights. Which knot was holding it closed? Her loose blouse, useful to hide the weights on land, billowed in the current. She couldn't see the knots. With both hands, she lifted her shirt hem and pulled the garment over her head. The water's greedy clutches swept it away.

Her bottom bounced against the seafloor, sending up a cloud of silt. A surge of bubbles forced themselves from between her lips. She clamped her mouth shut. The air escaped from her nose instead. Her tortured lungs burned like they might explode.

Her left foot scraped stone, and she tried to stand. To push toward the surface. The rock slid out from under her as the tide carried her out to sea.

She was so stupid. Why had she thought she wanted to die? And like this, as fish food? Eyes burning in the salt water and straining in the light, she searched for the right knot. Her fingers were numb with cold. Tingly. More air trickled from her nose. Her lungs cried out for her to take a breath.

The light grew dimmer. With both hands, she pushed at the belt, trying to squeeze it down around her hips. The rope stretched a little. Maybe she could shimmy out of it. Except the waistband of her capri pants thwarted that idea. She flicked open the button and slid them down her legs, taking her panties with them. Kicking, she released the fabric to the tide.

Without her consent, her lungs sipped a draught of water, and she doubled over with a cough. Then her lungs were full. There was no air to cough. Her naked legs scraped along the rocky bottom.

Her vision was going dark from lack of oxygen. Or was the water getting deeper? A strange calm settled over her. Another school of fish blocked the murky light. She blinked. Maybe death wouldn't be so bad. Like falling asleep. And maybe her baby would be waiting for her on the other side.

Strong hands grabbed her arms above the elbows. A man with spiky hair and glinting eyes stared into her face. Someone had come to save her! She flung her arms about his neck. Or at least she tried. The water slowed her motion. Both her legs wrapped around his waist like she might climb him to the surface.

His eyes widened, metallic silver beneath a dark brow line. Smooth skin slid beneath her fingertips. His face drew closer, eyes boring into hers. A firm mouth found hers, and his tongue slid in.

She gasped, the lightheadedness of drowning turning into the twirling water-ballet of desire. Like a lure, the dancing tongue within her called on instincts she didn't know she possessed. Created a pulsing throb in her core, a need greater than air. She bent her head and matched the kiss, tangling her tongue with his and sending rockets of electricity straight to her core. Her entwined legs drew her hips against his. Ground against the hard line of an erection.

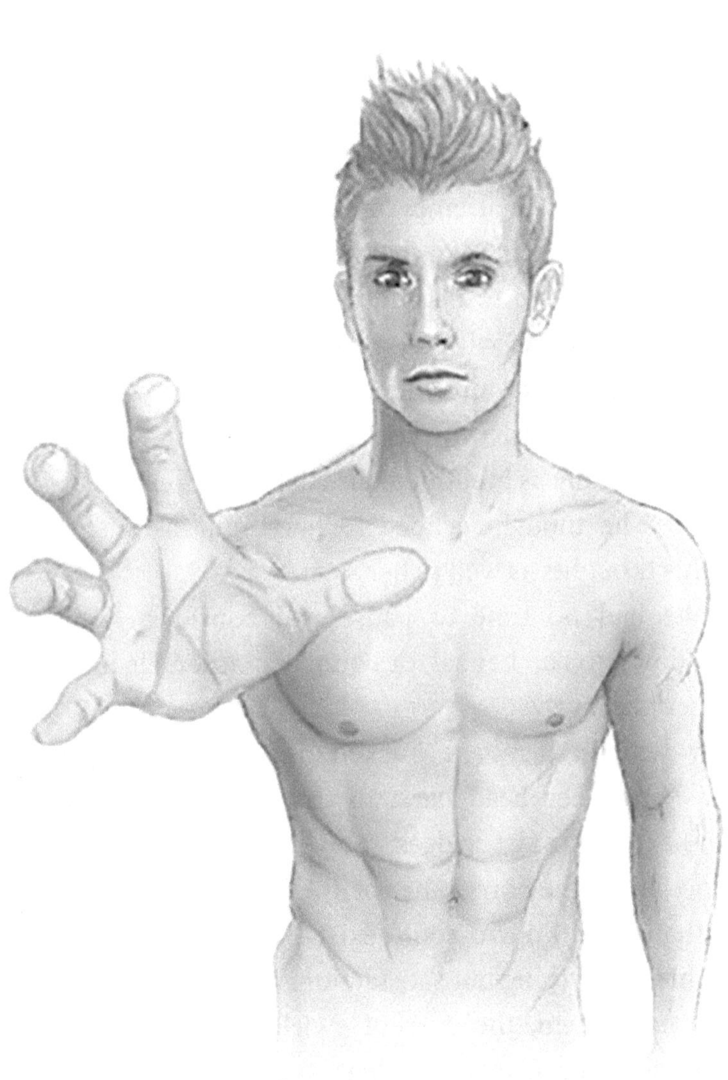

A drawn-out note—not quite a groan, not quite a song—surrounded her. Penetrated deep into her bones. He drew back, hands on her hips. The kiss continued in a teasing mockery of consummation.

For a split second, she wondered if this was the result of a final, dying fantasy. An attempt of her mind to protect her from the horror of death. But then the moment was gone, and all she knew was need. Need to be one with him. To feel him inside her. To cast away death with the very act that created life.

Legs still locked around him, she pulled him close again. Arched to meet him. Silently pleaded for more.

And as naturally as breathing, his cock filled her.

What...? The thought echoed in her brain, as if she were hearing his thoughts as well as her own.

Yet she had no time to pause and consider. His hands slithered down to cup her ass, drawing her closer. He undulated against her like a wave.

Dizzy with ecstasy, she bucked her hips in time to his rhythm. Threw her head back so the angle of their joining stroked her innermost ridges. Shivers rocketed down her thighs, pooled in the core of her belly. This was primal. A need greater than she'd known could exist. A demand blocking out all thoughts of anything but satisfaction.

All around them, the current swirled as he thrust. Pure instinct made her clamp her legs tighter about his waist. Nothing mattered now but the climax. The heady release of something larger than she'd ever experienced before. Heat flushed her, searing her from head to toe. Tumbling thoughts collided with each other inside her head. Sex. *Magic.* Heat. *Breath.* Life. *Yes!*

She screamed the last word, throwing her head back as her orgasm shook her.

The man's fingers dug deep into her buttocks as he joined her.

Eyes closed, chest heaving from exertion, she relaxed in his arms. Her heartbeat pulsed in her ears, and her limbs felt limp as jellyfish. Sex had always been bland with Eric. Clinical. She'd sought to please him but never found the ecstasy so many of her friends carried on about. Now she knew what the fuss was.

A muscular arm fastened about her waist, and a surge of water pushed her hair off her face. She opened her eyes, her breath catching in her throat. Then she stiffened. Breath? She was breathing. How was she breathing?

The weights she wore dug into her hip as he held her close against him. With amazing force, he propelled them through the water, focused on something ahead. Her gaze raked his spiked hair and naked shoulder. Down his back, his spine rose into a pronged fan. *A fin?*

She blinked, wondering if her eyes were playing tricks on her in the murky light. She was underwater. But breathing. She slid a hand across his shoulder blade and up the fin to the first bony prong. Craning her head, she looked down the length of his body. Salt water rose in her throat. Where legs should be, a silver tail ended in a billowing fin. *This guy has a tail.*

She'd just had sex with a merman. And now he was carrying her deeper into the sea.

THE FEMALE'S WARMTH coursed through his bloodstream like a drug. Zantu had seen her struggling and had meant only to check her body for salvage, a weakness of his inherited from his father. The glint of gold around her throat had made him dare to approach. Then she'd wrapped herself around him like a squid. A very hot squid. His cock had erupted from its sheath like a narwhal's horn through ice, ready to claim her heat before his brain even had time to process the act. The irrevocable act.

And now the green-eyed beauty owned him, body and soul.

Unlike the more promiscuous mer-females who would search out and copulate with anything with a penis, mermen bonded for life. A merman who bonded was doomed to a life of misery as his mate strayed again and again. He would raise the children, coddling them like a father sea horse until they, too, left him. Most mermen died of broken hearts.

Zantu gritted his teeth and tightened his grip around his

new mate. He'd felt her stiffen, likely to flee into the arms of another man now that she'd taken what she wanted. But Zantu wasn't about to let that happen. He was determined to find a way to bond her to him as tightly as he was bonded to her.

He would find a way to harness this capricious female heart.

The woman struggled in his grip, flailing uselessly as he dove over the first chasm toward the nesting grounds. Her nails dug into the flesh on his shoulder, and her naked legs slid along his tail.

Legs.

He'd never imagined bonding to a human. Mermaids seduced men all the time, but mermen, lacking a female's seductive skills, avoided contact at all costs. Many a tale warned of humans hunting mermen for sport.

As the woman struggled, the bush covering her female parts brushed his hip, hot and inviting. His cock stirred again at the invitation. He'd been told the bond would be strong when it happened, but the draw he felt was as inevitable as the tide. He adjusted his grip so she was beneath him, looking up, her eyes fixed on him. She opened her mouth as if to speak, but no sound emerged. Was she mute? Perhaps she was out of oxygen? The magic in his kiss should have enabled her to breathe as easily as a deep-sea dweller until the moon went dark. Then the magic would have to be renewed, or she would drown. At least that was what the mermaids said about the men they seduced. But perhaps a merman's kiss wasn't as strong?

After glancing forward to be sure he was on course, he dipped his head toward her and covered her mouth with his. Her lips were incredibly soft, working against his as she continued to try to speak. Her hands crept over his shoulders and slid along his dorsal, sending shivers across his skin.

Desire rose in him again, and he crushed her tighter against him, all thoughts of forward momentum banished as he plunged his tongue between her blunt teeth, twirled, and thrust. His shaft once again unsheathed itself, ready for another bonding.

Her legs fluttered, and he curled his tail up and between them, pressing his hips to hers. Her heat was waiting, slick and hot. Her legs around him tightened like a trap, and her soft breasts burned against his chest. Her mouth tasted like sunlight-dappled waves.

What am I doing? The thought wasn't his. Depths, he was truly done for. Only the strongest of bonds allowed a merman to hear his mate's thoughts. The only bond more rare was when the female could hear the male.

He opened his eyes. Maybe... Her lids were closed, her lips swollen with kisses. *Stay with me,* he thought. She threw back her head, mouth forming soundless words, but her hands kept tight hold against his shoulders. Maybe she heard him. Maybe not. All he could do was hold her as close as he could as long as he could.

Crushing her against him, he trailed kisses down her throat. One hand found her breast and cupped it, teasing the nipple into a coral nub. She shuddered, and her nails dug into his back as her depths tightened around him. His testicles throbbed for release, but he refused to let the moment be over so soon. He drew back until the tip of his member just teased her folds. In his mind, he heard her whimper, plead for more.

Not yet. I'm not done with you.

She wriggled her hips against him, pressing her clit along his waiting length. Her tongue roved her lips, inviting him to taste, but he resisted, simply gazing upon her, fighting his own desire. To exercise such control was as heady as mounting her. The drive was strong in him, but not overpowering. How was he doing this? A merman was supposed to be unable to resist his mate's lust, even for a moment, as doomed to her whims as a jellyfish to the tide. If he could hold off like this, perhaps there was hope for him.

Then she opened her eyes, and her lips mouthed, "Please." He was indeed doomed. With a shudder he sheathed himself inside her, slammed his hips against her. She matched his rhythm, throwing her head back and rocking with him until his tail curled in the ecstasy of release.

He sagged against her, holding her gently and allowing the current to carry them where it would. For thirty-five years he'd avoided his bond-fate, sidestepping many tempting offers in the process. Of late, his biology had nearly toppled him into the abyss on several occasions. A raven-haired seductress with a voice like an orca's. A green-tailed enchantress with a golden dorsal fin he later learned had been tipped with love toxin.

And yet, now that he was bonded, he was relieved. No longer would he need to live in terror of other mermaids. Of traps and subterfuge. And perhaps with a human, he would be able to maintain some control. Maybe even shrug off the curse of his bond-fate.

A war raged inside his chest as he held his mate close while some distant, protected part of his mind plotted a way to be free of her.

But for now, he'd do everything in his power to protect her.

RIANNA FLOATED BONELESS as sea kelp, luxuriating in the afterglow of the merman's lovemaking. As primal as the act had been, she still thought of it as lovemaking. She could have sworn he'd whispered his devotion in her ear as they'd coupled. Or perhaps it was just her subconscious desire to be loved and cherished.

She opened heavy lids but could see nothing beyond the shoulders of the merman in the inky depths. Featureless. Maybe this was all a dream and she was dead. Could you dream when you were dead? Whatever the case, she never wanted to wake up. Not if death was like this. With a sigh, she wrapped her arms around the merman's waist and pressed her cheek against his shoulder. He smelled briny and herbal at the same time.

I wonder what his name is.

A voice like a song came to her. *Zantu.*

She giggled, bubbles tickling her nose. *Now I'm hearing voices. What kind of a name is Zantu?*

The palm he'd been stroking against the small of her back stopped. He thrust her away to look into her face, his hands like claws around her biceps. *You can hear me?*

His silver eyes flashed fiercely, and he grinned; every one of his pearly whites was sharp as a canine. How had she not noticed that while they'd kissed? For the first time, she was afraid.

Can you hear me? The sonorous voice again floated through her mind.

A shiver started in her chest and rattled outward through her bones. Her heart raced until her vision jostled with every pounding beat. She managed to nod at him.

He released one hand from her bicep and stroked her cheek.

She recoiled at the sight of the slight webbing between his fingers. A word formed in her mind as his gyrating tail caught her attention. *Monster.*

His hand hovered millimeters from her cheek, and she swung her gaze up to meet his, suddenly horrified that he'd heard. His mouth no longer smiled. His liquid-silver eyes gleamed like twin moons. *I'm sorry,* she thought, hoping he could hear her.

He sucked in his cheeks as if willing himself not to speak and dropped the hand from her face. *Come.*

His other hand slid down her arm to take her hand, and he turned away. With a powerful thrash of his tail, he pulled her along behind him, towing her like a bit of flotsam.

ZANTU'S JOY about the discovery of the reciprocal, telepathic bond tasted like seagull spatter on his tongue. She thought him an abomination? A monster? Of course she did. Her kind hunted his. There could be no love between them.

I'm Brianna, she thought to him, but he didn't answer. He couldn't. He had to find a way to break this unholy bond before he revealed all the secrets of the mer-kingdom to an outsider. Before she could rally her people to hunt them down in their nests.

Pumping his tail muscles like he was fleeing an orca's teeth, he plunged them through the tidal current toward the deeper water where he could hold her until he'd formed a plan. The swim would normally take him less than a quarter tide, but with his mate's extra weight, he couldn't move nearly as fast. He surveyed the waters ahead, wary of sharks and other predators who might take advantage of his handicap.

A trill of laughter caught his attention, followed by three scale notes and the underlying vibrations of a fish-harp. His dorsal fin flattened against his back. Mermaids. Melody lilted through the water, a familiar cadence, a magic to incite desire. He knew that voice. Loia. She'd tempted him before, nearly caught him in her net. But now he felt only the faintest acknowledgement of her song's power. His bond was set, and she could no longer influence him.

Fin flaring tall and straight, he readjusted his course to carry him directly toward the music. He couldn't wait to see her face when she realized she'd lost him.

In the center of a shoal of tiny, silver fish, he spotted the curvaceous indigo tail fin of the songstress. The fish darted and flashed in time to her voice, falling and rising and spinning around in a magical haze. Her hair billowed outward like a blueberry sea fan, while her breasts, pale as alabaster and tipped with violet-blue nipples, bobbed like lures. Luscious indigo lips sang promises of bliss.

His throat tightened. Her magic was strong. Even with his ties to his new mate, the mermaid's song pulled at him, burned through his blood, and made his sheath swell as his cock surged in time with the dancing fish.

She spotted him. Her golden eyes narrowed and her lips curved into a predatory grin even as she continued her song. Her fingers caressed the tines of a fish-harp cradled in one arm, pulling notes from deep within each gold-tipped tine while she crooned of love and desire.

His mate's hand tightened around his fingers; for the barest moment he'd forgotten she was there. His heart thudded against his rib cage. He would be safe from the song because of his bond-mate. He pulled her up beside him and hooked an arm around her waist, delighting in the flicker of jealousy that crossed Loia's face.

"Zantu, what have you brought me?" she sang. "A pretty little feast?"

He held his woman tighter. "I've found my bond-mate. You have no more power over me, Loia."

The net of fish encircling the mermaid lost cohesion for a moment then re-formed, hovering like a million tiny blades ready to strike. "You cannot bond with a human. Their lives are over with a flick of the fin."

"Only because you abandon them to drown, Loia, lovesick and broken."

The mermaid undulated her tail and thrust forth her breasts suggestively. "Why would you even want her? She cannot play hide-and-seek with you among the kelp beds. Or race you along the canyon deeps. Or sing while you orgasm to your very bones. She can't even escape when a shark attacks. A human is no fit mate for our kind. They're barely useful as toys."

"You don't know that," he snapped. A tiny fish brushed his arm, and he shrugged it away. "Mermaids don't take mates." But her comments had him worried. How *would* he protect a human mate when predators invaded?

"We take plenty of mates, Zantu." Her grin exposed every one of her needle-sharp teeth, as if ready to devour him. "We just don't limit ourselves to one. A pity you will never experience a true lover's passion, only the clumsy limbs of a land-walker. Or... maybe she would like to play, too?" Loia spun in place, whipping her head around to find him again as she completed her turn. Her genital slit had pulsed open during her spin, exposing the pink invitation of her vulva. "Human men like to watch each other copulate. I could show her—and you—what a real female can do with a man."

Something caressed the opening of his sheath, and he looked down to find two tiny fish rubbing themselves against him. He looked back up and realized the rest of the school had engulfed them like a net.

Loia licked her lips and ran her hands up over her breasts to tweak her indigo nipples, arching her back. One hand traced lightly down her center line to massage the swollen folds of her labia. Her scent floated to him in the wake of her net of minions.

In spite of his bond to Brianna, Loia's overt sexuality was getting to him. The teasing at his groin had nearly burst his cock from its protective sheath. His head spun, and all he could think about was letting his urges free.

Brianna batted at a fish near her face and pressed herself closer to him, turning her face into his shoulder. *I want to go home.*

Those words sobered him faster than the strike of a moray eel. She wanted to leave him. He wrapped both arms around her and began to back away from Loia's seductions. If he wanted to keep his mate, staying near Loia wasn't the way to do it. "Go find some other man to ruin," he called out.

Loia's pale skin went lurid. Her lips spread thin as she bared every one of her shark-like teeth. "You cannot keep her," she shrilled.

Brianna wriggled in his grasp, her legs slapping his fin as if she wished to swim away. Her slender shoulders felt fragile in his grip, but he refused to let her go. The scent of blood reached his nose. Inside his head, he heard Brianna scream, *My legs!*

He loosed his hold and saw her lower extremities surrounded by Loia's net of fish. A trail of pink-clouded water floated in their wake. They were biting her. The blood would surely draw every predator within a league of them. Rage rose up inside him, and he opened his mouth wide to emit a deep, repelling sphere of sound.

The fish scattered.

THE SUDDEN BARITONE note Zantu emitted, so different from the tenor opera he'd been singing to the mermaid, vibrated deep into Brianna's bones. He pumped his tail, and a sudden surge of water forced her to close her eyes as they left the singing mermaid and her biting pets far behind.

Brianna's skin itched and burned where the tiny fish had nibbled her with razor-sharp teeth, but he was moving too fast for her to check her wounds. She buried her face against his warm neck and hung on for dear life. The mermaid's mesmerizing performance had grown more bizarre with every note that passed the female's lips. The final lewd sexual display left no doubt in Brianna's mind about what the creature wanted. And the pesky, biting fish made it very clear she'd prefer Brianna out of the picture.

She'd been frightened by the merman's differences only a short time earlier; now what frightened her about him also made her believe he could protect her. She rubbed her thighs together in memory of him between them. Why did he want her, when he was pursued by a creature as alluring as that mermaid? Even Brianna had felt that pull, and she'd never been attracted to another female in her life. No wonder sailors were said to willingly plunge to their deaths in pursuit of the creatures.

Looking back over her shoulder, she sought the mermaid in the gloomy water, sure the fierce female would pursue, but her eyes were too weak to pierce the midnight depths. The world had lost its color and become murky shades of black and green. A school of small fish slithered past, spear-shaped sides seeming to turn as one. Ahead, filaments rose from the seafloor to create a shifting curtain patterned by other sea creatures darting to and fro among them.

Zantu readjusted his grip around her waist, the pressure of his muscular arms making her skin quiver. She could feel his heartbeat beneath her fingers as he carried her ever deeper into the water. The way his tail bumped her legs and pubic bone as he swam reminded her of their earlier coupling. Made her yearn for more. But he showed no intention of slowing for another dalliance.

Colorful sea stars and anemones passed by in a rainbow blur in the rocks below. He continued to shoot through the forest, past a big red-and-black fish with a gaping mouth, over an eel peeking from the rocks. The forest here seemed thinner, with more light reaching the seafloor. Or maybe they were in shallower water? She looked upward at the canopy of fronds swaying in the current but couldn't judge how far away they were.

Where are you taking me?

Where you'll be safe.

His words eased the tension in her chest. Until that moment, she'd harbored a fear that with his lust satiated he might develop another hunger. One that used his razor-like teeth.

He slowed and pushed her away to look at her. *I'm not a monster.*

Guilt flushed her from head to toe. This whole "hearing each other's thoughts" thing was weirding her out. *I'm... sorry. I just don't know anything about you or your kind.*

We stay away from humans. You're dangerous.

A chuckle of bubbles left her mouth as she thought of that. Here she was, who knew how many feet below the sea, held captive by a sharp-toothed, web-fingered, sleek-tailed merman, and he claimed to be afraid of her. Yet when she met his silver-eyed gaze, she realized he was completely serious.

⋙⋘

ZANTU CLUTCHED his new mate to his side and torpedoed toward the kelp beds where he and the other mermen maintained the nesting grounds. Brianna's unfiltered thoughts reached him in irregular and unpredictable waves, one minute with disconcerting openness, the next not at all. He had no idea why. Most clear was her fear. Her curiosity. Her sensual attention to his skin against hers. The connection was driving him mad yet reassuring him at the same time. Although she thought him a monster, she wanted him as badly as he wanted her—at least for now. Would her interest wane like the females of his kind?

Ahead, the kelp swayed rhythmically between glistening shafts of filtered sunlight. Zantu dragged her into the foliage without halting, sending sonic commands to the plants and the creatures among it to clear the way. Those unfamiliar with the forest would be quickly lost and confused among the stalks, but he knew the path as well as he did his own tail. Strands of kelp caressed his skin with familiarity, loosing bubbles in his wake. Brianna clutched his neck tight enough for him to feel her racing heartbeat.

The kelp opened up to reveal his small refuge beneath the sea. Like the others of his sex, he'd created a haven fit for a queen, in spite of his determination to remain free of a bond-mate. Nesting was a biological imperative for his kind, mate or no mate.

His home had a floor of round, multicolored stones and wave-polished shells and glass. Items he'd salvaged from shipwrecks and lovingly restored filled the shallow depression: a rosewood table with three matching chairs, a vanity with a tall mirror still clear enough to see a reflection, a rocking chair inlaid with mother-of-pearl. A human bed with a fancy carved headboard rested in an alcove, mattress replaced by a soft garden of sponges. At the foot, an ancient ironbound chest held more treasures from his years of salvage. Around the clearing's edges, he'd cultivated a garden of fine, edible seaweed, decorative sea fans, and rock outcroppings covered with clusters of indigo and green mussels.

But his finest creation rested in the center of the nest, awaiting the day Zantu truly lost his freedom. Supported by living fingers of coral, a bassinet rocked evenly in the gentle ocean current.

In his mind, Brianna's thoughts swam with perceptions too jumbled for him to decipher. Or perhaps she was learning to guard her thoughts. There would eventually need to be a filter, if nothing else than to spare the other of the distraction of receiving every detailed impression.

He deposited her in the rocking chair, the fishing weights around her waist keeping her solidly planted against its seat, and pumped his tail once to back away from her. Spinning in a cautious circle, he surveyed the wall of kelp surrounding them. Loia's minions should have been blocked by the kelp forest, but he could take no chances they—and thereby she—might follow him to his refuge.

Satisfied they were alone, he faced his new mate, looking her over with what he hoped was an unbiased eye. Her hair, much shorter than any mermaid's and not nearly as colorful, floated in a dark halo about her face, and her speckled green eyes reminded him of sunlight through kelp fronds. Sun-kissed arms and legs transitioned to paler skin over her breasts and torso. Her deep-coral-peaked nipples bobbed lusciously above her smoothly muscled belly, and the tuft of hair between her legs made his cock stir as his eyes drifted over her hips and down her legs to her tiny painted toes.

A human.

He'd bonded with a human.

Had such a thing ever happened in the history of mer-kind? Certainly mermaids seduced human men, but never bonded. Not with mermen and certainly not with humans. The reclusive, emotionally susceptible mermen stayed far away from females of any kind—at least until a mermaid caught him. Just Zantu's luck to be seduced by a human. What was she doing in the ocean, anyway?

His gaze returned to the coarsely knotted belt around her hips. The weights he recognized as those used by fishermen seeking trophies. Such men were never gentle, and he'd helped many swordfish and tuna escape those deadly lines. The rope had marred her pale skin with angry-looking welts, and small blue bruises covered her hips.

Pointing a webbed finger at her waist, he sent, *Why do you wear this?*

Her face flushed crimson, and she tugged helplessly at one of the knots. *It was a mistake.*

Her efforts made her breasts bob more furiously, and he fought to keep his cock contained within its sheath. *You wish it removed?*

Yes. She looked up at him with pleading eyes, and his attempt at cool objectivity melted.

Here. He located the knife he'd made from a large green piece of sea glass. Careful to face the razor-sharp edge away from her, he sawed the rope free and dropped it to the stony floor beneath the chair.

Freed of the device, she rose toward the sun-dappled canopy above them.

Snapping out a hand, he grabbed her wrist. He would not let her leave. Not so easily. She would abandon him eventually. That was inevitable. But before she did, he wanted to show her what it was to be a mate. What it was to be utterly controlled and owned, as he now was. He could control her but only beneath the water. As long as she was down here, she needed him.

He sent, *Why did you come to me?*

Her gaze returned to him, and once again a flush infused her cheeks. *It was an accident.*

This does not look like an accident. He pointed to the belt. *This was to tie you to the ocean. To bring you to me.*

She pressed her lips together, brow furrowing in pain. *No. That...* Her hands crept over her smooth belly to lace her fingers together. *I was trying to kill myself.*

He narrowed his eyes, gauging her sincerity. *Why would you want to die?*

Her shoulders slumped, her body sinking until her feet rested against the smooth stone floor. *It's a long story. A silly one. The weights were so I couldn't change my mind.*

Tell me.

I lost a baby.

Zantu's gills fluttered. Mermaids considered children a burden. Something to be abandoned along with their mates. Never did they grieve the loss of one. But Brianna wasn't a mermaid. Her thoughts pounded his mind in a wave of unfiltered longing.

He curled his tail around the back of her knees, drawing her toward him. *I'm sorry you are grieved.*

She brought her hands up between them to press stiffly against his chest, as if creating a wall, but didn't shove with any real force.

He embraced her, running his fingertips lightly up the smooth curve of her finless spine. Her heartbeat fluttered against his chest, and he was reminded of how fragile she was, especially here beneath the waves. *Please do not try to die again.*

Her stiffness eased. This close, he could smell her unique, sunshine-dappled-waves scent. Her skin slid like silk against his, and his sheath pulsed with his cock's desire.

Closing his gills, he gathered air at the back of his throat and lowered his face toward her neck. He pursed his lips and gently blew a stream of bubbles against her collarbone. She shuddered, surprised enjoyment vibrating through their thought connection. Encouraged, he added sound, a baritone come-hither call that should penetrate her very bones.

She threw her head back, hips thrust forward, and he took the opportunity to slide his fingers over her folds, discovering her clit waiting like a little clam. Her heat intensified at his touch, urging him to increase his rhythm. He pressed against her slickness and caressed the nub until it swelled and pulsed with fervent need.

Her hands slipped from his chest to wrap around his ribs. Nipples hard as tiny shells crushed against his flesh, and she bucked against his fingers. His cock had sprung free now, bobbing in time to her rhythm, yearning for her each time her hip made contact with the tip. He gritted his teeth and continued rubbing, determined to make her come before he plunged himself into her heat.

A tiny squeak slipped past her lips in a stream of bubbles as her body shuddered in release.

I will make you mine. He thrust the thought into her mind even as he pulled her hips to him. Her legs spread wide, allowing him entry, and he pumped his tail to carry them both to the mossy bed. He wanted her beneath him, held in place so he could grind his hips against her. So he could know her full depths with every thrust.

She settled into the sponges and lifted her hips to meet his rhythm, tiny gasps sending bubbles from her mouth to tickle his cheeks. He dipped his head to claim her lips, his tongue probing one set of lips while his cock probed the other. When she came again, he clutched her rounded buttocks and pumped one final thrust into her core. His shudders matched hers, leaving him exhausted.

Wrapping his arms around her, he allowed himself to fall into sleep.

BRIANNA WOKE TO groggy darkness. She stretched and rolled over to look for the bedside clock. Her movements were awkward, slow motion, unsupported. *What the...?*

Memories flooded back to her like a bore tide. The pier, the weighted belt, the water... the merman. *Merman?* That part must've been a dream, an escape for her mind before death took her. This must be death. She stared into the deep black, the weight of the entire ocean pressing against her. Nothingness. She hadn't thought it would feel so... alone.

A muscular arm snaked around her, and a voice sounded directly in her head. *Go back to sleep, my angelfish.*

She screamed—or squeaked, the sound muffled by water—and struggled free of the embrace. *Oh God, oh God, oh God.*

A short burst of sound, and the world ignited in lavender light. Zantu's webbed hands reached to still her. Blue-violet light reflected from his silver eyes and gilded his skin, accentuating the perfect muscles of his torso. *What's wrong?*

Her initial bout of terror was replaced by awe. The strange illumination came from everywhere and nowhere all at once, creating an eerie sort of moonlight without a source. And then there was the godlike form of the merman leaning over her, face creased with concern.

A soothing song pulsed from his throat, calming her nerves. Looking past him, she realized the water surrounding them was studded with what looked like tiny purple diamonds. *It's so beautiful.* She reached out to try to catch one of the motes, but it slipped through her fingers as if it were air. *What are they?*

Zantu wrapped his arms around her, nuzzling her neck and sending a stream of bubbles through her hair. *Humans call them plankton.*

Can you turn them on and off?

His chest vibrated with sound, and the water went black.

Oh, no, leave them on! She clawed forward, searching for him. Terror of the darkness, the unknown threatened to crush her.

You asked me to turn them off.

She located one of his biceps, wrapped both hands around it to pull him closer. *No, I wanted to know if you could.*

Again, he sang the motes awake, and Brianna looked up into a face full of amused tenderness that made her heart skip a beat.

He leaned in to press his forehead to hers. The odd-colored light made his eyes hard to read, but his voice in her head was full of all the sincerity she needed. *I will keep you safe. Always.*

She reached up to caress his cheek, enjoying the smooth skin along his angular jaw. God help her, she believed him.

At that moment, her stomach growled.

And I'll keep you fed. His chuckle matched the curve of his lips.

A craving for nachos filled her. Or maybe fried chicken. She licked her lips. What did mermen eat? Raw fish? She'd never been a fan of sushi. Even rare steak made her queasy.

Don't worry, little angelfish. We're mostly vegetarians. Sit. He pulled a chair away from the rosewood table and gestured.

So far, she'd only moved through the water with his aid. Now, left to her own mobility, she floundered over and took a seat. Luckily, he wasn't watching.

He'd taken a knife to the edge of the clearing and was cutting seaweed and other unidentified items, placing them into a huge half-shell bowl. She watched him work, the muscles of his back and arms bulging and rippling with his movements. His powerful tail flexed with muscle as well, each move through the water accomplished with mere flickers of effort. This had been her first chance to really look at him without him looking back. She wanted to reach out and touch the delicate-looking fin at the end of his tail. Examine what she imagined were tiny scales covering his body. Find out exactly where he hid his cock when they weren't making love.

I can show you if you like.

Her skin heated with embarrassment even as her pussy tightened. She'd forgotten he could basically hear her every thought.

He looked over his shoulder at her and winked. *Don't be embarrassed, little angelfish. I like to know what you're thinking.* In a flash of movement, he somersaulted through the water to face her and set the half-shell down on the table. *What do men look like in your world?*

Not like you. The tremor in her thoughts embarrassed her even more, but she refused to look away from him.

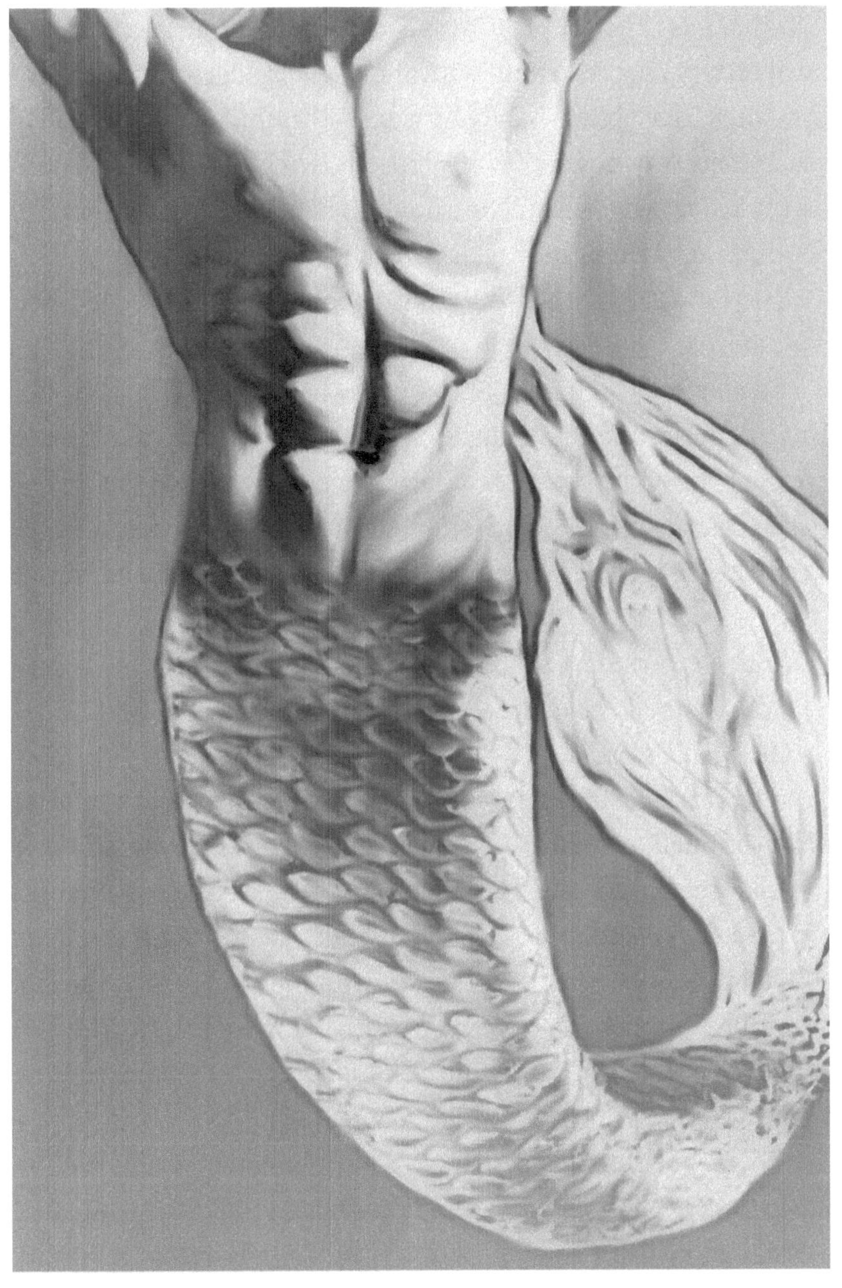

What's so different? He moved closer, hovering mere inches away, six-pack abs flexing with the tiny circular movements of his tail. His webbed hands spread across his ribs and slowly made their way down over his hips, drawing her gaze like a lure to the place where his cock should be—a bulge, there beneath the skin, covered as if by well-fitted clothing.

His thought reached out and caressed her. Compelled her. *Touch me.*

Swallowing, she reached out a hand and brushed her fingertips across the bulge. A note like a sigh of pleasure coursed through the water. Emboldened, she placed her entire palm over the lump, surprised by his heat. By the softness of his skin. She'd expected scales, but he was as smooth here as he was on his torso.

Scales are for fish. Desire colored his thought.

What are you, then?

Am I not a man?

She caressed the throbbing bulge, the crevice between her thighs immediately hot and slick. Fish or man, she wanted him.

Like magic, the skin beneath her fingers bloomed open to reveal a dark, throbbing cock. Her fingers squeezed the velvety hot thickness of him, coaxing a glistening pearl from the tip. Without thinking, she leaned forward and took him into her mouth. He tasted of salt and musk and every bit as male as any man she'd known.

He groaned, hands settling on her shoulders. *What are you doing to me?* His thought was thick with lust.

Delighted with the ability to "speak" while pleasuring him, she circled her tongue around the head of his dick. *Making you mine.*

His hands on her shoulders tightened. *Do not mock me.*

The urgency of his emotions touched her through their link like never before. Exposed and raw. His desire shone bright and full but was shadowed with a mix of anger and resignation she didn't understand. She wrapped her hands around his hips and pulled him closer to her, tilting her chin to take him more deeply into her mouth.

He groaned, his fingers digging into her shoulders as she sucked deeply. Against the back of her throat, she felt his release. After a shuddering moment, he disengaged and pulled her from the chair to squeeze her against his chest. *I will not let you leave me.*

The statement threw her off guard. Surprised her. She hadn't thought of escaping from Zantu, not since that awful episode with the mermaid. Despite the fact she was in the depths of the ocean. His promise to protect her made her feel safe. Nurtured.

He crushed his lips against hers. Her hands flattened against his ribs, her breasts tight against him, as he devoured her with deep, rolling thrusts of his tongue. If she'd been standing, she would've been weak at the knees. As it was, the water allowed them to twist and dance with each other without needing support.

His cock thrummed in a hard line against her belly, and she once again found his tail parting her legs. She slipped a hand between them, grabbed hold of him, and guided him inside her, yearning for the pressure of him, the fullness. The rippling muscles of his abs and the water slicking her skin ignited every nerve cell in her body with need.

Sliding a hand down her back to cup her ass, he pulled her firmly onto his rock-hard length and pressed himself into her core. He held there, deep and pulsing inside her while he ground against her clit. His tongue teased over her teeth and gums.

She wrapped her legs tightly around him, the edge of her climax rising above her like a wave about to engulf them both.

His teasing rhythm kept the wave hovering just out of reach. *You're mine.*

Please, please, she begged, unable to form a coherent thought.

Tell me you are. The hand on her ass squeezed, pressing him deeper into her folds with excruciating pleasure.

She threw back her head and bucked her hips against him, searching for release. *I'm yours. Please!*

Satisfaction dominated his thoughts, and he drew back only to pound immediately into her, again and again, until the wave broke and sent her spiraling into dizzying relief.

✦⋖ ✦⋖ ✦⋖

BRIANNA'S HEAD thrummed with what reminded her of morning birdsong: trills from her left, bass-throated hoots from high to the right, and an eerie rising and falling tenor undertone she realized was coming from Zantu.

He sat on the shell-strewn floor at the edge of the clearing, tail curled to one side, as he appeared to be tending the fine fronds of bright-green eelgrass growing there. Sunlight cut sharp angles in the kelp swaying above their heads, filtering gold light down into the clearing.

Still not believing everything that had happened yesterday, she sent a tentative thought. *What is that noise?*

The ocean's salute to the sun, my angelfish. Come, breakfast awaits you.

She sat up, realizing he'd moved her to the bed some time

during the night. Tiny bubbles rose from the sponges and caressed her sides. She stretched and looked around.

Her gaze fell on the table, where two bone china plates had been set along with what looked like two solid-gold forks. A half-shell bowl waited in the center, brimming with seaweed and whatever else Zantu had deemed edible, much of it floating free of the bowl but enough remaining within to be considered a meal. Her stomach quivered, still nervous about what he might consider tasty. But by now she was hungry enough to eat almost anything.

She pushed herself from the bed, aiming for the table, and discovered if she relaxed, she could walk, albeit in slow motion. The stones and shells beneath her toes were surprisingly rough, but solid enough to give her purchase, and she made it to the chair without floundering too much. She sat and admired the place settings.

Are those real gold? She reached for a fork.

They were my father's. Zantu joined her, sliding himself into the chair next to her. *He found them in a sunken ship many years ago.*

You had a father? The thought was out before she could think about how stupid she sounded. She covered her mouth, even though the words hadn't come from her lips. What a rude question. She'd never thought of mermen having families. Come to think of it, she'd never thought about mermen at all until yesterday.

Of course we have families. Well, fathers and siblings, at least.

Curiosity nibbled at her thoughts, and she fought to control it, but it was like only a sieve existed between their minds. *What about your mother?*

He used a smaller shell to scoop what looked like seaweed

salad onto her plate, his thoughts obviously guarded. *Mermaids do not care for children.*

She frowned, unsure what to make of that bit of information. *So they have a baby and abandon it?*

He shrugged. *Fathers take care of the young.*

Are there a lot of other mermen? She looked around at the wall of kelp, as if the words might make one appear.

Zantu's hands paused briefly, then he pushed her plate in front of her, his silver eyes intensely regarding her. *Do not concern yourself with other merfolk.*

Brianna tilted her head, a small smile tugging the corner of her mouth. Was that jealousy she detected? *Afraid I'll run off with another merman? Or maybe a mermaid—*

Do not tease about such things.

The seriousness of his thought sobered her. Reminded her of her own vows of marriage, strengthened by her oath to her brokenhearted father to never follow in her mother's footsteps. She clenched her hands in her lap and stared at the seaweed salad. *I can't stay with you. I'm married.*

In your world, that means very little.

Her ire rose. *What do you know about our world? I take my vows very seriously.*

Even as she sent the thought, the hypocrisy of her words stopped her. The truth was, she'd abandoned her loyalty to Eric the moment she'd decided to jump. She'd chosen a coward's way out. And Eric was now as alone as her father had been. She might as well have divorced him.

Zantu placed a webbed hand over hers. *For a merman, a mate is for life.*

She looked at him out of the corner of her eye. *I thought you said mermaids didn't stick around.*

His jaw muscles twitched. *Even so, a merman will only ever take one mate.*

The way he thought *mate* held so much more meaning than could be put into words. Adoration. Certainty. Grief. And in spite of the contradictions, she knew exactly what it meant. The hopefulness of a word that could never truly be fulfilled. The inevitable loneliness of a life with the wrong person. Trapped in a marriage to a cold fish like Eric…

Her gaze shifted past Zantu's shoulder to the cradle resting in the middle of his nest. A baby cradle in a merman's lair. Had his mate left him with a child? Why else would he need a cradle? A twinge of jealousy invaded her as she pictured him with a gorgeous mermaid like the one they'd encountered yesterday. Then her gut squirmed. Why was she here? To raise a child in lieu of its missing mother?

A soothing series of notes permeated the water, stopping her thoughts. *Brianna, you are my mate.*

She met Zantu's gaze, blinking in confusion. *Me? What?*

You claimed me when you seduced me.

Seduced you? You're *the one who kissed* me.

The barbs of his dorsal fin darkened from blued silver to inky midnight. *I kissed you only to give you enough life to reach the surface. You're the one who… who… wrapped your legs around me and made me yours.*

Indignation drove her to her feet and sent her floating slowly upward. *Are you calling me a whore?*

He grabbed her wrist and pulled her back to the bottom beside him. His metallic-silver eyes bored into her with disconcerting intensity. *I don't know what a whore is, but from your tone, I believe it's a bad thing. So no, I will not call you a whore. But I don't want you to mistake my objective in saving you.*

Your objective? She tried to jab a finger toward him, her ire doubled by how slowly she was forced to move her hand. *You've made me a slave!*

We don't keep slaves. His grip on her wrist tightened, becoming almost painful. A series of deep clicks resonated through the water while his chest flexed widely like the hood of a cobra. *If anyone's a slave, it's me. I've avoided mermaid songs for thirty-five years, only to be captured by... by a human!*

She yanked her hand free of his grip. *If you feel that way about humans, why didn't you just let me die?* Even as she said it, she regretted it.

He blew a violent string of bubbles and rose to hover above the table. *Maybe I should have. But now I am bound to protect you. I could no more let you die than I could kill our child.* With a flick from his tail, he was next to the coral-supported cradle. *A merman's driven to nest, mate or no mate. To prepare. To care for a baby in spite of overwhelming heartbreak. When you have our child, I'll be ready to care for it, whether you're here or not.*

His words hit her like a rock skipped over the water, only sinking in after the momentum had played out. He'd said "our child." Could a human and a merman...?

I don't know. He responded to her half-formed question. *Mermaids carry half-human children. Abandon them with one mate or another. I imagine our union will produce the same.*

He spoke as if a child were a foregone conclusion. Could it be? Her fingers strayed to her abdomen. She and Eric had tried so hard... Her hands hooked into claws. She knew that wasn't true. Over the last twenty-four hours, she and Zantu had coupled more times than she and Eric had in the last two months.

The real question was not if it was possible, but did she *want* it to be possible?

Her gaze returned to the man before her. His silver tail brushed the pebbled floor while his torso glinted in the filtered morning sunlight. He was her mate. A mate for life. A mate who wanted children, had sworn to protect her, and had created a love nest for her before he even knew who she was. Leaving him would be the biggest mistake of her life. She walked toward him, attempting to be graceful in spite of the water's resistance. *Do you want one or two?*

A jolt of elation reached her through their bond—a bond she now recognized as special. The kind mates should have. He drifted to meet her, his silver eyes alight with fire. *As many as you will give me.*

She threw her arms around him and kissed him.

ANTU CRADLED HIS mate in his arms after making love again, free-floating in the center of the clearing. She rolled over to snuggle her back against him, and he flexed his tail to maintain contact around her bottom and legs. *You've curled up like a little shrimp,* he teased.

Through the mental connection, she huffed indignantly. *I'm not sure I'll ever get used to floating around all day. Can we go lie on the bed?*

He pushed her hair aside to dot tiny kisses behind her ear. *Mmmm, I just realized you have something to offer no mermaid does.* He slid one hand along her spine and cupped her bottom, fingers following the crease to discover her still-slick opening. *We can do it from behind.*

Brianna stiffened, her skin trembling with tiny vibrations. Fear, not excitement. He halted his caress. *Does that position offend you?*

Are you sure I shouldn't concern myself with other merpeople?

The worry he'd made a faux pas suggesting a new position was flushed away in a brine of adrenaline. Already she was thinking of other men. Yet her thoughts weren't full of lust… *Why do you ask?*

I think there's someone watching us.

Releasing his embrace, he whipped around in front of her, eyes scouring the kelp wall she'd been facing. Had Loia tracked them down after all? When his vision revealed nothing, he loosed a sonic query, reading the bounce-back for any irregularities. He knew this kelp forest like he knew his own fins.

A flash of turquoise silver caught the edge of his song. Familiar colors. Familiar shape. The tension in his shoulders and dorsal fin relaxed. He sang a playful coo, an invitation. "Ebby, come out."

From the floor between two crustacean-covered rocks, a tiny face appeared. "Hi, Uncle Zantu."

"What are you doing? Where's your father?" The sonic query should have revealed the larger shape of the merman or at least elicited an answering song. Perhaps his brother had spotted Brianna and fled.

The merchild remained partially hidden in the rocks, large eyes even more gigantic as they rested on Brianna. "What's that?"

Of course the child would be frightened, and Brianna's thoughts weren't exactly calm at this moment, either. He pulled his mate from behind him by the hand, singing and thinking at the same time, "Ebby, this is Brianna, my mate. Brianna, meet my nibling, Ebby."

Ebby slithered out from between the rocks, mottled

turquoise skin shifting to blend with the darker greens and purples of the mussels behind.

Oh my God. A baby. A real live mer... what are merchildren called?

That. Merchildren. Zantu smiled.

Snagging the bit of silk from the cradle and wrapping it about her hips, Brianna approached the child clumsily and settled to her knees against the stone-and-shell floor. *Is it a boy or a girl?*

Merchildren are sexless until puberty, Zantu sent, only half-listening to her. Ebby was far too young to be wandering the kelp alone. Where was Rubac? Had something attacked his brother's nest?

"Now you'll be broken like Dad?" A thumb crept into the child's mouth.

Zantu ignored the unintended barb. "Where's your dad?"

"With the new baby. I'm hungry."

What's it saying? Brianna's undercurrent of thoughts thrummed with eagerness to touch the child, but she held back. Which was good. Merchildren were wary of females. He didn't need Ebby fleeing into the kelp. He made the effort to think as well as sing his interactions with the child.

"New baby? So Didra's there?" Mermaids often arrived at a mate's nest pregnant, seeking a safe place to give birth before wandering off again in search of more lustful prey. And mermen, in spite of themselves, lived for those gestational interludes.

"No. She left." Ebby's song shifted to a higher key of worry. "Now Dad won't get up, and I'm hungry."

Dread filled Zantu's chest. Mermaids might not be the best

mothers, but they stuck around to nurse their newborns for a few weeks, at least until their mates had lined up a local sea lion or otter mother to provide milk. If Didra had split early, Rubac would not only be fighting depression, but struggling to feed a new child. Entire merfamilies had met their end for this very reason.

"Brianna, Ebby's hungry," he both said and sent the thought. "Would you mind getting some food?"

While Ebby followed Brianna to the table, Zantu patrolled the edge of the clearing, sending a long-distance note to his brother to ask if he was okay. No answer echoed in return, so he called upon the nearest señorita fish to carry a message that Ebby was all right.

Ebby's high-pitched protest drew his attention to the table. "I said don't touch me!" The spines on the child's dorsal fin splayed like sharpened claws, and the mottled turquoise tail had darkened to gray.

Brianna held one hand out, thoughts full of curiosity, acting as if she hadn't heard. *Your tails can change color?*

The child's angry. Zantu propelled himself over and put a hand over Brianna's. He should have warned her to keep her distance. "Ebby, calm down. She didn't mean anything."

I didn't mean to cause trouble. Brianna clasped her hands in her lap.

"Is she deaf?" Ebby backed toward the kelp.

"No," Zantu made a point of both speaking and thinking the words. "She's a human and hasn't yet learned our language. Why don't you help me teach her? She won't touch you again, I promise."

Ebby paused.

"Let's start with your name." He looked at Brianna and pointed to the merchild, saying, "Ebby."

Brianna made a face and recoiled slightly. *You want me to sing?*

Like this. Taking her hand, he pressed it to his breastbone. The note vibrated from him once again.

Wrinkling her nose, Brianna opened her mouth and emitted a pathetic trickle of noise.

Ebby giggled.

I can't sing. Brianna crossed her arms and slumped in the chair.

Pull from here. His hand brushed Brianna's nipple as he sought a spot below her breastbone, and he had to forcefully redirect his thoughts to the task at hand. Her enjoyment of his touch filtering through their mental connection didn't help.

With an inner sigh, she sat up. This time her sound was a bit stronger but still pitiful and far off-key.

He joined Ebby in laughter while Brianna glowered. *You just asked a starfish to rub your belly.*

I told you, I can't sing.

You just need practice. Try to make it lower, he thought, again repeating Ebby's name.

Squaring her shoulders, she let out a long grunt that rose and fell.

"Oh!" Ebby dashed to the nearby rocks and disappeared.

Zantu swallowed back dismay. "You just tried to summon a school of barracuda."

Fear laced through the thought connection, and she clung to his arm, looking around. *I did?*

"There are none nearby, thankfully." How could this be so difficult? Ebby's name was an easy note. A baby name. He throttled his thoughts, hoping none of his frustration leaked through. "Ebby, come out. There's no danger."

"I want to go home."

"I know. I'll take you soon."

"I can go myself."

"I don't want you out there alone."

What's the child saying?

Ebby's small quick form was already darting away, keeping low to the rocks.

"Ebby!"

The child's trickle of sonic guidance clicks faded in the distance. The child should not be roaming the forest alone. And then there was Rubac's condition to consider. And a new baby. Zantu needed to be sure everyone was all right.

He turned to Brianna and caressed her cheek with his fingertips and leaned in to brush his lips against hers. *I need you to stay here. I must check on my brother.*

Can't I come? I'd love to meet him.

Mermen do not bring their mates to another's nest. It's forbidden.

Why?

I don't have time to explain. You must trust me.

Before she could argue more, he slithered between the kelp toward his brother's nest.

⬥⬥⬥

BRIANNA HOVERED in the nest's gentle current, unsure what to do next. She hadn't been able to follow Zantu's conversation with the child, but she could only assume the merchild was in danger. Their singing exchange had sometimes contained notes barely within range of Brianna's hearing, and she wondered if there were other notes she hadn't heard at all. She'd tried to send her thoughts to the child the way she did with Zantu, but there'd been no response. Then she'd wondered if maybe they had to touch each other first. Bad idea, apparently. And now her tone-deaf singing had driven the child off for good. She prayed Zantu found Ebby before anything bad happened.

To kill time, she explored the clearing, admiring the way he'd integrated human items with ocean-based needs. The sea sponges for a mattress, the mother-of-pearl inlays on wood. When she bored of that, she tried to nap, but without Zantu to be her anchor, she felt exposed. Alone.

She was on the bottom of the ocean. Naked except for the scrap of silk she'd pulled from the cradle. At least she didn't need air. For how long? She wished she'd asked him.

From beyond the thick kelp wall, a constant humming and chirping reached her, as if she were in a forest full of birds and insects. She supposed the fish and crustaceans were the birds and insects of the ocean.

Curious, she put a hand through the fronds and pushed them aside, as if peering through curtains. A bright-orange fish met her gaze, seemingly as curious about her as she was of it. It wriggled there, looking at her expectantly. *I don't have any food for you, little guy.*

A mottled brown-and-white fish with a spiky dorsal darted up and nipped at the orange one.

Hey! Be nice!

The mottled fish darted side to side then hovered in front of her face, bulbous eyes moving independently of each other to look everywhere but at her.

The small orange fish returned, this time with a friend, and once again the brown fish shot out to attack it. The orange fish let out a pitiful cry, and Brianna found herself pushing through the kelp to come to its rescue. *Stop it!*

All the fish scattered.

Clear of the nest's confinement, she took the opportunity to survey the kelp forest. A rock wall covered with vibrant purple-and-pink mossy growth drew her attention. Unable to resist, she floundered forward to take a closer look. The wall teemed with fish and other creatures. A purple-speckled octopus bubbled out of a crack in the rock to slither down the wall and away as if indignant about her visit. A golden-shelled snail plodded a trail over an outcropping while small red shrimp darted across the surface around him. *You know how clumsy I feel in the water, I bet,* she thought at the snail.

Something stung her foot, and she jerked her knees up, realizing she'd stepped on an anemone. The sting burned like crazy. She grabbed her foot to look at the red welt striping her ankle. Twisting to keep from touching another anemone, she flapped her arms and legs and managed to gain some altitude. Without Zantu here, it seemed her body naturally wanted to be on solid ground rather than float. She'd have to pay better attention.

A small shark zigzagged by, startling her. She gulped, wondering if there were any larger ones lurking about. Putting her back to the wall, she decided she should return to the nest. Plus, her foot hurt like crazy.

She spun to retrace her steps and realized she wasn't entirely sure how. Layer upon layer of kelp all looked alike. How far down the wall had she travelled? *Stupid Brianna. He told you to stay put.*

The mottled fish with the dorsal fin nudged her hand. She pulled away, regarding it. After the anemone, she was extra cautious. But it merely hovered there, eyes rolling every which way as if it were a sentinel tasked to guard her.

Maybe she could find the crack with the octopus again and go from there? She fluttered her legs in that direction, limbs growing tired from the effort of staying off the bottom. What she wouldn't give for a life vest right now.

She glanced at the canopy above. If she surfaced, would she be able to breathe air again? And if she did, would she lose her ability to breathe water? She could barely remember why she'd wanted to drown herself—was it only yesterday? Now she had a sea god for a lover. A mate. She could imagine eternity, safe in his arms. And why not? Eric already thought her dead. Going back would solve nothing. She'd been given a new chance at life. At love. And, perhaps, at motherhood.

She kicked her legs again, searching for a familiar landmark along the wall. What if he never came back?

She banished the thought. He had to come back. They were mates. Of one mind. The missing mental connection felt like a hole inside her. Out of curiosity, she mind-called, *Zantu?*

Only silence.

Overhead, the curious orange fish appeared again, as if inviting her upward. Was it singing to her? Maybe she should swim up to the top of the wall and get a better vantage point.

She kicked her legs, propelling herself upwards with none of the grace Zantu could call upon. The mottled fish followed her, keeping close to her left ear, its song a funny little cicada buzz.

At the upper edge of the rock, the current grew stronger. She kicked harder, trying to keep close to the wall. The kelp forest up top was impossible to see through, but she thought she saw something move. Something large. Sharks returned to mind, and her heart accelerated to dizzying speed. She stopped kicking and allowed herself to sink again. She should just return to the seafloor and walk along it like before, sea anemones or not. Up here she felt out of control.

A broken leaf spun through the current and caught her across the cheek to flap over one eye. She clawed it away. When she could see again, the mottled fish was no longer in sight. Kelp fronds bumped her legs, grabbing her as she struggled against the current. The more she kicked, the more tangled she became.

Panic seized her. She thrashed against the restraining strands. While the kelp held her legs, the current continued to push against her torso, and she found herself lying on her back, staring at a wave-tossed slice of blue sky. Leaves covered her eyes, bound her right arm to her side, locked her legs in place.

What sounded like a laugh reached her, but she could no longer see. Without thinking, she screamed, the sound rising from deep in her gut. She knew it was louder in her head than in the water, but what if she'd just called another school of barracuda? Or a shark?

She clamped her lips together and sent, *Help!* with all the force she could muster. *Zantu, help!* How was he going to find her, so far from where he'd left her?

Water stung her eyes and nose. The kelp felt like it was crushing the breath out of her. She struggled against her bonds, wondering if she'd die down here after all.

ANTU FOUND RUBAC lying on a mound of sea sponges, a newborn curled on his chest. The nest was a more traditional merman's nest, with none of the human detritus Zantu loved to collect, other than the toys he brought for Ebby. The merchild was already there, glowering from behind a dollhouse.

"Brother?" Zantu approached the prone merman through a seaweed garden eaten down to stubble.

Rubac opened his lime-green eyes. "You've come."

"Ebby showed up at my nest complaining about a new baby."

"Didra said she'd be back." His voice held a minor key that boded ill for any merman. "But I know she won't be."

Zantu wanted to find the golden-tailed mermaid and strangle her with her own yellow hair. "Need help getting milk?"

Rubac waved a limp hand heavy with rings and what he called his prayer bracelet through the water. "There's no point."

Zantu took a closer look at the baby. The tiny nub of a tail lay limp across his brother's chest. A shock of ebony hair floated loosely in the current. But skin that should be mottled with newborn color remained pasty. Had Didra left because the baby was dead, or was it the other way around? His chest ached at the loss. "Rubac, I'm sorry."

"Will you take Ebby for me?"

Zantu's throat tightened. Mermen were very good at deluding themselves that their mates would be back any moment. Good at focusing on the children she brought them, in spite of a broken heart. Until his heart had enough. And once a broken heart fell apart, there'd be no return. Zantu couldn't allow his brother to just give up. "Remember when Dad left you in charge while he went to find medicine for that cut on his tail? How it felt to think he might not come back, and how we'd gone searching for him? Don't you think Ebby would do the same?"

"I knew he'd come back. I just wanted to go exploring." Rubac's mouth twitched upward, as if he wanted to smile but couldn't.

Sweeping the floor with his tail, Zantu kicked a flurry of small shells and debris at the merman. "I'm serious. Think about how we felt. You want Ebby to feel like that?"

Rubac's reply held a key of despair. "I need you to help so I can try to elevate the baby's soul."

If Zantu's throat had been tight before, now his entire chest felt as if it were about to cave in. His brother's love of mer-myth and magic could sometimes be entertaining, but in this case, it would likely prove deadly. The myth of elevation said a great blue whale could free a mer-soul from the cycle of the sea. But blue whales only lived out in the wild deeps, far from the safety of the kelp forest. Zantu and his brother had braved it several times before Ebby was born, Zantu seeking salvage while Rubac spoke to the smaller whales and other creatures. Back then they'd had nothing to lose but themselves.

"Now's not the time to go chasing myths." He reached for the limp form on Rubac's chest. "Why don't I take care of the baby? You stay with Ebby."

Rubac's arm closed tighter about his dead child. "I have to try."

"A living child needs you. You can't take risks like we used to."

"That's why I need Ebby to stay with you."

"Ebby needs *you*, brother."

"You love Ebby, and you don't have a mate yet, so—"

"Uncle Zantu has a mate now," Ebby sang from behind the dollhouse.

The heart-wrenching drama with Rubac had almost made Zantu forget about Brianna. He hoped she wasn't too frightened. Although he'd verified no predators were near, every muscle in his body suddenly burned with the need to get back to her. Yet his brother needed him as well and just as badly. He was torn between two worlds.

Rubac rose from the mound of sponges and stared at Zantu. "You've been caught? When?"

"It's a long story, and I don't have time to tell it now. But I can't take Ebby. I need to know you won't abandon your child to pursue a myth."

"She's a human," Ebby threw out, holding up a long-legged, naked doll. "No tail."

Rubac blinked, frowned at the doll. He turned again to

Zantu, his lime-green eyes now shrewd with curiosity. "Human?"

"I told you, it's a long story." Zantu pulled away, relieved by his brother's apparent return of clarity. "She's waiting for me at my nest."

"Waiting? Oh, you *have* been deluded." Rubac put a hand on Zantu's shoulder. "I'm so sorry. I thought you might be one of the lucky ones and escape the bond."

"Human women are different."

"You're serious." Rubac settled back onto the sponges. "You've bonded to a human."

"Indeed."

"I want to hear all about this."

His brother's innate curiosity gave Zantu a bargaining chip. "Promise you won't abandon Ebby and head off to the deeps, and I promise to come back in a day or two and tell you."

Rubac seemed to think for a moment then nodded his head. "I won't abandon Ebby."

Zantu blew out a string of relieved bubbles. Once he was more secure about leaving Brianna in the nest, he could come back to fulfill his promise. "Thank you. I need to get back to Brianna. She's never been alone." He pushed aside the screen of kelp to exit the clearing. "Remember your promise. I'll see you in a few days."

"You too, brother. Good luck."

Zantu slipped through the stalks, relieved by his brother's return to his senses. At least he hoped Rubac was okay and wouldn't abandon Ebby for a myth. But Zantu had other responsibilities than his brother right now.

ZANTU SENT OUT A THOUGHT, unsure how far the link might travel. He'd lost contact not far from the nest.

Nothing.

The brown-spotted sculpin he'd left to watch her was supposed to come find him if there was trouble. Not the best guard fish but more reliable than the capricious orange garibaldi fish who often served mermaids just for fun.

He jetted through the kelp, pulsing his sonic query ahead to clear the way. The kelp thinned as he exited Rubac's territory and reached the ledge down to his own. He jackknifed over a lip of rock, shooting straight for his nest.

Shoving through the thick wall of kelp into the clearing, he smiled in anticipation. He'd never had a mate to come home to before. Inside the nest, he looked around, and his smile faded. *Brianna?* She was nowhere in sight. He added a sonic query.

Gone.

Of course she'd left him. That was what women did. He'd hoped a human would be different, but obviously not. Why would he believe she was any different from any other female? Yet a dark cloud of doubt enshrouded his soul. His nest was far from land. How could she expect to strike out on her own and reach safety? There were predators, riptides, mermaids, and other dangers. Without fins or tail she'd be at the mercy of the current. He had to make sure she was safe, even if she had left him.

He slid out of the nest and searched for the sculpin guard. Missing, of course. Creating a song for the simple creatures in the area, he asked the whereabouts of the human. As one, the creatures pointed toward the rock wall nearby. An orange garibaldi giggled and darted away, trailing a few friends.

A flutter of panic leaked through Zantu's mind. He darted

after the garibaldi through the rocks and between kelp, calling ahead with both mind and sonar.

Even with the current, she shouldn't have drifted far. Where was she?

A brown-speckled sculpin poked its head from behind a sea fan on the floor, its mind relaying the feel of rising toward the surface and the pull of the stronger current. Sculpins were bottom dwellers, and the creature's own instincts had overridden the directive to watch Brianna.

Zantu should have known better than to trust a sculpin to report trouble. Cowards, every one.

Another panic wave rippled through Zantu. Was the feeling his own or something he was receiving from Brianna? Speeding toward the surface, he called with both voice and mind. *Brianna!*

The panic in his chest grew stronger, and now he recognized it wasn't all his. A word whispered through his mind. *Help!*

Brianna! Where are you?

As he entered a thick section of kelp, the words grew stronger. *I can't breathe. God, hurry!*

He spun in place, searching the surrounding forest. He could detect nothing awry. The mind connection gave him no sense of direction. *Can you sing to me? Call me!*

No! There's something nearby. I'm afraid. The kelp— her thoughts were muddy, but the panic remained sharp and clear.

Summoning a song deep in his core, Zantu formed a command to every creature within range. "Protect my mate!"

The water churned with activity as nearby creatures passed the message along: low foghorn calls from a nearby black jewfish, buzzing from a school of perches, and low against the ocean floor, the ba-ba-ba of a few sea bats. And then a high bark from a sea lion, a warning about invasion of territory. Zantu homed in on the call, racing between the stalks until he spotted the whiskered face of the local sea lion male. He'd interacted with the creature before, and it tolerated Zantu in what it considered its domain.

"What is it?"

The sea lion bared its teeth with unusual aggression and responded with the note sea lions used to warn competitors away.

Zantu tilted his head to look out of the corner of his eye submissively. "You know me, brother. I'm not here to hurt you or your family. I'm looking for a human."

The beast circled him, the whites of its eyes showing starkly against sleek brown fur. It grunted a story about a mermaid playing games, using the kelp to trap and drown his harem's babies.

Stomach churning, Zantu ground his teeth. A mermaid would find Brianna even more fun to toy with than baby sea lions. "Take me there."

The big animal somersaulted once and shot through the kelp to an area shorn from its holdfasts to create a floating mat of greenery. Thick stems tangled in the canopy, yanking more stalks loose as the current continued its relentless path. In the distance, the shouts of the sea lion's harem met the taunting giggles of a retreating mermaid. The big male bellowed and sped in that direction.

Zantu coiled himself to follow then spotted glints of skin amidst the tangle of kelp. A naked foot peeked from within the mat. Realigning his trajectory, he tore through the mass toward his mate.

I'm here, he thought as he yanked the stalks and debris free. Pushing aside mats of flat leaves, he searched for her face.

Her thoughts had drifted into a hazy calm. Almost nonexistent. He tore a leaf aside and found her eyes staring at him. Through him. *No!* Immediately, he placed his lips over hers and released a stream of bubbles into her mouth. *Brianna, breathe!*

Her body bucked, the kelp still binding her limbs. She couldn't die. Again he kissed her lips, trying to recall exactly how he'd done it when they'd first met. It was one thing for her to leave him, return to the surface. Go back to her life there. Knowing she lived, he, too, could live on. But if she died in his arms, he'd have nothing to live for. *Please, Brianna. I love you.*

Free me, she thought.

The ache in his gut twisted sharply. Wrenched him to the core. Reminded him she'd left the nest, swum to the surface to seek escape. Even now, she sought to be free of him. He wished he could mimic that desire. The bond he'd thought to find a way to break had only strengthened as time passed. He was as trapped by the bond as she was by the entangling kelp.

Clawing at a handful of stalks, he tore them loose. Another handful. Unleashing himself on the inanimate plant matter, he shredded away thick stems and fronds and let them drift away on the current. "You shouldn't have left me," he growled, his thoughts a boiling stew of emotion she probably couldn't decipher. He wasn't even entirely sure what he felt except that it hurt beyond anything he'd ever thought possible. He wanted to hurt her and hold her at the same time.

The moment he jerked the last bond free, she wrapped her arms around him and buried her face against his shoulder. *Oh, God, thank you.*

His frenzied emotions dissolved like salt in water. Embracing her, he savored the feel of her warmth against him, the sunshine scent of her skin that had so captivated him. How could she hold such control over him? It didn't matter. He was hers, now and forever. And she was alive.

Don't leave me again. She gripped him tighter.

She was toying with him, of course. Using him when she needed him only to throw him away the next chance she got. His chest ached, as if the mate-bond might squeeze the life out of him. He tried to read her thoughts, but his own were too stormy to see past. *I thought you wanted to be set free?*

I wanted free of the kelp. *Did you think I meant free of you?*

Why else would you have tried to reach the surface?

She pushed away from his chest to look into his face. *I didn't. You were gone so long, and I got bored. There were these fish fighting, and I thought I'd break it up. I know it was stupid. I should have stayed put. The current sucked me away. I couldn't find the nest again. Then I hit the kelp and, and—* Her thoughts catapulted over one another, saturated with raw terror. *I thought I was going to die.*

A wave of relief rolled over him. And guilt. The connection of their thoughts couldn't lie. *I promise never to leave you alone again.*

He curled his tail up to caress the sensual curve of her bottom with his fin. Her legs still fascinated him, and the way she could embrace him with both her arms and legs during lovemaking drove him mad with lust. She sighed within her mind at his caress and spread her thighs. Her mind radiated trust. Commitment. Love?

His cock bulged and thrummed against its sheath, demanding release, demanding the satiation of her heated core, but he held back. He wanted to savor every moment he could. To make her want him as badly as he wanted her. He roamed his hands along the curve of her hips, thumbs grazing the slight hollows of her hip bones until they found the downy mound of fur between her legs. So soft, so hot, the mound pulsed as he cupped his fingers over it, slipping between those sensual legs.

She traced her hands over his arms, up his biceps, around his neck. He dipped his head to kiss her, fingers massaging her labia even as his mouth plied her lips open to receive his tongue. Her fingers reached the top edge of his dorsal fin and traced both sides of it down his spine to his hips. His cock sprang free. Still he ignored it, enthralled by the erotic gyrations of her hips against his hand.

Leaving her lips, he found a breast, taking her nipple between his teeth to nibble gently. Her fingers clawed into him, her mind spiraling with both pleasure and pain. He'd need to be cautious using his pointed teeth against her tender skin. Still massaging her slick nub, he moved to the other breast and drew the nipple to a barnacle-hard peak before tracing kisses along her belly.

She bucked and strained against him. He wrapped his other hand around to cup her ass and dipped his head between her legs to replace his fingers with his tongue. She tasted as good as she smelled, and bucked harder against him, her thoughts yearning for penetration.

As you wish, he sent, and plunged a finger into her. Her interior ridges quivered around his finger. He slipped a second inside and discovered that crooking his fingers while plunging her depths sent her into a cascade of pleasure. The shared mental connection to her shuddering climax nearly had him spilling his seed into the surrounding water.

Keeping hold of her sides, he slid up her length to find her mouth with his again. His cock entered her core as easily as an eel returning to its den, smooth and graceful and a perfect fit. She sighed in mental satisfaction and lifted her face to kiss him.

I love you forever, he thought as he sent his seed deep within her.

*L*IKE A BABY otter, Brianna lay atop Zantu's chest, while yards below them the kelp canopy undulated in deceivingly benign patterns. She reached up and broke the water's surface with one hand, the droplets on her fingertips refracting the setting sun into tiny rainbows. Drawing her hand back into the ocean's embrace, she ran her fingertips along the rippled muscles of Zantu's abdomen. The thought of going back down through the kelp to his nest terrified her. Being apart from Zantu terrified her. Everything about this ocean terrified her. More than terrified her. As both adrenaline scare and coital passion subsided, she realized she was angry as hell. *How could you leave me alone like that?*

Zantu hugged her closer, his tail rhythmically sweeping the water. *I'm sorry—*

She shoved at him, flailed as he released her, then clung to him and pounded his rock-hard chest instead. *What if you hadn't made it back in time? Did you realize I'd stop breathing?*

I left a sculpin to watch over you—

A fish? You left me in the care of a fish?

A mistake, I admit. He grabbed hold of the fist she'd been pounding against his chest. *I don't know why you had trouble breathing. The breath bond is supposed to last until the new moon. Perhaps that mermaid broke it.*

A new fear took root in the pit of her stomach. *Breath bond? Is that a spell? What if it gets broken again?*

I won't leave you again. His face was hard with resolve. *Not until I know how to keep you safe.*

His evasive answer shifted her fright into suspicion. *That's not what I asked.*

As long as I'm near, I can renew the bond.

She stared upward at the darkening sky. *You can't possibly guarantee you'll be at my side every moment of every day.*

His mind was a maelstrom of ideas until he settled on a tentative thought. *My brother might know of deeper magic.*

Her fist tightened beneath his palm until her nails dug into her flesh. *I'm not letting you leave me alone again.*

No. I won't do that.

What then? she asked, hoping mermen had some way to communicate over long distances yet knowing they didn't. If they had, he could have simply called his brother the first time.

You'll come with me. In spite of the wall he'd tried to erect between their mind-connection, horrific images flashed across her vision. A frenzy of mermen tearing one of their own limb from limb. Blood filling the water. Horrific silence as they departed, leaving the dead to feed the fish.

She gasped, salt water catching in her throat. *Who are those mermen?*

Zantu's chest rose and fell in a sigh. *Remember I told you taking a mate to another's nest is forbidden? The punishment for breaking the pact is death.*

Her heart was beating so fast she thought it might explode. *But... even your brother?*

My brother's not like other mermen. He'll hear me out. The words he sent were steady, yet she could detect a falseness to his confidence.

Why such harsh punishment? she asked.

Most mermen are solitary creatures, avoiding both maids and men alike. His arms tightened around her. *Unfortunately, weaker mermen have been known to indulge a mate's desire and reveal the locations of fellow mermen's nests. Any merman not mate-bonded would likely be forced to mate, no better than a slave. Any who rejects her faces her wrath, not only toward himself but also his children. Entire families have been destroyed by a single mermaid. A nest is supposed to be a sanctuary. A safe place, hidden among the kelp away from predators and mermaids. Revealing a nest's location is one of the gravest sins. Carrying out punishment is one of the few times mermen will gather together.*

She swallowed, unable to erase the violent images from her mind. *I don't want you to get hurt.*

Rubac and I share a special bond, closer than other brothers. We spent many years together exploring the wild deeps for treasure and knowledge. When Didra caught him I thought our relationship would end, but he's strong. He trusts me to visit his nest. To care for his child.

What if you left me at the surface? She squeezed him tighter, pressing her face against his chest. *I could tread water there and breathe until you got back.*

His already-dark thoughts became stormy. *The surface is not safe. Predators can see you from below, waves can bury you from above.* And other humans could find you and take you away.

He didn't say the last part, but it carried across his thoughts unbidden. She stroked her fingers along his dorsal lovingly. *I do not want to leave you, my love.*

A shiver passed over his skin, and guilt soured the mind-connection. *I'm trying to trust you. But all I've ever learned of women tells me otherwise.*

From what little she'd learned—and seen—of mermaids, she knew he was fighting an uphill battle. She wanted him to trust her. Believed he would in time. And she had to admit, the idea of fending off sharks or trying to keep her head above crashing waves sounded as unlikely as surviving a journey to Rubac's nest. *If the surface is out, there must be another option. Where'd Rubac learn about the magic? Can we go there?*

Bubbles streamed from his nose. *The wild deeps would be more dangerous than taking you to Rubac's nest. I think Rubac will understand the special circumstances. Especially since you've already met Ebby.*

Her thoughts returned to the merchild and the reason Zantu had left the first time. *Is Ebby okay?*

Ebby's safe for now. My brother's the one who concerns me. Zantu's thoughts blurred and wavered with uncertainty.

Why?

His new baby is dead. Most likely stillborn. He's...

Stillborn? The mind-connection with Zantu popped and seemed to fizzle, as if shorted out. An unexpected tsunami of memory slammed into her. The first sound of her baby's heartbeat. The smell of new paint in the nursery. The sensation of that first fluttering kick from deep inside her. And then the day she'd realized the kicking had stopped. The pain of fruitless labor and delivery. Blessed unconsciousness from blood loss.

And finally, Eric standing in the hospital doorway telling

her he'd already "taken care of things." She'd been unconscious five days, and the ashes had already been scattered.

The sting of water in her nose and throat yanked her back to the present. Water squeezed from every side, forcing the breath from her body. She realized she was gasping, and there was no air to be found.

Zantu's hands grasped her face, and she felt his mouth against hers. Her lungs eased immediately. His kiss was tender, gentle. Infused with love rather than lust. An anchor in her storm. He tilted his head and traced kisses along her jaw, his hands stroking her back as if gentling a horse. *I believe I understand now why you came to me,* his mind whispered to hers.

She might not have a physical voice, but her thought was choked with pain. *He took her from me. I never got to say goodbye.*

I'm so sorry. He gathered her in his arms.

Maybe it was because of the mind-connection, but the genuine shared grief flowing from Zantu's thoughts was stronger than all the combined words of comfort she'd received from family and friends. Definitely more than she'd received from Eric, who couldn't understand why she wasn't grateful to escape the chore of a funeral. She broke down and sobbed against her mate, truly cried as she never could with Eric. Zantu held her tight, saying nothing, because he didn't have to. It was enough that he was with her. Enough that he wanted with all his heart to make things better.

She cried from the pit of her soul, and the ocean accepted her tears as its own.

⚜⚜⚜

AFTER COMFORTING BRIANNA'S GRIEF, Zantu carried her

through the night-dark kelp. Her thoughts were sorrowful but solid. Something inside her had changed, as if brackish water had been washed away by an incoming tide. She'd been through a lot—even before he'd met her. How lucky he was to have a mate who not only wanted to stay with him, but also wanted children. Children they would raise together. The anxiety he felt about approaching his brother's nest was caught up with a desire to share news of his lucky pairing. Who would have guessed a human would make such a perfect mate?

He pumped his tail and carried them toward Rubac's nest. Hopefully night would mask Brianna's proximity while he talked to his brother. Some silly part of him hoped he could get away without Rubac ever being the wiser about having his nest revealed. Another part hoped his brother noticed and wanted to meet his mate. He'd always wondered how a merman could be so weak as to take a mate to see other mermen, but now a part of him understood the draw of wanting to introduce your bond-mate to your brothers.

Brianna clung to his shoulders, thoughts numb with exhaustion. Adrenaline kept him moving. He sent sonic queries ahead to guide his path. A merman was never blind as long as there were landmarks for echolocation. One danger of the wild deeps was the vast expanse of water with nothing physical to orient himself with except the current. He prayed his brother had the answers they needed, because a trip to the wild deeps would be unthinkable with Brianna in tow.

He reached the thick wall of kelp surrounding Rubac's nest and unhooked Brianna's arms from his neck. Guiding her hands to a barnacle-rough stone, he thought, *Stay exactly here. I'll be just on the other side of this kelp. If I need to bring you into the nest, do not make eye contact. Do not interact. Most importantly, do not make physical contact of any sort. You saw what happened with Ebby. Pretend you're invisible, okay?*

She nodded into the darkness, which he felt as a slight ripple of water.

He stroked her cheek with his knuckles and then brushed her lips with his. She was too beautiful to ever be invisible, but his brother was already mated and should be immune to most female charms. Thinking of her charms ignited a fire low in his belly, and he had to rein back his desire. Now was not the time nor place.

Turning from her, he pushed aside the thickly woven kelp. Normally he'd have announced himself before entering, but he wanted to forestall Rubac's sonic query. Once Zantu was inside, Rubac's shorter query would hopefully miss Brianna's presence outside.

Moving past the kelp, he approached the mound of sponges Rubac normally rested on. He knew the layout from previous visits and moved with confidence to within an arm's length of the bed. "Rubac, it's Zantu."

No answer. Not even the shush of water against fin as Rubac or Ebby stirred.

"Rubac? Ebby?"

Still the clearing remained silent. He chirped another query and read the bounce-back. Nobody was home. He sent a louder query, verifying the other objects in the nest. Ebby's toys were right where the child always left them, and the mound of sea sponges was undisturbed. Nothing seemed out of place.

Zantu's heartbeat sped up until it pounded in his ears. Something wasn't right. He returned to where he'd left Brianna, relieved to find she was where he'd left her. *There's nobody home.*

Where do you think he went?

He rubbed a hand through his hair. All he could assume was that Rubac had taken the baby's body to inter it in the reef at the edge of the wild deeps. Why his brother had decided to do it at the edge of nightfall was a mystery. *Probably the baby's funeral.*

Oh. Her thoughts grew dark, her own loss a sharp background full of scars. *Shouldn't you be there, too?*

Her concern for his brother in spite of her own mental state touched him. *Funerals are rare, and very private when they happen. Most merfolk die in seclusion, and the dead are undiscovered until their bones have already scattered to the sea. When a loved one does find a body, it's taken to the edge of the reef and tucked into a crevice.*

The idea of Rubac at the edge of the reef, where the kelp dropped off and the wild deeps began, made Zantu nervous. Especially at night, when large predators rose to hunt. Ebby wouldn't be able to keep up the same pace Rubac did. The child would have to rest. Yet sleeping would be impossible with the current continually flowing out to the deeps.

He sent a long-range query through the kelp. A flutter of night-feeding damselfish but nothing else. The forest felt too quiet. He didn't like being outside the protection of a nest. *We'll wait inside. I imagine he'll be back in the morning.*

Won't he be angry to find us here?

Probably. But I'm not taking chances sleeping outside with you. He elbowed aside the kelp curtain and pulled her through. The current inside the nest was much weaker, and he relaxed his grip around her waist. *Do you want to rest on the bed, or would you prefer to float?*

Her fingers tightened around his forearm. *I can't see a thing.*

Exhaustion from the day's activities all seemed to drop on him at once, weighing him down like a bottle swamped with seawater. He could have called on the plankton to light the place, but it seemed easier to simply make the decision. *I think we'll rest on the bed tonight.*

He carried her to the tuft of sea sponges and relaxed, allowing their combined weight to settle them into the cushioning surface. Brianna turned to spoon herself into his embrace, her sleepy thoughts full of contentment, lulling him to sleep.

He murmured a lullaby into her hair, "You are my sunken treasure."

She sighed and snuggled closer. The gentle trickle of water over his skin soothed his sore muscles, and he fell into a deep sleep.

RIANNA BLINKED AWAKE in the darkness but this time with no confusion or fear. A predawn chorus of fish played a soothing background melody, and she snuggled closer into Zantu's warm embrace. She was delighted to feel his morning erection pressing against her bottom. His mind was blank with sleep, his body hers to explore, so she reached a slow hand around behind her and sought the throbbing shaft that'd woken her.

Sequestered in its sheath, his cock responded to a little coaxing from her hand. He flexed his hips toward her but didn't waken. Keeping her mind purposefully blank so as not to wake him, she wrapped her fingers around his heated shaft and pressed her thumb over the small slit at its head. Her pussy tightened with desire as she imagined his cock inside her. Seeking lower, she found his testicles hiding within the sheath. She massaged the tender sack, rolling the orbs between her fingers.

Zantu pressed his hips harder against her and crushed her in the circle of his arms, not enough to hurt but enough to immobilize her. A low growl rose from his throat against her ear. *Good morning, my little angelfish. Or should I say devilfish?*

The vibration sent shivers deep inside her, creating an ache that needed to be filled.

His hand sought hers still wrapped around his cock, encouraged her to squeeze and press his shaft downward. The tip grazed her ass, and she rubbed herself over it. *Depths, woman. We're on my brother's bed.*

So?

He slid her higher along his body until her opening was poised directly over his cock, the head teasing her lower lips. Both his hands found her breasts, fingertips pinching her nipples until they stiffened.

She arched her back, thrusting her hips against him to take him in, but he resisted, keeping the tantalizing head just at the opening. He sent, *I want to kiss your lips.*

She started to turn, but he held her facing away.

Not those lips. He lifted her farther up along his chest, skin sliding against skin, strong hands guiding her by her hips. His chin grazed her spine, making her back tingle. When he reached the top of her buttocks, she felt his tongue caress the upper edge of her crack. Both his hands encircled her ass cheeks, spreading her wide. One thumb crept inward to circle her anus. She puckered, yearning for more no matter his intent.

Thumb massaging with gentle pressure, he slid his face lower. She gasped as he thrust his mouth between her legs. His tongue slipped along her quivering folds, ending at the throbbing nub of her clit. The pressure of his mouth sent shudders of pleasure deep into her belly.

At some point they'd floated above the bed and now free-floated in the water. She flailed, seeking something to grip, something to ground her as he worked the sensitive button of flesh with his tongue and teeth.

Hold onto your breasts, he commanded. *Pinch them for me.*

She clutched her own flesh, pinching until the electric jolts of sensation from his mouth met the matching ones from her nipples.

His mouth covered her pussy, tongue circling every crevice before plunging deeply into her. She arched, aching for more. *I need you,* she thought.

And then he began to sing.

The deep vibrations worked into her bones, filled her as surely as if he were fucking her. The sensation grew to enormous proportions, demanding release, and yet she yearned for the moment to last forever. Every muscle tightened, unable to escape his song. The thrumming, pulsing cadence worked her very core until the crescendo rolled over her in a great spasming release.

With a single purposeful move, Zantu pulled her down, and his cock settled deep into her folds.

She moaned, rising through another crescendo toward climax. His hands on her hips held her tightly against him, his body rocking hard. She widened her thighs and wrapped her calves around behind him, straining to take him deeper. She wanted his cock to touch her soul. To make him come so deep he melded with her forever.

A gasp left him as he clutched her tightly, driving his seed deep inside her.

ZANTU STARTLED awake to early pink sunlight reflecting through the kelp foliage above the nest. He'd fallen asleep almost immediately after making love, arms cradling his mate like a precious pearl. Wondering what had woken him, he gently released her and slid from the sponge bed. Rubac would have taken refuge during the night, but with morning light, he could return at any moment. Zantu hoped his brother never found out they'd made love in his nest, but even if he did, that moment with Brianna had been worth it.

The usual fish song trickled through the water, nothing apparently amiss. He didn't want to send a sonic query to Rubac and risk waking Brianna, so he decided to gather breakfast instead. The overharvested seaweed gardens would offer little for a meal, but Zantu didn't want his angelfish to start the day hungry.

Rubac didn't utilize human artifacts much, and Zantu had to search among Ebby's toys to find a beautiful cobalt-rimmed bowl. Taking the bowl to the outer edges of the garden, he searched for edible leaves and pods, leaving the newest seedlings in place for future meals. The garden was in even worse shape than he'd originally thought. How long had Rubac lain here grieving, leaving poor Ebby to fend for food alone?

He decided to take a quick patrol of the outer nest, both for food and to scout out anything of concern. Perhaps he'd find a clue about where Rubac and Ebby had gone. Much as he told himself things were probably fine, his brother's state of mind hadn't been exactly stable when Zantu had left him.

Outside the nest, sunlight danced and glittered across the forest floor as the current tossed the canopy above. A nearby garibaldi let loose a string of notes that sounded like rain against the water's surface. Farther out, a moray eel clacked its teeth before retreating into its den. Zantu found a small patch of red dulse and bent to pick the fronds.

Something brushed against his dorsal fin. He turned to find a small yellow señorita fish looking at him, its tiny mouth pursed as if it had something to say. "What is it, little one?"

"Sorry, brother," the little fish recited—señorita fish were excellent at parroting back a song. "Elevation called. Sorry, brother. Elevation called."

Zantu stared at it in shock. His brother had gone to the wild deeps anyway? What about Ebby? Depths. He must've taken the merchild along. The fish had been left as a messenger to Zantu in case Rubac didn't return. The fish darted into the kelp, job apparently done.

Dropping the bowl, Zantu raced back to Rubac's nest. Brianna rolled over at his arrival, stretching in a languid arch he didn't have time to appreciate. *I have to go after my brother. He took Ebby to the deeps.*

Why? She sat up to look at him.

There is a myth, a type of funeral called an elevation which can free a soul from the cycle of the sea. It can only be done in the wild deeps with the aid of an ancient blue whale. He went to her, taking her in his arms. He realized he'd never told her about the deeps, only sought to protect her from them. *The deeps are past the kelp forest, where the sharks and squid and other predators live. There are no landmarks to guide by, only the strength of the current, which can challenge even a merman's stamina. I can't take you there. And I can't leave you here.*

She grabbed his arms and pushed away from him. *What the hell are you suggesting?*

It dawned on him that he was suggesting releasing her. Setting her free.

Oh, no you're not. We're mates, remember? Whatever we do, we do together. Besides, land's in the opposite direction, and you don't have time to dawdle. I'm coming with you. Just give me a knife or something to help fend off the predators.

The determination in her thoughts about drowned him. He'd been trying to believe she wanted to be with him, but some part of him had been waiting to prove she was lying. That, like any mermaid, she'd leave him without looking back. But at this moment she was digging through Ebby's toys, looking for a weapon. Planning to accompany him on a journey that could kill them both.

Any reservations he may have had about her washed away.

Yet that knowledge didn't eliminate the problem at hand.

He searched through Rubac's small statues, jewelry, and other mythic artifacts but couldn't find anything that might serve as a weapon. Looking up, he saw Brianna brandishing a long pole with a net on it wider than his shoulders. *I can use this to push things away or tangle them up.*

In spite of the fear gripping his insides, he smiled. *My ferocious little angelfish.*

CHAPTER TEN

ZANTU CLUTCHED BRIANNA tightly against his chest and exited the kelp forest. They'd been swimming for hours, heading toward the great chasm where predators hunted other predators, often merely for sport. The sudden lack of foliage, coupled with the immediate drop into nothingness, always made his stomach flip. His most recent trip to the deeps had been when he'd followed a trail of cargo containers washed overboard during the last autumn storm. Then, he'd run into a raven-haired seductress prowling the area and nearly lost his freedom. Now he'd be risking something much more precious.

He sent out a sonic query to test the dark waters. The song would not only provide him bounce-back information on what was ahead, but it would also frighten away any mindless hunting squid. Sharks and whales were another matter—much trickier to coerce—but he'd deal with them if the need arose.

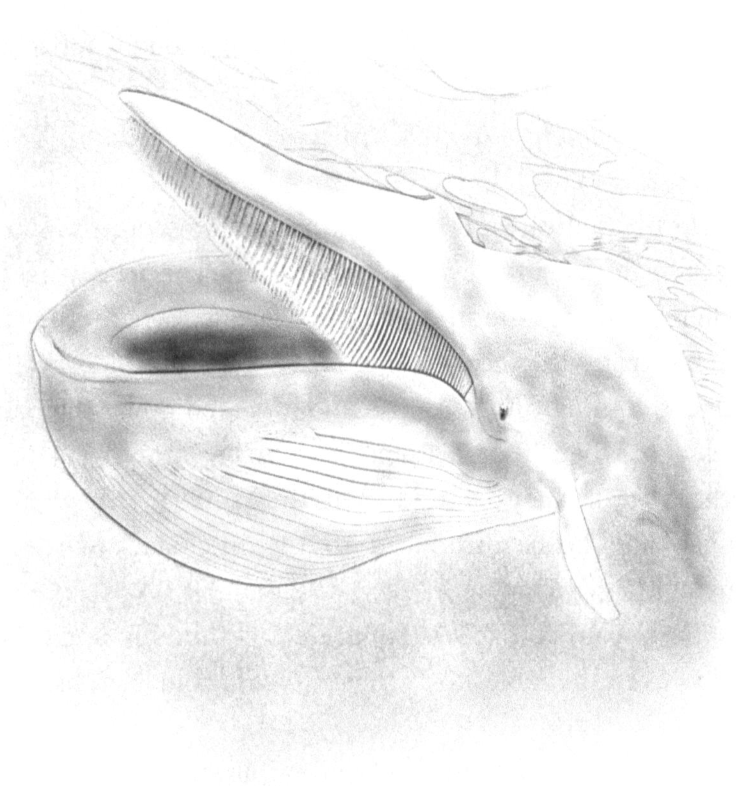

How are we going to find them? Brianna asked.

He pointed to a dusky cloud of krill interrupting the milky light reaching from the surface. *See the krill? We look for that. Whales follow krill, and Rubac's looking for whales.*

He emitted a short burst of song, searching for the gigantic animals. Nothing.

I can't see anything. The tremor in her thought reflected his own nervous fear.

There's nothing to see. Whales haven't found this swarm yet. We'll keep looking.

He pressed onward, farther and farther from the safety of the kelp forest into ever deeper water. The true wild deeps didn't begin for another quarter league, where the colder waters from the north joined and pushed underneath the current coming off the kelp reef. He'd been down that current ages ago, when he and Rubac had first ventured out of their father's nest. They'd found their first sunken ship there, and Rubac had been introduced to the intelligent whales who carried the sea's myths.

"Sink you, Rubac," he muttered within his song. Would Ebby even be able to survive those cold depths? Would Brianna?

A drumbeat reached him from far ahead. Then a low moan dropped its pitch through the water.

Brianna's fingers dug into his shoulder. *What's that?*

He gave her a short squeeze of reassurance, his own pulse loud in his ears. *Blue whales.*

A warning thump beat the water as the whale sensed their presence. "Go play your games in another pool," the whale's ponderous voice cautioned. "You've caused enough trouble for one night."

Zantu slowed. "I'm not here for games. I'm seeking my brother and his child. Have you seen them?"

A dark form moved between them and the surface. Zantu kicked his tail to resist being thrust downward in its wake.

"Ah, merman," the whale grated, its barnacled body stretching forever into the darkness. "I thought you were a maid. Your females have delighted in inciting a frenzy among the nearby sharks."

Zantu resisted the urge to send a sonic query into their surroundings. Sharks were bad enough, but now he'd have to watch for mermaids as well. "Have you seen another male? He would have asked you to assist with an elevation."

The drumbeat sound approached again, and a great mouth, open as if to swallow them whole, appeared. "An elevation? How odd." The mouth brushed by, revealing the black orb of an eye, a dark moon to counter the pale sun outlined above the surface.

Brianna remained surprisingly calm in the midst of the inspection. Excited but not frightened, even daring to reach her hand out to brush the whale's scarred hide. *Can you understand it?*

The eye regarded them while the voice continued to groan through the water. "What's this? A human?"

Nerves jangling, Zantu thrust out his chest and swelled his song to potent volume. He wanted there to be no doubts about how far he'd go to protect the human at his side. "My mate."

The whale blinked and seemed to sigh. "I've not seen a mated human in over a century. You have much to learn. But now," the whale sang in a heavy tone, appropriate for a funeral, "I believe I hear your brother."

In the far-off distance, Zantu could barely detect the

familiar notes of his brother's sonic query. The whale answered with a moan that seemed to shake the very ocean, and drifted off to swallow more krill.

"Rubac!" Zantu called, moving to intercept.

You've found him? Brianna clutched him with one hand, and the netted pole with the other, struggling to keep from losing it in the water's resistance.

Ahead.

They left the whale behind, Zantu querying madly to discover Rubac's location. His brother's song had stopped, but the higher, more uncertain chimes of Ebby's song grew louder. "Uncle Zantu!"

Zantu raced ahead, drawn to Ebby's voice. Finally, he saw Rubac's form.

Alongside the unmistakable curves of a mermaid.

Zantu halted his momentum. *The whale said there was a mermaid around.*

Oh shit. Brianna brandished her net in front of her, looking about. *I still can't see a thing.*

I don't see Ebby. A sonnet trilled to his left, accompanied by the notes from a fish-harp. He spun, only to spot the disappearing flash of an indigo tail. *Depths. There's more than one.*

He turned back toward Rubac and thrust forward, hoping to at least find safety in numbers. The mermaid teasing his brother had yellow hair and a golden tail. Didra.

"Oh, you've come to our party!" she chimed, clapping her hands. "Rubac's such a bore."

"Where's Ebby?" Zantu shouted. To his relief, the tiny figure materialized through the krill-speckled water. The child held back a distance, avoiding the mermaids and watching.

A duet behind him sent him spinning around in time to pull

Brianna beyond the reach of a raven-haired mermaid. Her dark tail caught the light as she passed by, first iridescently green and then swirling violet. A section of her tail fin was missing, the jagged edge puckered with old scar tissue. She cooed, "I've heard about you, Zantu."

Her partner was familiar, nimble fingers plucking a fish-harp's tines. "Loia."

She laughed while her accompanying veil of fish shimmied and shifted around her in time to her harp. "I warned you a human was no fit mate for a merman. Especially a big strong merman like you. She'll never be able to keep up with our games."

Brianna's knuckles were white around the net pole, every muscle in her body tense. *What's she saying?*

Threats. Behind him, he heard the tiny susurration of skin against water as Didra shifted position. His brother remained eerily silent, eyes hooded, tail fin limp. There was no sign of the stillborn child. "Rubac? You okay?"

No answer.

The raven-haired mermaid swooped up from below, rubbing her scarlet nipples along Zantu's length. Brianna recoiled, arching away from the contact and throwing him off-balance, but he caught her and pulled her against him tightly.

An arm's length away, the mermaid backflipped to face them again and rolled a small dart between her fingers. Immediately, Zantu knew what was wrong with Rubac. Love toxin.

The mermaid's voice chimed with deceptive playfulness, her scarred tail fluttering with mesmerizing iridescence. "I wonder what would happen if I used this on her?"

He swelled his chest. "I will kill you if you touch her."

Brianna's thoughts spun like a water spout, her attention

first on one mermaid then another. She poked the net at Loia. *We're surrounded.*

Fingertips tickled the tips of his dorsal fin, sending a shudder through his blood as Loia's lilting melody of desire began. "Oh, are we going to have fun now."

He twisted to bat the hand away. Loia's veil of fish enveloped them. Summoning his sonic blast, he sent them scattering. The scent of blood filled the water. Brianna's blood. He had to get her out of here. Get Ebby out of here. Fast. His brother… his brother would have to fend for himself. Coiling the muscles of his tail, he lurched forward between Rubac and his mate. "Ebby, swim home!"

Something nipped his side. For a moment he thought it was another of Loia's fish. He brushed a hand over the spot to flick it away and found the dart lodged there. Depths. He'd been hit with the toxin. Jerking it free, he continued his momentum, barely registering Ebby's tiny figure matching his pace several yards away. The fog of the poison was already taking hold. His muscles ached as he tried to force them to keep working. To get his mate to safety. The grip he held on Brianna slipped, her skin scraping along his side before he caught her again.

She clung painfully to his neck, her feet kicking in a pitiful attempt to help them swim. *Zantu, what's wrong?*

She hit me with a love toxin. Soon I'll be paralyzed. He didn't know what to do. His gaze scoured the blank expanse of water for anything, anywhere he could hide Brianna. His grip slipped again, and he realized his tail was twitching ineffectually against the current.

"Uncle Zantu, what about Dad?"

Sink it, Ebby was in danger here, too. Not from the mermaids—Didra wouldn't allow the others to harm her own blood. But she wouldn't ensure Ebby made it back to the safety of a nest, either. Ebby would be abandoned. "He'll be fine." He prayed he wasn't lying. "I'm going to be paralyzed soon, like him. You have to get back to the kelp forest. Take Brianna."

"I don't know the way."

He opened his mouth to tell the child how, but his voice had succumbed to the effects of the toxin. His arm now refused to keep hold of Brianna, and she clung to him as if he were a dead piece of coral.

Zantu?

You have to show Ebby how to get home. At least his mind-connection still worked.

How? I don't know the way, and I couldn't tell Ebby even if I did.

Keep the current to the right and in front of you. Stay out of the cold layer—it'll suck you to the bottom very quickly. If it does touch you, keep it hard to your right and swim upward as fast as you can. Ebby wriggled into view, turquoise eyes confused and frightened. He hoped somehow the merchild would trust Brianna.

The laughter of mermaids tinkled toward him like hail against the surface.

Kiss me, he thought.

What?

You have to let go now, and I want your breath-bond fresh. The thought of her drowning was almost as paralyzing as the toxin. All he could hope was that she broke the surface before the spell ended.

No! They'll rip you apart! The terror clawing through her mind was stronger than it had been while she'd been trapped by kelp.

If you don't, both you and Ebby will die.

Brianna's gaze cut to the merchild, then her lovely face crumpled in anguish. *I don't want to leave you.*

I know. He sought to make his thoughts calm. To reassure her. *But you have to. You have to save the child.*

She bit her lips together then nodded. Grief reddened her beautiful green eyes. Taking his face between her hands, she placed her soft lips against his. *I love you.*

The toxin didn't take away his ability to feel, only to move, and he was thankful in this instance to have one last memory of her. *And I love you, my angelfish. Now swim. Get back to shore if you can.*

She released him and turned to the merchild. Ebby's tail flashed with alarming colors, unable to settle on a single camouflage. The child's attention flicked to Brianna then back to Zantu. "I'll take care of her, Uncle Zantu."

Ebby reached out a tiny webbed hand and took Brianna's, pulling her away into the dark waters.

❤❤❤

BRIANNA GRIPPED Ebby's hand and kicked to assist their momentum. The mermaids' songs echoed through the water, trying to lure her back. She wondered if Ebby felt the pull, too, or if merchildren—being sexless—were immune. The possible biological reason for a merchild's androgyny made a lot of sense right now.

The song's pull doubled her reluctance to leave Zantu and forced her to use every ounce of will to keep moving away. If it hadn't been for the merchild, she would have stayed by her mate's side, fought each murderous mermaid with every ounce of strength left in her body. She prayed he could find a way to escape. To find her again. He was stronger than any man she'd ever met.

Ebby dragged her along, using the current to aid their momentum. Now it was time to turn against it. To head back to the kelp beds. Brianna pulled against the child's grip and pointed with her free hand into the distance, keeping the water's flow slightly to her right as Zantu had instructed.

Ebby's eyebrows rose at Brianna's nonverbal instruction. The merchild blinked twice then nodded and changed direction.

Brianna let out a sigh of bubbles, grateful the child wasn't going to argue. Zantu's last wish had been for Ebby to reach safety, and Brianna would do everything she could to make that happen, even if she drowned in the process. She kicked with all the stamina she could muster. But exhaustion was already setting in. The drag created from the net was stronger than she'd previously realized, perhaps because they were now going against the water instead of with it. Poor little Ebby wriggled ferociously, but it didn't feel like they were making much progress.

A cramp seized her right calf, and she doubled over, awkwardly trying to massage it without letting go of the net. The tiny teeth marks left by the mermaid's swarm of fish continued to trail blood.

Swallowing, Brianna searched the surrounding waters. Hadn't Zantu said something about predators? Once, she'd watched a nature show about giant squid, with green-and-black video of a man-sized creature latching onto a diver's faceplate. The scrape and crunch of its beak biting the plastic still resonated in her memory. Zantu'd used his song to check for predators, yet Ebby moved through the water silently. Brianna hoped it was another survival trick, like the androgyny that made them immune to mermaid songs.

Overhead, the sun's orb seemed weaker, and the water had grown decidedly cooler against her skin. She reoriented toward the surface and aimed the net like a prow. Her leg threatened a new cramp, but she persisted in kicking until Ebby noticed and shifted direction. The downward pull was even more relentless than the outward current, and it seemed forever until a sudden flush of warmer water gave Brianna an extra burst of energy. She kicked like mad toward the sun.

Suddenly Ebby froze and spun to look behind them. A tremble passed between their connected hands, and Brianna squinted into the dark. Shadows. Moving shadows. Had the mermaids found them? The sharp curve of a dorsal fin cut through the waters.

Sharks.

Seriously? Sharks? She felt like she was playing a part in the worst horror movie ever. She clutched the net tighter, realizing how silly and useless a thing it would be.

The creatures moved sinuously toward her, toothy mouths open to taste the water. A large one was in the lead. When a smaller one moved abreast, the giant shot sideways to bite at it. Another midsized shark passed the fight, dead set on engaging its prey.

For the first time, Ebby let loose a wide arc of sound. It was nowhere near as authoritative as Zantu's thunderous voice, but it still had some effect. The sharks veered away, all but the largest one. The monster merely seemed pleased to ditch the competition.

Brianna released her grip on the child's hand. Tried to shake free so Ebby could escape. But the merchild didn't let go.

Instead, Ebby gave Brianna a headshake to negate the idea. Did the little one have a plan?

The shark's mouth formed an oval of deadly teeth. Brianna pointed the net at it, hoping to at least force it to keep its distance. The shark was more agile and intelligent than she imagined, nosing the net aside so it could slide along the pole. At the last moment, Ebby jerked Brianna away. The beast's sandpapery side grazed Brianna's foot, leaving a burning welt in its wake.

Ebby turned, little tail churning water, and emitted another blast of song. The shark ignored it and circled back. The merchild's hold on Brianna tightened, shaking wildly. Brianna realized the child was no match for this beast, no matter how brave.

Gathering her strength, she jerked her hand free of the merchild's. She grasped her net with both hands and swung it down between her and the shark in a maddeningly slow arc. If she could lodge it in the creature's mouth, at least Ebby might be able to get away.

Ebby cried out again, and the shark twitched to the right.

Directly into the loop of the net.

The creature bolted forward, face in the net, and the hoop caught against its dorsal fin. Brianna's head rocked back at the sudden speed, her grip on the pole slipping slightly. The net seemed to both anger and confuse the beast. It twisted and rolled, trying to free itself. Brianna hung on like she held a tiger by the tail.

Ebby darted in front of the shark's nose, luring it along. The creature pulled determinedly, slowed by Brianna's weight. At first Brianna thought the merchild meant to use the shark to head home. Instead, Ebby turned into the current.

Back toward Zantu and the mermaids.

It appeared they really were going to take the tiger by the tail.

ANTU CLOSED HIS eyes and tried to ward off the effects of Loia's song. Her hands caressed his chest and arms, her endless song complimenting his physique, promising pleasures untold. One hand found his sheath, attempting to lure his cock free.

Then a second voice joined hers, battling for supremacy. He opened his eyes a slit. The raven-haired mermaid undulated in the filtered light, her iridescent skin shifting with mesmerizing color. Her crimson nipples pointed as sharply as the dart she'd hit him with. Her genital slit gaped suggestively, and he felt his cock respond with a will of its own.

Loia screeched in complaint, sending her veil of fish at the newcomer.

The dark one screeched back, "It was my dart that felled him!"

The water churned with foam and bits of slaughtered fish as the two engaged in a physical competition. The iridescent one spun and smacked Loia in the face with her scarred tail fin, drawing blood. Loia's hand flew to her mouth, and she reeled backward, her fish-harp sinking from sight.

The dark one rippled toward Zantu, a predatory grin on her lips.

Loia recovered and shot forward, mouth open to bury her pointed teeth in the other's shoulder.

And then a flash of gold as Didra slipped past the fight to press her coral-brown nipples against Zantu's chest. Her song in his ear was subtle, quiet, and deliciously inviting.

His cock surged against her genital slit. The helplessness from the love toxin clawed at his soul. Burned through his blood. Raged against the injustice of one sex that held so much power over the other. His fingernails bit into his palm as he commanded every muscle to fight the promise of pleasure.

Another angry screech, and Didra was ripped from him. Flashes of indigo, gold, and iridescent-black fins created an intoxicating dance. The water grew cloudy with fish parts and blood. Furious mer-song escalated as each mermaid attempted to outdo the other, their notes coalescing into a single, primal melody of lust.

His racing heart pulsed in his head, the tempo overriding the music in the churning water. He clenched his fists, focusing on the sensation of his fingernails biting into his palm. Perhaps the toxin was wearing off. If only he could slip away now, while they were busy competing with each other.

Out of nowhere, something slammed into the midst of the brawl. He barely had time to register the predatory shape of a massive shark—with a human trailing it like a lamprey...

Brianna? he sent.

There was too much chaos for him to sense anything in

return. The cloudy water reddened with more than fish blood, and the mermaid's screams no longer carried a hint of seduction. *Brianna!* he sent. Surely he'd been imagining things? How could she be controlling a shark? Under the best circumstances, even mer-song couldn't exert much control over the beasts other than inciting them against each other. Brianna couldn't even sing.

He twitched his tail, pulling forth every bit of strength he had to fight off the waning toxin and regain mobility.

A voice reached him. Not through the water, but in his mind. *Zantu!*

Brianna? Where are you? I told you to run!

Out of the gory cloud emerged a small merchild followed by a clumsy, flailing human. The ravenous crunch of bones from within confirmed the shark was otherwise occupied.

Brianna's thought echoed with feverish energy. *We're here to save you.*

"Where's my dad?" Ebby cried.

Zantu was gaining strength by the moment and turned to point in the direction he remembered leaving Rubac. Ebby took his hand and began hauling both him and Brianna that way. As the toxin left his system, he joined the child's efforts.

He sent out a query and was answered by a weak version of Rubac's familiar song. Ebby released them and darted forward. Zantu took the moment to draw Brianna against his side. *You should not have come back.*

She wrapped her legs around him and buried her face against his neck. *I thought I'd lost you.*

How the depths did you wrangle a shark?

All I did was hang on. Ebby's quite the little scrapper. Her trembling body told him a bigger story.

He embraced her, savoring the scent of her hair and skin. His imagination churned with other more likely outcomes. *You got lucky this time.*

Rubac appeared through the hazy water, tail movements still uncoordinated from the effects of the toxin. Ebby held his hand, leading the way.

Zantu looked over Brianna's head to greet his brother. "What were you thinking, Rubac? The deeps are no place for a youngling."

"You refused to help." Rubac hung his head. "And Father used to bring us out here. Ebby wanted to come."

"I wanted to see a whale." Ebby looked into Rubac's face with a youth's oblivion to mortality. "But we lost the baby."

A part of Zantu felt sorry for his brother. "What happened?"

Rubac covered his face with both hands. Ebby wriggled up to give him a hug. The child answered for him. "Didra dropped it into the deeps."

The pity in Zantu's soul intensified, but there was nothing to be done. "The child is at one with the sea again. That's all anyone can ask for."

Gripping Brianna tight against him, he led the way back to the kelp forest.

⋘⋘⋘

Zantu carried a sleeping Brianna back to his nest and laid her on the sponge bed. He spent the night holding her, stroking her, making love with her, etching each moment into his memory so it would last a lifetime. He wanted her at his side forever, but if today's incident had taught him anything, it was that Brianna didn't belong in the ocean. She couldn't sing. She couldn't even hear the full range of notes the ocean carried. And even if the breath-bond could be made permanent, she couldn't defend herself; the net had been a lucky moment, one not likely to be repeated.

She belonged on land.

If she stayed with him in the ocean, it only meant death for them both. And while he'd die for her in a heartbeat, the thought of her dying because of his selfish need to keep her close was unacceptable. The only place she'd be safe was back among her kind.

He knew she would fight his decision. Resist his plan to send her back. How odd that he was about to execute the very thing he'd feared from the outset of his mate-bond.

At the first notes of the morning chorus, he lifted her gently and carried her out of the nest. Each coral-covered stone they passed on the way toward the shore felt like an added weight to Zantu's soul. He broke the surface as golden fingers of light glinted across the wavelets of the cove he'd chosen for her. His lungs felt tight with more than unaccustomed air as grief threatened to turn him back. He forced himself onward, knowing this was the only way to keep his mate safe. The pebbled beach was vacant in the morning light, but a small boat rested on the shore, and a house stood in sight of the water among wind-twisted trees on a rocky hill.

She roused as his tail scraped the rocky bottom, her sleepy thoughts reaching for him, seeking comfort.

Zantu? Where are we?

He set her feet against the floor. *You must go home, my angelfish.*

She groped for him, fingers slipping against his shoulders. *Wait! I don't understand!*

He gritted his teeth and dove beneath the waves, swimming fast and far out to sea.

Don't leave me! Zantu!

Her cries followed him clear to the edge of the wild deeps.

ZANTU CRUISED the watery interface where the cold northern waters met the current off the kelp beds. Since abandoning Brianna, the dark waters of the wild deeps seemed to call his soul. He'd spent the last four moons scouring the bottom for treasure. His nest was crowded with human items, from gilded picture frames to unidentifiable plastic machines.

But none of it was the human thing he wanted.

He circled the long metal box from a cargo ship that had lodged on a ledge. This one appeared undamaged. The lower current's cold water had seeped into his bones, and his fingers were stiff as he lifted a chunk of basalt to bash the lock. Merpeople didn't have the layer of blubber that kept whales and other sea mammals warm in northern waters, and he'd already been down here past his usual endurance. But finding human artifacts was the only thing that interested him since leaving Brianna, so he kept at it.

The rusty metal lock crumbled under the impact. Once it was removed, he put a shoulder beneath the bar securing the door and pushed. The latch gave with a rusty, hollow grating sound, as did the hinges as he opened the door. He squinted and sent forth a sonic query to judge the contents.

Mounds of rotted textiles.

Disappointment sank him to the stony outcropping. Ruined

by the sea. That seemed to be the story of most things human down here. Broken. Decayed. Unable to survive.

The familiar drumbeat of a whale reached him, and he realized he'd been resting too long. His joints were stiff with cold, and his heart seemed to struggle to beat. Going to sleep seemed like a good idea.

The whale thumped the water, calling to the krill it sought to consume. Whales were one of the few creatures, fish or mammal, to have words in its song. Rubac swore they were the keepers of myth and still grieved over the lost opportunity to elevate his child.

Zantu thought about his last meeting with one, when Brianna had been by his side. The creature hadn't denied the magic of elevation, so maybe the myth had some truth.

But it had said something else, too. Something just now returning to his memory. *I've not seen a mated human in over a century. You have much to learn.*

Zantu frowned, blood pumping a little harder. What was there to learn? Was there something he'd missed? Gathering his strength, he forced his cold muscles to carry him upward toward the whale's song.

He found the whale circling near the surface, its massive, scarred body black against the light.

"Great whale," Zantu called. The frigid waters had sapped him of his voice, and the whale took no notice of the small visitor, continuing its wide-mouthed sweep through the clouds of krill. He tried again. "Great whale, I have a question."

The whale continued to ignore him, thumping the water.

Zantu bolstered his song. "Please, I have a human bond-mate. I need your help."

The whale's thumping paused, its barnacled body slowing its loop through the swarm. It turned its great black eye upon him. "Bond-mate?" the creature grated. "How did this happen?"

The story flowed out like a riptide, of how he'd happened upon her, how she'd proven herself loyal, how he'd been forced to set her free. The retelling left Zantu mentally exhausted.

The whale resumed its circle through the krill. "If she cannot be with you, why do you not join her?"

Zantu's mind spun. "Join her? How would I do that?"

"Humans and merfolk separated ways not so very long ago in the timeline of the world. You can breathe air, can you not?"

Although mermen avoided the surface, Zantu had indeed breathed air a handful of times and knew that to be true. "Yes, but breathing air is only one piece of things. She lives on land. With legs."

The whale's drumbeat call sounded like laughter. "Have the merfolk truly lost all knowledge of their magic? As you can give the gift of the ocean with water breathing to her, she can give the gift of land to you."

Zantu's mind reeled. "Do you mean legs?"

"True bond-mates compromise to be together. Sometimes one gives more, sometimes another. It is the way of things if they wish to be together."

"I could live on land," Zantu said, rolling the words around as if tasting the idea.

"Indeed," the whale sang and swiped its tail to pursue the retreating cloud of krill.

"Wait! How?"

But the whale didn't stop. Its words floated back in an echo of song. "If you're bonded, you already know."

Zantu wasn't sure what that meant. But he meant to find out. Reenergized with new hope, he aimed himself for the surface.

CHAPTER TWELVE

SURROUNDED BY THE scent of rotting seaweed and salt, Brianna rose from the damp stone and snapped shut the picnic basket that'd held her lunch. Facing the sea, she brushed bits of sand from her cotton capri pants. As always, the slate-gray ocean whispered to her, waves kissing the shore with promises never kept. Sometimes the water cleared the beach, leaving pristine pebbles glinting in the sun. Sometimes it left lines of garbage. Today the beach was clear.

She called with her mind as she did every time before she left the cove, *Zantu!*

As usual, only silence in return.

Perhaps her therapist was correct. Her time in the ocean had been a hallucination. Her mate a myth.

As if in disagreement, the child within her rolled, a sensation like tiny bubbles. She placed her hand over her barely rounded belly. "Don't worry, little one. I know I'm not crazy."

Upon her forced return to land, she'd climbed the stairs to

the small house. The driftwood-gray structure had obviously been vacant for a long time, but the door was unlocked, and inside she'd found some old clothes. After a short walk down the dirt lane, she'd reached the highway, flagged down a car, and made it back to town.

Within the week, Eric had signed her divorce paperwork without question. Soon after, she'd discovered she was pregnant. The idea of raising a child alone broke her heart, but she knew there'd never be another man in her life. Zantu was her mate and always would be.

She'd bought the small cliff house overlooking Zantu's beach and taken a position at the nearby marine research center. Granted, she was only a bookkeeper, but being near the fish and other creatures felt like home.

And, sometimes, she swore she could hear them singing.

Placing her sandaled feet carefully over the uneven beach stones, she headed toward the stairs up to the house. The tide was coming in, and although she sometimes dreamed of throwing herself back into the ocean's embrace, she knew better than to hope to be saved a second time. Plus she now had another life to consider.

The brisk breeze at her back seemed to call her name as she walked, stones crunching beneath her feet. *Brianna...*

She paused, cocking her head and closing her eyes to accept the wind's caress. She often dreamed like this, her name upon her lover's lips, the sensation of the word along her skin.

Brianna...

She opened her eyes. This wasn't the wind. *Zantu?*

The baby rolled again, fluttering within her as if dancing to a song.

Brianna, I need you.

She spun to face the sea, nearly turning an ankle on the uneven stones. A silver tail splashed the water near the cliff.

"Zantu," she whispered, the air in her lungs refusing to move. Then, full force, she screamed, "Zantu!"

Heedless of her shoes, her clothes, her footing, she flung the picnic basket aside and ran into the waves. "Zantu, I'm here!"

A head appeared above the surface a little closer than before, silver hair blending with the gray-clouded horizon, then was gone.

She stopped as the water reached her waist, sandals slipping over the lumpy bottom. Waves lifted and dropped her. Had she imagined him? She watched the water, every ounce of her being calling to him. *I'm here!*

A length of silver materialized beneath the mirrored water in front of her, and then Zantu's naked gleaming torso rose.

"Oh my God." She stepped forward, slipped, fell into his arms. She threw kisses across his face, gulped water as they both went under, found his mouth to kiss.

He pushed her away, upward to the surface. *No.*

Gasping and choking, she clawed her hands against his shoulders, feet scrabbling to find the bottom. *Why are you here then? Please don't leave me again.*

He rose to face her, helping her stand. She gripped him tightly around the neck. Wrapped her legs around his hips. *I won't let you go. You have to take me with you.*

Chuckling against her hair, he shifted his hands down around to support her bottom and began moving to shore. He stumbled once but caught himself. He was *walking* to shore.

Brianna nearly let go. *"What..."*

I'm here for you, angelfish. It's your time to share magic with me.

Rising out of the water like an ancient god, he carried her toward the cliff.

"You're human!" She found herself speaking the words as she thought them. Still in shock, she lowered her feet to the ground to make him stop. *"Are you really here to stay?"*

"Yes." He used his real voice this time instead of only his mind. The word, although accented, was clear and deep and sexy as hell.

She stepped back, her gaze roving over his broad shoulders to his well-muscled stomach and lower, to where his member stood at half-mast amid sparse silver curls. Where his tail had been he now had perfect, athletic legs. Her attention returned to his cock. "You're naked! And you're a man."

His cock twitched in response, rising to attention. "Yes, I am."

Tempting as he was, she forced her gaze back to his eyes. They were as silver as she remembered, his lips just as luscious. She raised one hand to trace a finger over the soft skin.

From down the beach, a child's voice snapped Brianna out of her lust. While her little cove was generally secluded, it was by no means private. There'd be time to explore Zantu later. Lots of time.

"You're going to need some clothes." She shrugged out of her windbreaker and wrapped it around his hips. It didn't cover everything, to her chagrin and delight, so she had to skew it sideways to hide the most important parts.

"Why do you get to undress and I have to dress?" He tugged at the knotted fabric, and she slapped his hand gently.

"You've got a lot to learn about humans."

"I'm looking forward to it."

She took his hand and led him past the curious stares of two children toting kites along the windswept beach. *Well, you're going to get to learn from the ground up—Daddy.*

His moment of confusion was followed by a joyful shout that echoed from the rocky cliffs and drew giggles from the nearby children. He swept her into his arms and spun her as she giggled.

Together they climbed the stairs to their nest overlooking the ocean. She'd found her mate. Her true love. The father of her children.

the Merman's Quest

CHAPTER ONE

Madison adjusted the focus of the binoculars again, concentrating on the white-capped waves breaking against the reef while maintaining her balance on the boat's rocking deck. She'd been following a pod of dolphins for almost three days, only to lose them yesterday before she could get close enough to verify her find—a wild hybrid cross between *Pseudorca crassidens* and *Tursiops truncates*. Only a single hybrid of this species had been born in captivity, and no one had ever provided solid proof of one in the wild before. She needed evidence. Photos for one thing. But even more important, she needed tissue samples. DNA proof would be irrefutable, and such a discovery would help erase the blemish on her career.

The small cruiser caught a wave sideways, and she adjusted her heading to face the rolling water. Working the vessel alone while also performing research was tricky, but after last year, she wasn't about to rely on anyone else's assistance again. *Steller*

"

sea cow my ass. Extinct for over two hundred and fifty years, the beast might as well have been a mermaid. And she'd bought into it, hook, line, and sinker, putting her full reputation behind the "data" her grad students provided. Now she was on her own, funding this trip out of her savings in hope of salvaging something of her reputation. *I'll show them all.*

She checked the depth finder—ninety-eight feet—then slipped on her polarized sunglasses to again scan the horizon. How was she supposed to manage over a dozen research assistants, verify every scrap of data, and meet the university's publishing schedule for tenure? Those damned assistants claimed it was a prank taken too far, but she was the one who'd had to shoulder the repercussions. The embarrassment of the peer-reviewed journal's scathing feedback, the media hype "debunking" her find, all of it had ruined her career. She'd lost her position at the university and her grant funding. Even her off-and-on boyfriend—a vet at the marine research center—didn't want to be associated with her.

Noting her GPS coordinates, she angled toward a darker area where the kelp canopy nearly touched the surface. The green water slapped against the hull, sending fine salt spray into the air. She loved the sea. Loved the smell, the rolling of the deck beneath her feet, the bite of the cold water against her skin. Although the sun beat down on her head, the winter breeze made swimming unpleasant, or she'd have stripped down and rinsed three days of salt-grime off her skin.

Where was the dolphin pod? She searched for the familiar dark bullet shapes below the waves. They had to surface soon. Her two precious biopsy darts were ready, if only she could get close enough.

The equipment had cost her a significant portion of her savings, as had the boat rental, and her rental agreement was nearly over.

She cut the engine, hoping the pod would show itself. This particular pod seemed more skittish than usual, without the usual dolphin curiosity about boats. They stayed just out of range of her darts, as if they knew exactly how close she needed to be.

Something splashed to the boat's aft. She turned, the small deck requiring no more than three steps until her thighs hit the inboard engine casing, and searched the glinting water's surface. The glare off the water made anything lurking beneath difficult to define, even through polarized lenses.

The splash again, this time slightly starboard. She shifted her attention in time to see a dolphin-sized, bright-green tail fin slip back into the water. *Green?*

Dolphins were shades of blue, gray, white or brown. Never green. Was it covered in algae? Maybe it was a carcass, bobbing to the surface as it rotted. Yet it hadn't moved like something dead...

She reached into her pocket for her camera, holding it ready while scanning for movement. She waited ten minutes. Twenty. Nothing.

Whatever it had been, it didn't seem to be coming back.

⽕⟨⽕⟨⽕⟨

RUBAC DOVE toward the sea floor, leaving the boat's shadow far behind. Excitement at finding a human woman alone had easily been overshadowed by trepidation about his quest. His heart raced and his muscles ached with tension. He rubbed the mother-of-pearl vision rod piercing his nipple, hoping to regain confidence. The prophetic vision he'd had while slumbering in the crook of the great whale's fin no longer seemed as straightforward.

His brother had always laughed himself silly at Rubac's mystical musings, his belief in kindred spirits, his premonitions. But Rubac knew what he felt, what he saw, what he needed. He needed this female. She would be his salvation. Would free him of his slavery to a mate-bond he'd never chosen —a soon-to-be fatal tie now that his mate was dead.

Then why was he hesitating?

He came to rest between two large sea fans, using them to escape the current while he thought. The ingrained habit of avoiding females held him weighted to the sea floor. *She's not a mermaid,* he reminded himself. *You're here to take her life, not the other way around.*

When he'd first received the premonition, he'd believed the hard part would be finding a vulnerable human female. But then he'd happened across this opportunity the very next day. Assurance his guiding spirit was real. Now he was faced with the actual quest. The quest's final requirement posed no problem in his mind; killing a human would be easy once he had her in the water. The part causing his hesitation was the first part—the part where he had to seduce her. Not so easy for a bonded merman, dead mate or not.

Unlike mermaids, who used and killed mates with abandon, mermen bonded for life. A mate-bonded merman was doomed to a life of misery as his mate strayed again and again. He would raise the children, coddling them like a father seahorse until they, too, left him. Most mermen died of broken hearts. But after Rubac's child had chosen her gender and left the nest, he'd refused to languish away. Instead, he'd sought a quick death, venturing far into the wild deeps where he'd discovered the secret to freedom.

Another fear surfaced. What if he couldn't perform? A mermaid would rip a failed lover apart—literally. Were human females as ruthless?

The light reaching him from the surface wavered and darkened as the boat passed overhead. She was hunting him, now. The irony wasn't lost on him.

A lone human female on the ocean wasn't exactly common. This might be his only chance. Completing this quest would sever the agonizing mate-bond already spiraling him toward death.

He grasped the small sea harp hanging from a cord about his neck. It matched the one his bond-mate had used to lure him into mating. Into becoming her slave. Long, pale tines rose from the curved shape of what had once been a sea sponge. He'd dived a quarter league into the bottom of the wild deeps to harvest the fragile creature. The delicate exoskeleton could be coaxed to produce an irresistible melody. Perhaps a song would not only seduce this human, but increase his own libido as well.

A tingle of guilt threaded his bloodstream. He'd been on the other side of this magic. Knew the helpless cessation of will she would experience. Mersong spoke to the primal core within every creature. It was the magic mermaids used to seduce sailors. She would be utterly powerless against it.

Do it or die. He was doomed either way, so might as well give it everything he had. Stroking his fingertips along the tines, he rose toward the surface.

*M*adison stowed her camera and ducked back under the pilot canopy to reengage the engine. Whatever she'd seen—if it'd even been real—was long gone, and she needed to find that dolphin pod today or shell out another chunk of money for the boat rental. The engine sputtered to life and then backfired and died. With a curse, she shut everything down and moved to the engine compartment to adjust the choke.

A high, sweet note bounced across the water like a small child's laugh. *What was that?* She stopped and searched the waves. The note shifted into something like a sultry oboe or saxophone holding a long note accompanied by a compulsive rhythm like a heartbeat. Was there another vessel nearby playing music? She couldn't see one.

She closed her eyes, taking a breath of sweet, salty air before opening them again to search for the song's source. The sun glittered like diamonds across the water's surface, forcing her to squint. Was that a man swimming toward her?

He disappeared below the surface, and the song thrummed through the deck against her feet. The pulse crept up her legs in delightful shivers to concentrate in her core. *God, that feels good.* Next thing she knew, she was standing at the gunwale.

A dark haired man surfaced about six meters away, closely trimmed beard dripping water. He had the broad shoulders and lean, muscular torso of a speed swimmer. A spiral shell earring curled through one earlobe, and a large sliver of mother-of-pearl pierced his nipple in one well-sculpted left pec. He stroked a mesmerizing rhythm over a white pronged object hanging from a cord about his neck, seemingly unperturbed about being adrift at sea. What struck her most, however, was the lime-green shade of his eyes. A sense of vertigo blossomed in her stomach, and she yearned to escape the rocking motion of the deck. She leaned against the gunwale to steady herself.

"Hello? Do you need help?" She didn't know what else to ask. He was too far out to have come from shore.

He opened his mouth, and the shockingly physical melody that had driven her to the side swelled louder.

Her core tightened with surprising intensity, deliciously orgasmic. The scientist in her distantly wondered if orgasm by auditory stimulation was even possible. Then stopped analyzing and allowed the sensation to sweep her along as if it were a curling green wave. Her nipples pebbled against her shirt and warmth pooled deep in her belly. She gripped both hands on the lip of the gunwale, legs trembling.

The man dove, revealing what looked like a lacy green dorsal fin along his spine. A bright green tail followed, the billowing fin sending a shower of water her direction. She blinked, regaining a fleeting moment of scientific curiosity. *Had that been...? No way.* Then the song changed back into that bone-deep rhythm, rising through the deck, through her legs. Pounding against her pelvis as if a man thrust deep inside her.

Inhaling sharply, she threw back her head, lost in the ecstasy. The tide of primal sensation overwhelmed her logic. Every inch of her skin thrilled with electric desire, and she ached to be touched. Now.

Her hand crept to her breast, fondled her nipple to an aching peak. She needed more. She needed this man, who was somehow calling up her basest emotions. Leaning over, one hand on the gunwale while the other still pinched her nipple, she peered into the water. Where'd he gone?

His face appeared directly below, rising to meet her. A pair of lime-green eyes bored into hers with a come-hither purpose to match the vibrations in her bones. She stretched forward, heeding the call.

He broke the surface and met her lips with his. The contact sent her spiraling into climax. Her grip on the gunwale fell slack, and she plunged past him into the icy water.

◆◆◆

THE HUMAN'S lips met Rubac's in a jolt like an electric eel.

Stunned, he dropped back into the water, thoughts colliding like flotsam caught in a riptide. His cock prodded the opening of his sheath, as if waking from a long dream.

What was that all about? Was it part of the quest? The human contact had been nothing like the connection he'd expected.

129

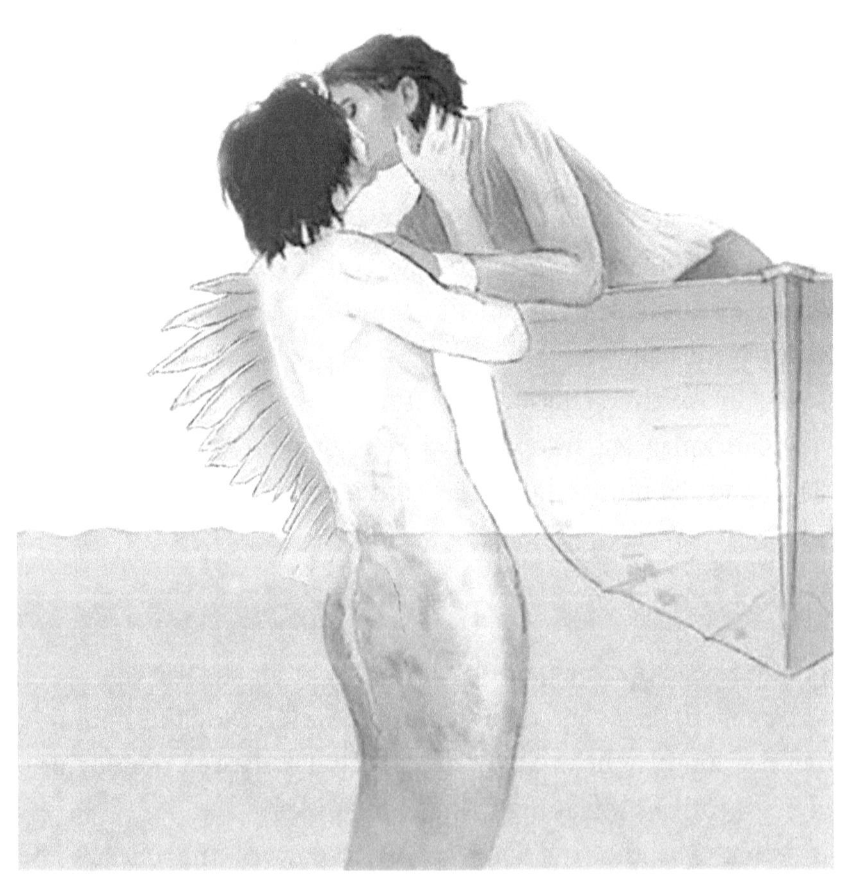

When the mermaid had captured and bonded him, he'd felt a tightening, as if his whole body was constricted by kelp strands. A chain tying him to his bond-mate for eternity. What he'd just experienced with the human felt more like the exhilaration of riding a sailfish as it cleared the water.

Then he realized her limp body was sinking past him, limbs askew. A thin wisp of blood trailed her wake.

He jackknifed and caught her, carrying her limp form to the surface. She must've hit her head when she fell. Should he take her to his nest and finish what he'd started? It seemed wrong to take advantage of her when she was unconscious. Doubly wrong after mesmerizing her with song.

Wrapping an arm around her waist, he hauled her to the boat. The back of the vessel had a platform next to the motor, and he managed to leverage himself up. He clutched her to his chest and pulled her onto the deck where she sprawled on top of him. Her shoulder crushed the sea harp between them, shattering the delicate tines.

His entire body tightened. Without the harp's aid, his task would be more difficult. Maybe impossible. Definitely more dangerous.

Rolling out from under her weight, he pushed himself up on one elbow to look at her. Although lacking a mermaid's exotic flair, the human seemed attractive enough. The contours of her breasts pressed against the fabric of her shirt with nothing in between, and the curve of her waist rounded pleasantly to her hips.

She lay sprawled and uncomfortable-looking across the hard surface. How did these humans stand it, being weighted like this all their lives? He passed a hand over her heart, verifying her life aura still occupied her body. There it was, a yellow glow mixed with rich brown and pale orange. The information in that glow intrigued him; she was a seeker of knowledge, like him.

He pulled back with a shiver. He should finish what he started or flee before she roused. But curiosity compelled him to examine her just a bit longer. He'd only been this close to a human once before, a brief interaction when his brother had been captured in a mate bond by one. Rubac sometimes spied on the couple from a distance as they walked—his brother walked!—on a beach, but he'd never approached. Now he allowed himself to inspect the close details of this human's skin. He liked the simplicity of her short, wind-rough hair, generous lips, and smooth, flat nose. A small gold stud gleamed from the crease of her nostril, complimenting her velvety brown skin. The wet fabric of her button-down shirt molded against her breasts, her hard brown nipples begging for his caress. Her flat stomach descended to a V where her legs met, and he found himself curious about what he might find there, so different from a mermaid's vulval slit.

She stirred, and he dragged his gaze back to her face. Large brown eyes blinked at him, and with the wall previously created by her sunglasses gone, he found himself falling into the depths of her soul. A warm and curious comfort, like finding a kindred spirit after being eternally alone.

"Who are you?" Her aura was tinged with confusion and the pink threads of attraction.

Without thinking, he lowered his face and kissed her.

The stranger's lips moved against hers so skillfully, Madison didn't think. She closed her eyes and responded. Her hand clutched his biceps, his muscles bulging as he supported his weight above her, skin warm and slick with seawater. Lingering heat from her orgasm flared again. His body pressed against hers, and she found herself arching toward him, drawing him closer.

He responded by curling a hand through the hair at the back of her neck and tilting her head to deepen the kiss. His mouth tasted of salt and a hint of ginger spice as he plunged his tongue between her teeth. Her panties flooded with an explosion of heat between her thighs.

She sucked in a breath, stunned at the insane reaction her body had to him. This man was a complete stranger, and she didn't even care. In her whole life, she'd never been kissed like this, ignited like this. She didn't want it to end, refused to go back to the logic that usually ruled her life. For once she felt primal. Unpredictable. Wild.

Raking her hand off his biceps, she clawed at his ribs, finally settling on his hip. His erection pressed insistently between them, and she wanted him like she'd never wanted anyone before. She crushed her pelvis against him, delighted by his groan against her lips. His hand left her neck and cupped her ass, kneading it a moment before sliding up her side to find her breast. Sensation rocketed through her nipple, as if it had been aching for his touch all her life, and orgasmic electricity shot downward to pool in her abdomen.

Her right hand, partially trapped between them, snaked lower to brush the head of his cock, surprised to find him already exposed, already naked. The throbbing member pulsed at her touch. She wanted to see him. Wanted to experience him with every sense. She opened her eyes and was met by unnaturally lime-green eyes in a face that could serve a Greek god, with chiseled brow and dark, stubbled beard.

He pulled back, broke the contact of their lips, and stared down at her. Reason niggled its way into her brain. *Where had this man come from?*

She reached up to touch his cheek, and alarm fleeted across his face. With both hands he shoved away from her. A whoosh of cool air separated them like a knife. He rolled, grabbed the nearest gunwale, and disappeared over the side. She was left blinking at a lingering impression of a bright green tail.

Bolting upright, she knelt to peer over the side. *Tail?* But she'd been kissing a man. The two images didn't belong together. Mermen didn't exist.

Yet her lips still tingled from his kisses.

RUBAC PLUNGED through the water like a harpoon from a hunter's hand, a tether of lust trailing behind him. Why had he fled? It shouldn't matter if she knew what he was. He needed to kill her anyway. If he wanted to be free of the mate-bond, he had the second part of his quest to finish. But for some reason, the question in the human's eyes, the shift in her aura, had broken through his driving need. Reminded him of who he was.

What the human thought of him mattered. He didn't want her to see him as a monster. Even if he was about to be one by killing her.

How could his entire being now hunger for a woman who was not his mate? For a human? Was this insatiable urge what mermaids felt all the time, what drove them to seek out new lovers again and again in spite of a dedicated man waiting at home? Yet he didn't want other humans. He wanted the one right above him. Halting his descent, he rubbed his fingers over his meditation bracelet, seeking calmness. Seeking guidance. The desire boiling within him made him feel like an animal. His quest wasn't supposed to be like this. It was supposed to be a chore. A burden. Done quickly and forgotten. Yet here he was, lurking beneath the boat's shadow while his balls throbbed with need inside their protective sheath.

Settle down. You simply haven't been around a female in a while.

How did mermaids do this on a regular basis? Would it be like this every time he met a human? A note of anger ripped from his throat, sending a nearby school of señorita fish scattering. He was breaking apart. He wanted this woman more than anything he'd ever wanted in his life. Depths, why did he want her so bad? It had to be the damned fish harp song. It had captured him as much as it had the human. But the song was over, the fish harp broken. Its affects should be long finished. Why wasn't it fading?

Swimming in a tight circle directly beneath the hull, he fought the urge to surface. To caress those perfect breasts and kiss that warm brown skin. To sink his cock deep within her heated core. His entire body thrummed with need. *You're going to get yourself killed,* he thought. She'd seen him. Was likely waiting with a weapon. Her kind was dangerous. Apex predators. They'd hunted merfolk since the sundering of Atlantis. Mermaids hunted their men in return. There was no love between the species. Why was he drawn to her so strongly? He felt as if the fish harp had been used on him instead of by him.

Dread pooled into his stomach. What if it had? What if instead of freeing himself, he'd just lured himself toward a second mate-bond? Impossible. Mermen bonded for life to a single mate. No, it had to be the strength of the fish harp's song. That was all. He would approach her again, this time without magic, and finish the quest. It was either that or succumb to his impending deterioration toward insanity and death.

Seducing the human without magic would be tricky, however. Simply swimming up and having his way with her was not a safe option. He'd have to appeal to her other desires—assuming she didn't have a weapon. He knew from her aura she sought knowledge. She'd have questions about him and his kind. Perhaps he could lure her with that. Get close enough to pull her into the water...

No. He rubbed his index finger over his vision rod. Pulling

her in would frighten her. He didn't want to rape her. He wanted to seduce her. She needed to be comfortable. Confident. He had to take himself to her world. Allow her to see him. Touch him.

He'd have to seduce her using himself as bait.

$\mathcal{M}$adison remained frozen, staring at the water where that perfect specimen of a man had disappeared. A fantasy with abs like a washboard, shoulders like a gymnast… and a tail like a fish.

Her head swam and her legs felt almost too weak to stand. Had any of that really just happened? Lifting a hand to her forehead, she felt the lump there. She'd had worse. Certainly the injury wasn't enough to cause hallucinations? Strong hallucinations could elicit a physiological response. Her fingertips moved to her lips, tracing her swollen flesh while she examined the smear of blood on her palm from three tiny pinpricks. His fin had been sharp. Both were real enough.

A breeze off the water sent a rush of goosebumps over her skin through her wet clothing. On trembling legs, she rose and moved into the semi-protected space around the pilot's chair. Before stripping down, she scanned the surrounding water, but the glittering surface refused to reveal its secrets. She shivered again, needing to get warm.

Peeling out of her pants, she dropped onto the swivel seat in only her panties while she wrung seawater from her clothes. Doubt crept in. Mermen didn't exist. Every nerve in her scientist body denied the possibility, in spite of her tingling lips and bleeding hand. She flung her clothes over the seat next to her to dry. Yet if it had been a dream, it was the most realistic dream ever. She yearned to feel his body against hers again and finish what they'd started.

Ducking into the tiny cabin under the boat's foredeck, she struggled into fresh clothing, her skin sticky with saltwater. She'd definitely gone over the side. And somehow gotten back on board. There could be no scientific explanation for that. So exactly what had happened? And why had the stranger kissed her, gotten her all excited, only to flee?

Back on deck, she approached the side where the man or whatever he was had disappeared. The chopping waves still held no sign of him, be he human or merman. A human would've had to come from somewhere—gone to somewhere. But there was no land in sight, no vessels. An underwater habitat? A submarine?

She bent over the edge to look. The memory of a bearded face and disconcertingly green eyes rising out of the depths toward her about knocked her backward. She remembered the pulsing song that had seemed to center directly in her vagina. And she definitely remembered the ravenous impulse to consummate the promise of that song.

Straightening, she ran her fingers through her damp hair, eyes unfocused as she searched her memories. "Worse than a drunk girl at a college frat party," she murmured, shaking her head.

She recalled the thick pressure of his cock against her hip, the velvety surprise of his nakedness beneath her fingers. Of course he was naked. Mermen didn't wear clothes.

She licked her lips, realizing what she was thinking. What she couldn't deny. She'd kissed a merman. She darted a look around the boat, half expecting a grad student to pop up and say "gotcha." But of course she was alone. This discovery was her own. It was real.

Her heart thundered against her ribs. A hybrid dolphin would be chump change compared to documenting a merman. Unprecedented. Yet claiming the discovery of a merman would make her more of a laughingstock than she already was if she didn't gather irrefutable proof. She took a moment and logged her coordinates on her GPS. Would he come back? Why had he come to her in the first place? Certainly not just for a kiss. He had wanted something, but what?

About all she knew of mermaids were old wives' tales of them seducing men to watery graves. Yet he hadn't taken her with him over the side. In fact, he'd pulled her out of the ocean and put her back on deck. She would've surely drowned without him. No, he couldn't mean to harm her. He just wanted…

Her pussy tightened, thinking of what he wanted. Or was that what *she* wanted? After all, he'd left without finishing what he'd started. Why? Tiny electric jolts pricked her nipples as she remembered the absolute magic of his kiss, the tantalizing grip of his hand on her neck, on her ass, cupping her breast. Good Lord, if she kept thinking like this, she was going to need to finish what he'd started by herself.

Research. She needed to focus on research. Proving the existence of a merman would be the find of the century. She needed to keep her wits right now, not be thinking of her vagina. She had to plan her strategy. Not think about how good it would feel to wrap her legs around his hips, press her breasts against that sculpted torso…

Stop it. She picked up the biopsy gun and tucked it into her waistband. Stuffed her small camera into the breast pocket of her shirt. She had to be ready for anything. Her data had to be comprehensive. Tissue samples. DNA. Maybe she could devise a way to capture the creature if it came back, a net of some kind...

She froze, realizing what she was thinking. Was he a creature, or a man? Part of him was definitely all man. She was about to set a precedent for how he was treated by the rest of humanity.

Maybe I should just fuck him. How's that for precedent? Her pussy tightened in agreement.

But seriously, if he did come back, what was she supposed to do?

Talk to him. Could he talk? If he could, she would film the conversation. Document first contact. Well, second contact, but who was counting?

Grabbing a folding chair, she settled in to wait for her fantasy lover to reappear.

Madison didn't know how, but she was looking directly at the spot when he resurfaced. He rose silently, cautiously approaching from about a hundred feet away with the afternoon light behind him and the water glittering all around. Swallowing, she pulled her camera from her pocket, aimed it, and hit record. Then she rose and approached the gunwale.

"Hello!" Her voice wavered, and she swallowed again. Could he speak English? Could he speak at all? He was magnificent, broad shoulders, glistening tanned-gold skin. But from here she could see no tail. No sign he was anything other than human.

He paused his approach around thirty feet out. "Greetings." His deep voice rolled across the water like the promise of a storm.

Thank God, he can speak! She checked the camera's view screen to be sure she was capturing him. "My name's Madison. What's yours?"

"Rubac."

"Are you… what are you?"

The wind had picked up with the falling sun, and his torso rose and fell with the roll of the sea, yet never exposed what lay beneath. "Your kind would call me a merman."

Waves slapped the hull loudly. She prayed the audio was capturing his words. "Can I… can I see you?"

He smiled, then bent into a dive. A spiked green dorsal fin cut the air, followed by an emerald tail. She gripped the gunwale to support her suddenly weak legs. The roll of the deck had never felt so unsteady. "You're real."

"Now it's your turn," he said, drawing nearer.

She frowned. "My turn? What do you mean?"

"I want to see you," he rumbled. The cool bite of the breeze alerted her that her panties were wet. They grew even wetter when he commanded, "Take off your shirt."

For the first time, it occurred to her that this man could mean her harm. She was alone out here. Her stomach tightened and her free hand flew to cover her chest. "Are you…" She swallowed. "Why?"

He dropped his gaze, as if shy, and sank into the waves until only his head was exposed. "I am curious about you, too."

She licked her lips, gaze remaining on him. He was curious, too. Fair enough. What was the harm in showing him? She'd never had issues with her own body. Didn't wear a bra unless she had to. Wasn't wearing one now, in fact. She could edit the audio out of the video later, and no one need know what she'd done. Besides, she wanted his eyes on her. Wanted a lot more than that, actually.

Setting the still-recording camera on the gunwale, she looped the wrist strap around a fishing pole grommet and then stood to face him. The bite of the evening breeze made her hyper-aware of her own skin as she lifted her shirt slowly over her head. His hungry gaze sent tiny thrills racing along her sides and pooled in a mass of heat in her belly.

To her gratification, more of him appeared above the waves, water running off his arms and ribs in glistening rivulets. His nipples were hard, perfect circles in the center of nearly square pecs. Damn, she'd never seen a human man who could rival his chest and abs. She wondered what the lower half of him really looked like.

She allowed the fabric to slide sensually off her arms and fall to the deck. Her nipples hardened as if inviting his hands to tease the peaks. Jutting her chin, she said, "Your turn."

He smiled and put both hands behind his head, then leaned back until he floated face up on the surface. His shining green tail stroked the water with leisurely sensuality, the fin at the bottom a wide, rippling fan. Yet in spite of the fascination his tail had for her, what caught her most was what lay just below his navel, rising from a slit where his tanned abs merged into his bright green tail. His engorged cock seemed to pulse in response to her attention. He stroked one hand along his length and she shivered.

She forced her gaze to his face, her pussy aching in primal reply to his display. Her breathing quickened to little panting gasps. *Focus, Madison. You're a scientist, not a teenager looking for a hookup.* Shaking her head, as if she could clear it of hormones, she remembered the camera. She readjusted its view and tightened the loop of the wrist strap around the grommet. Her gaze returned to the magnificent creature in the water, abs and chest glistening in the sun and muscular tail leaving a wake behind him.

And then she realized—no matter how spectacular the footage, it would never be believed without accompanying data. Photos could be manipulated. She'd need skin samples at the very least. DNA. Blood. Her biopsy gun was still tucked into her waistband. *The moment you draw it, he'll flee.* Maybe she could convince him to come on deck with her and even freely give a sample or two. *Break the ice. Ask him some questions.*

"So, Rubac. Do you come here often?" Great. She was resorting to B-rate pickup lines.

He drifted closer until he floated right alongside the hull. "I am a long way from home."

"What's your usual habitat?" Better. Keep it scientific. But his engorged cock was damned distracting.

"Merfolk range the entire ocean."

"I've lived much of my life on the ocean." She crossed her arms. "I've never seen one."

He shrugged. "We choose not to be seen."

"Why choose to be seen now, then?" She narrowed her eyes, mistrust skittering up her spine. "And how do you know my language?"

"We sing many songs under the water. Communicate in many ways." His tail flicked, and he did a barrel roll, then ducked under the water. Quick as lightning, he reemerged closer to the boat. "What else would you like to know?"

Her heart increased to a thunderous pace. "Will you come on deck and let me look at you?"

His lips spread into a grin. "Take off your pants. Let me look at you first."

A shiver rolled through her. He wanted to keep playing? Fine. She'd play. She splayed both palms over her naked belly in what she hoped was a sensual manner and inched them inward to unfasten the button at her waist. His lime-green eyes followed her hands hungrily. She opened the zipper and slid one hand into the opening, cupping herself, making an intentional whimper of pleasure as her fingertip contacted her throbbing clit.

His mouth parted slightly, tongue peeking forth. Just imagining that tongue on her clit made her insides tighten. His gaze lifted to meet hers. "Off," he said.

She pushed the waistband down around her hips, suddenly self-conscious of her plain cotton panties. Would a merman notice her lack of sexy lingerie? Her pants pooled around her ankles, and his gaze raked her up and down greedily. *Guess not.* Swallowing, she said, "Okay, they're off. You said you'd come aboard."

He swam to the aft. Realizing she needed to capture this moment on film, she dragged her gaze from him and grabbed the camera, focusing it on the gunwale. The boat rocked beneath his weight, and a muscular heave of his shoulders lifted him with surprising agility. He cleared the edge, bringing along a surge of seawater.

The deck wasn't very spacious to begin with, and she was standing close, intending to capitalize on the proximity to document him. His flashing tail doused her with water. Worse, it tagged the camera, ripping it from her hands and flipping it over the side. "No!" she screamed, flailing for it. But it was too late. The camera and all its documentation sank out of sight.

She turned to see him poised as if to roll backward into the sea once again. His triceps and lats bulged, tail fin pressed flat against the deck. His green eyes bored into her with uncertainty.

She forced herself to smile and held up both hands in peace, even though her insides roiled. The video was gone, but she had the real deal right in front of her. An opportunity to get much more than footage. *Don't scare him away.* "My fault. I should have given you more room."

His arms relaxed, and he eased to a sitting position on the deck with his back against the inside hull. His jewel-bright tail stretched toward her, fin resting only inches from her toes. This close, its bright green looked almost fake. She let her gaze travel up from his fin to where his crotch would be. His cock had receded back into its sheath, but the bulge remained there as evidence of its location. She realized she'd been focused on that spot too long and glanced up to see his lime-green eyes full of mirth.

"You may touch me if you like."

Flushing, she squatted to run her fingertips over his fin. It twitched beneath her touch, the edges curling up around her hand in a return caress. Her skin tingled at the contact, so innocuous, and yet somehow suggestive at the same time. "I can't believe I'm touching a real merman."

"I can't believe I'm being touched by a real human."

The deep timbre of his voice seemed to caress her very bones, eliciting a primitive response she could no more have controlled than she could control her heartbeat. She became acutely aware of her bare breasts, of a heat between her legs, of an itch that needed scratched. Like a sailor at sea too many days in a row, she was ready. Yearning to impale herself on his waiting shaft. And this merman was so very male. Broad chest, washboard abs, and those eyes.

Those eyes that beckoned her come hither at this very moment.

She found herself on her hands and knees, straddling his tail as she crawled up his length. *I want to see where fish meets man,* she rationalized. And his jewelry. She'd always been a sucker for a man with piercings. She kept her eyes on his, drawn forward until she straddled his hips.

Stopping her crawl, she ran her fingers across the mother-of-pearl pin in his nipple.

The merman sucked in a breath, clasped her arms, and drew her into another mind-blowing kiss.

CHAPTER SIX

The moment the human touched his fin, Rubac knew he had her. Her aura had been pink with interest since the moment he'd arrived, but now it spiked with desire, bright scarlet flashes through the gold of her curiosity. He hadn't even needed to use his song. She wanted him.

And he wanted her.

But when she'd stroked his vision rod, his desire had spiked into something deeper. It rose with fury like a summer storm. Any control he thought he'd had vanished. Cupping her face with both hands, he delved into her mouth. She tasted of sweet kombu and a hint of coconut, reminiscent of his days as a single merman when he'd been daring enough to swim close to the volcanic islands around the equator.

She settled her weight on his hips, her heat spreading through his sheath and into his cock. Leaning into him, she matched the intensity of his kiss. He let his hands fall to her hips, kneading her soft flesh. The feel of her legs around him drove him mad with lust. Lifting off the deck with one hand, he flipped so he could lie atop her, flattening his hands on the deck to either side of her shoulders. Her small breasts brushed his chest, and she wriggled to match her pelvis against his. She stroked her palms up his ribs and around his triceps, while her heels digging into his backside made his cock surge against its protective sheath, seeking the call from between her legs.

Without breaking the kiss, he slipped one hand over her nipple, tweaking it as he cupped her naked breast. She arched against him in encouragement. He dropped his caress lower, over her ribs to the curve of her waist. Traced the swell of her hip. He slid his hand between where their hips met, finding thin fabric blocking her opening. He cupped his palm over her mound, curling his fingers toward the heat between her legs.

She whimpered, straining against his hand, fumbling her own down to his waist. She pushed the fabric aside and urged his fingers beneath. Her cleft was slick and ready, her clit engorged and pulsing. He circled the nub gently, her heat drawing him down between the folds and back up again. His cock pulsed insistently where it met her hip.

Still kissing him, she rolled her panties down around her thighs, kicking her legs free. Her pink and crimson aura burned with passion. Engulfing him. Consuming him.

Even if he'd wanted to stop, he couldn't. Her hunger controlled his entire being. What he'd believed would be his triumph had leveled him once again to a slave. His cock was ready, and her legs entrapped him, drew him close. Forced the length of his cock along her slippery opening. Her lower lips seemed to kiss him, promising him the pleasure of her depths. The soft down covering her mound, so different from a mermaid's utter smoothness, added a layer of sensation that about drove him over the edge.

She cupped his face, guided his head downward to a breast. Her dark areola was rigid, nipple engorged and waiting. Careful with his sharp teeth, he licked her flesh, eliciting a small gasp from her. Her back arched. He took first one, then the other between his lips, careful not to break any skin. She shuddered, the cleft against his cock surging with moisture.

"I want you," she pleaded.

Drawing back, he allowed the head of his shaft to tease the opening to her welcoming depths. Her eyes met his, the rich brown irises nearly obscured by black pupils. She nodded, the pressure of her heels digging into his backside, urging him onward.

He plunged forward, the ecstasy of their joining a surging tide that rose like a tsunami in his blood, unseen but inevitable in its power. He buried himself deep inside this woman, this human, rising only to plunge again and again. His building climax rose to almost painful levels, awaiting the crest ahead.

She met him thrust for thrust, her aura shifting from scarlet to purple to radiant white as she stretched for climax alongside him. They both seemed to climb the same wave, reaching the top hand in hand to catch the rolling edge that would drive them forward into rapture.

Her heat pulsed around him, milked him of his seed in a shuddering release. He collapsed to his elbows to lie exhausted over her, heated skin against heated skin. Her breathing matched his own, rough and spent with passion.

He pressed his forehead to hers, his mind muddled with desire. "Beautiful," he sang the word in her language. A yearning to take her beneath the waves and show her this passion again, this time buoyed by the current, rushed through his blood. To show her his nest and fill it with all the treasures and baubles her heart might desire. To sing tales of the sea to amuse her. She had already begun to make him forget how much his heart hurt at the loss of the bond-mate he'd never loved, the child he'd likely never see again. He wanted to defend her and protect her and make her happy. This human made him want to live again, just like his prophetic vision told him.

Then he remembered his quest. Now that he'd seduced her, he had to finish things. Her warm scent filled his head as his fingers tightened into helpless fists against the deck. He was not supposed to feel this way. Killing was supposed to be the easy part.

Muscles trembling, he forced himself up, cursing the weight of his own body. She stared at him, a small crease denting the skin between her eyebrows. "What is it?"

He couldn't face her now. Look into her eyes. Know he was about to betray her. Nerves on fire, he grabbed the nearby gunwale and launched himself back into the sea.

*M*adison rolled over, body suddenly chilled without his warmth, and struggled to her knees to look over the side. Gone, like the stereotypic man after a one-night stand. Was that all he'd wanted? Her chest ached.

So much for scientific research. Her photos were gone. She hadn't gathered skin or blood samples. What was wrong with her?

Her pants lay in a puddle near the engine compartment. Heat flushed her as she remembered sliding them down her thighs, seducing him in. The wind prickled her legs with goose bumps. *Get your head on straight,* she told herself. *First things first, get dressed.* Thinking would be impossible until she established a baseline of comfort.

She picked up her jeans. The wet denim would be worse than being naked. Ducking into the hold where she'd been sleeping the last three days, she pulled out a clean pair of panties. Halfway into them, she paused.

She hadn't taken tissue samples, but there was one bio-sample she had access to.

The warmth still trickling down her thighs.

Her throat felt tight as she opened her biopsy kit for a sterile swab. How could she be so stupid? Unprotected sex? Who knew what kind of diseases mermen carried. And what about pregnancy? Was that even an issue? Her brain spun with questions she had no way to answer.

She ripped open the sterile swab and hesitated. Somehow taking a sample off herself felt like a betrayal. Like she was claiming rape after having completely consensual intercourse. Plus, how was she going to explain the procedure she'd used to gather that sample? *I seduced a merman onto my boat and ravaged him to gather semen for sampling.* Talk about a laughingstock.

Yet the sample would be legitimate whether he was man or fish. Hell, it might be her only sample.

She swabbed herself and placed the sample in an isolation tube before stowing it away. The thought of using her sex life for scientific purposes made her nauseous. He might come back. The thought was silly, she knew. Like waiting for a call the next day that never came. But there was always a chance. Never before had she felt a connection like this to a man. And Rubac had really seemed to be into her, too.

She only had the boat until tomorrow. Should she wait here for him to return, or was she being stupid? Her scientific brain told her to cut her losses. But her heart told her to wait until tomorrow. Nobody had mind-blowing sex like that and just moved on, right?

Rubac had to come back.

THE SEA COOLED Rubac's heated skin and calmed the blood surging through his veins. How could he go through with killing her? *That's why it's a quest,* he told himself. *It's not supposed to be easy.*

But if he killed her, he'd be no better than the mermaids he detested.

He couldn't bear the thought of the human's—Madison's—blood on his hands. She wasn't a deadly predator. She was a seeker of knowledge, like he was. A guest in his ocean. And her aura was as compelling to him as the cleft between her legs.

He floated without purpose, allowing his thoughts to float with him. His time on the surface had dried his skin, and the sun had left behind an uncomfortable prickle. He lifted his arms and spun a lazy spiral through the water, reveling in the current against his skin. The weight of his aura was lighter than it had been in decades, since before being trapped in the mate-bond. He suddenly felt like he could enjoy the sea again.

Sucking refreshing water through his gills, he raced toward a school of señorita fish, circling them until they formed a small silver ball. Diving to the rocky bottom, he teased a flounder from its resting spot in the sand before turning sharply upwards to tickle a sea bass on the belly. It rolled over begging for more.

He'd never felt more alive.

He rolled to his back and gazed upward at the dark speck of the boat at the surface. He searched for any remnant of longing for his dead mate and found nothing. His aura truly felt free. Did he really need to kill a human to break the mate-bond? Or had intimacy been the key to it all?

He felt free. Therefore he was free. The idea brought a smile to his face, and he picked up speed to head back to the kelp beds. Perhaps the whale oracle had purposefully misled him. If the quest had included only seduction, Rubac would have likely never even pursued it, fearing the end would be impossible. Making the seduction merely one step toward a goal had given him a different finish line to focus on and allowed him to complete the task.

Which hadn't really been such a task after all. His cock stirred at the memory of Madison's soft curves and her inviting deep brown eyes. He might even consider engaging her again. He stopped swimming and stared at a dark rock jutting from the sea floor.

Despite his depression when his mate used to leave him, he'd never looked forward to reuniting with her. Sex with her, although pleasurable, had always been a chore. The encounters left him drained, his soul weak and fragile. After her visits, he'd taken days to recover. Mermen believed the post-coital weakness was merely loneliness and yearning for a mate who'd left. But what if it was something more? What if his mate had consumed a small piece of his soul to fortify her own every time she'd visited? Chipped away at his life force until he could no longer survive without her? Had this human encounter renewed his life force?

He held out a hand and squinted to observe his own aura. The usual deep gold-orange spread in a wide band over his skin, veined in strong violet pulses of vitality. Never had he seen his own colors with such clarity. He let out a burst of happy song, startling a nearby school of gobies. He'd broken the bond!

Then another thought occurred to him. This rejuvenating power had to come from somewhere. He hadn't made his soul whole again all on his own. What if he'd stolen this supplemental life force and left Madison as empty and exposed as he'd felt every time his mate left him?

Had this been what the whale meant when it told him to sacrifice the human?

The joy of realizing he didn't need to kill Madison soured. If what he imagined was true, he'd been no better than the mermaids he detested, leaving a lover drained and broken.

The boat's shadow was nowhere in sight now, the once-bright sky deepening over the surface. He recalled the magnificent colors of the human's aura, the bright orangey-yellows that told him she was a seeker like himself. Anxiety twisted his gut, a protective feeling flooding through him like he'd only ever felt for his children. He didn't want to be like his dead mate and the other mermaids, leaving lovers empty and suffering.

Letting out a stream of bubbles, he swept up toward the rolling waves, tail fin thrashing as fast as his muscles allowed. He had to be sure Madison was all right.

CHAPTER EIGHT

Madison adjusted the radio and went to set the anchor. Damn rental place. Keeping the boat another night would forfeit part of her deposit in return for the delay. How she was going to pay next month's rent was beside the point. This had to be the most foolish move she'd ever made—even more foolish than believing in Steller sea cows. But her heart couldn't accept another defeat.

She brought her sleeping bag up from the hold, kicked off her shoes, and arranged a folding chair so she could keep watch over the ocean while she munched on a protein bar and downed an energy drink. She didn't like the things, but she needed to stay awake. The sun was falling into the ocean, creating brilliant neon colors across the horizon. Luckily the moon would be over half full tonight. With her camera gone, she'd have to rely on her phone camera to document images. It only had basic low-light capabilities, and she'd be lucky to get any decent images at all.

She hadn't entirely decided how to proceed if the merman showed back up, but she wasn't about to regret not being ready. One of the biopsy darts rested in her lap, and her phone was on a strap looped around her neck. No way was she risking losing that. She settled into the chair with the sleeping bag bundled tight around her to ward off the evening chill.

Her forehead ached where she'd hit it against the boat, and she had to stop herself from fiddling with the scab. To keep her hands busy, she unloaded and reloaded the dart gun. Took a flash selfie to double check the camera was working, then erased it and turned the flash off for night distance photography. Zipped and unzipped her sleeping bag around her feet to find the perfect temperature balance.

The ocean gleamed blackly beneath a gajillion stars, awaiting a moon that, at the moment, was only a glimmer on the horizon. Today had been a long day, first rising early to chase those dolphins, then the excitement with the merman. What had happened to those dolphins? She wondered if the merman had scared them off. What did mermen eat, anyway?

The thought brought a naughty alternative to mind, and she wondered what his mouth would have felt like eating her out. Her body heated with the thought. Damn, she wanted him. Again. She slowly licked her lips while her nether regions tingled at the memory. This was going to be a long night.

A splash brought her out of her chair. Her heart revved up a notch at a thump against the hull. *He's back.* Breathing hard, she took a step back, aiming her phone—and tripped against her sleeping bag. Her legs went out from under her, and her rear-end hit the deck in a painful jolt. The biopsy dart flew from her grip, but at least the phone remained around her neck.

The moon's low position against the horizon outlined the shadow of a man's head and shoulders peering over the boat's side.

Cursing herself for turning the flash off, she fumbled in the dark with the settings. She hadn't anticipated getting him this close so fast.

A baritone voice cut through the night. "Your aura is pale. I apologize."

Her finger hovered over the camera button. "Apologize?"

"That I took from you."

She lowered the phone, not wanting to scare him off with the flash. If she took a picture now, all she'd get was his human half over the gunwale, anyway. "What did you take?"

"You do not feel it?"

She shook her head. "Feel what?"

"Your aura is diminished. I do not wish to leave you damaged."

Aura? What the hell was he talking about? She unzipped the sleeping bag and slipped free, never taking her eyes from the merman. His head dipped below the gunwale like he was about to leave. She reached out a pleading hand. "Please don't go!"

He slowly rose back into view, the deck heaving beneath his weight.

Rolling onto her knees, she crept closer. *Keep him talking.* "How many of your kind are there?"

"Few." His voice grew husky at her approach. It reminded her of their earlier encounter, weakening her legs with remembered bliss.

"Will you come back on deck?"

He hesitated, his shadow motionless in the moonlight. Then

he vaulted over the edge as he had this afternoon, sending a shower of seawater over her head.

She could barely breathe. Her hands were locked around the phone and yet seemed unable to move. *He's four feet away, for Christ's sake! Take the picture!* Still she waited. The thought of scaring him away with a photo made her feel hollow inside.

"Why did you come to me?" She inched forward, her breathing shallow.

The waves lapped at the hull rhythmically as he seemed to consider. His voice thrummed low enough to vibrate the deck supporting her. "I needed a cure." He stretched a hand toward her breast, stopping just short of touching her. For a moment she swore his whole body flashed deep violet. He dropped the hand. "I will not take from you again, Madison."

He turned to grasp the gunwale.

Sure she would lose her chance forever, she lunged. Her hands wrapped around his hips and her weight dragged him back to the deck with a bone-jarring thump. Quickly, before he could recover, she scrambled to pin his arms. "I'm not done talking to you."

He flexed, easily lifting her upward, as if to prove she couldn't hold him. Then he relaxed, lying there unresisting. The moon had risen high enough to pour light onto the deck, and his eyes glinted at her with fiery green and purple light. She was suddenly very aware of her crotch resting against his firm abs.

A slow smile lifted the corners of his mouth, and the tip of his tongue slipped out to caress his upper lip. Damn, this man was the most sex-charged creature she could ever imagine. She breathed out a sigh. He lifted his chin as if reveling in a tropical breeze. His voice rumbled from his chest and straight into her core with shocking intensity. "You are a confusing female."

Her grip on his arms trembled, like her bones wanted to turn to jelly. "Well, you're an intriguing male. Please tell me you won't leave until we're done talking."

"I'm apparently at your command." He arched one eyebrow.

Loosing her grip, she remained straddling his torso.

He shifted beneath her, lowering his arms so his palms rested on her hips, and his thumbs circled the sensitive hollows on either side of her abdomen. Eddies of desire rocketed down her thighs. *Don't be sidetracked by hormones again.* He was being disingenuous at best. Answering her with ambiguous riddles about auras and shit. She hardened her heart, cutting a look across the deck to search for the biopsy dart she'd dropped. It lay lodged against one leg of her folding chair several feet away.

"Your aura changes color as frequently as a cuttlefish." He seemed amused by her. "Tell me what you seek now, Madison."

Her gaze snapped back to him guiltily. Swallowing, she decided to tell him the truth. "I want to document you."

"What do you mean?"

"Write a story about you." She considered how she might tactfully request a sample of his flesh.

"Ah." He nodded approval. "You keep the myths."

Her pulse pounded in her throat. "Not myths. Science. Truth." Proving merpeople existed would first and foremost have to disprove the myth. And with her reputation, the scientific world would seek every opportunity to debunk her. No matter how much data she gathered, there would be those who insisted it was a hoax. Yet how could she not try, with a specimen right here in her hands? Between her legs... She shook her head to clear it. "If you'll let me take a tissue sample, I can try to prove you're not a myth."

His hands clenched her hips. "You want humans to hunt us again."

She dropped her hands to cover his, horror chilling her veins. "No! Never hunt."

"I cannot let you write a story about me." Faster than she could respond, he flipped her over and lay atop her, face mere centimeters from hers. Now it was her turn to have her hands trapped against the deck.

For whatever reason, she wasn't afraid of him. If he'd wanted to hurt or kill her, he could have done it long ago. His proximity ignited tiny fires in her nipples. She resisted the urge to wrap her legs around him. "What are you going to do?"

A throaty growl tumbled from his mouth. "I do not wish to harm you."

"Then help me," she begged.

"I cannot give you what you ask."

She grimaced, angry at herself for the burning tears rising into her eyes. "I have to go back with data to publish. I can't continue to be a laughingstock."

His grip on her softened. "You were not out here to find me. Perhaps I can help you finish what you started."

"Only if you know where to find a wild hybrid dolphin."

"You mean K'kee'ei." The name was a perfect imitation of a dolphin's chatter. "You wish to hunt dolphins, then."

Although he kept his weight off her chest, she found it suddenly hard to breathe. "You know the dolphin I'm talking about? I don't mean to harm it. Only record its parentage."

"A genealogy?"

"Of sorts, yes."

"You will not harm her?"

"No. I only want photos and measurements." Hope

reignited. The scientific community would more easily accept documentation of a new hybrid. Perhaps with Rubac's help, she could capture video footage to go with the hard data of tissue samples. "And a skin sample. That might sting, but won't actually cause harm."

He seemed to consider her for a moment. "Your aura is truthful." He rolled off her, staying close but no longer preventing her from moving. "If you promise not to tell the story of my visit, at first light I will help you find K'kee'ei."

A smile lit Madison's features, and any trepidation Rubac might have had about helping her melted away. She reached out and rested a hand on his chest, the contact warm and inviting directly over his heart. Her voice was husky with excitement as she said, "Really? Thank you."

Her touch set his blood on fire, igniting instincts he had no business feeling. He still feared damaging her aura, stealing her spirit. But she let out a breathy moan, her gaze raking his lips and downward... Desire for her exploded into need. His urges couldn't be denied, not when his chest tingled from the contact of her hand and his craving to feel more of her wrapped around him consumed him.

He curled his fingers behind her neck and opened his mouth to her, exploring her with his tongue. His other hand found her breast, the cotton top rough against his palm. He shoved the fabric up to reach her bare skin. He needed more. He slid his hand around her ribs and over her lower back, into the back of her pants to cup her bottom. She moaned against his mouth.

Deep in his soul he fretted that he was making a mistake, stealing from her, taking more than he could give. He pressed her backward against the deck, stretching over her, cradling her head as she toppled backward to the hard surface. She looped her arms about him and hooked both legs around his hips, allowing his cock to settle against the hollow of her heat. The move assured him she didn't sense a drain. She wanted him as much as he wanted her.

He broke the kiss and skimmed his lips across her jaw until he reached her ear. Catching the tender lobe between his teeth, he gently nibbled. A shudder ran through her body. He hummed deeply, touching her aura with the vibration of his voice, and another shudder ran through her. He moved his hand to her cloth-covered sex, relishing the dampness soaking through.

His cock jerked, jealous of his fingers. He wanted to lose himself in her. But he needed to slow it down, make sure he gave as much or more than he took. That was the key to this joining. Ensuring the lovemaking was a sublime exchange of energy circling in a never-ending flow of pleasure between them.

He again slid his hand beneath the waistband of her pants, this time in front, and pushed aside the thin panties covering her lower lips. She was slick and ready, raising her hips to him with urgent need. He circled her opening. The heat and warmth there made him growl in anticipation. He pushed two fingers into her body and she gasped.

Her hands fluttered down to unfasten the clasp, to shove the restrictive clothing off and away. He pulled free and rolled aside to watch her fumble with the fabric, amusement tumbling amidst his desire.

She turned back to him, gloriously naked legs now free, the downy mound of her sex exposed to his hungry gaze. Her eyes shifted down to where his cock waited, free of its sheath, burning for her touch. But he needed to see to her pleasure first. To ensure she came away full and satiated. "Not yet. I want to watch you come," he said.

Her gaze flicked back up to meet his, a protest on her lips. He surged forward and claimed them before she could speak. His hand once again found her opening, seeking her slippery depths. He curled his fingers and stroked her core, reveling in the way her body shuddered and she tightened around him in juicy response. He added a third finger and pumped them into her body, stroking her until her arousal soaked his hand. Her breaths quickened. Each inhale lifted her breasts, pushing erect nipples against the thin shirt. In and out he slid his fingers, adjusting the speed and angle of his thrusts to carry her to the edge.

Each time her sex quivered and her breathing hitched, he changed the depth, delaying her release. He wanted her to be at full potential when she came. Her aura sparked and flared with crimson sunbursts as her arousal crested, reaching an almost blinding hot level.

"Rubac, please," she rocked against his hand.

Still, he wanted to drive her to higher heights. He replaced his fingers with his tongue. She tasted sweet and earthy, her folds melting with her own rich juices. He slid both hands beneath her bottom and kissed her deeply, exploring her completely. Her glistening short curls tickled his nose and surrounded him with her delicious scent. He focused on exciting her, watching the pulse of her aura across her skin.

"Say you're mine," he rumbled against her sex, and shook his head to increase the rhythm of his stimulation.

"Yes, anything. Yes!" She bucked and strained, and he clenched his hands beneath her butt cheeks to help her impale herself on his tongue.

He rumbled again, letting the sound creep up his throat, reveling in the way she shuddered in response. She was perfect. So perfect. He let the vibration of his voice seep into her sensitive lips and carry her higher.

"Oh, there, please, there."

He flickered his tongue inside her, feeling the slight change in the muscles of her core. She was close. Ready to tip over the edge. He wanted to join her. Withdrawing his tongue, he slithered up to bring them face-to-face, holding himself above her to look into her eyes. Her wonderfully melting brown eyes.

She once again flung her legs around him, straining her hips up to meet his thrust. He entered her, encasing himself to the hilt in her heat. Her breath escaped on a shaky sigh. Still looking into her eyes, he pulled back and entered again, slowly, purposefully. Deeply. In and out, hips meeting hips, he pounded into her, a steady drive into her tightening core.

Her aura flashed white and hot with the first ripples of her orgasm. His cock seemed to respond by swelling larger and harder, counteracting her pulsing core. He drove into her again and again, watching her arch her head back and surrender to the ecstasy, until his own release met hers in an almost surprising explosion of pleasure that left him reeling. He pumped his seed deeply into her, every muscle quivering, until he could hold himself no more and collapsed atop her.

She sighed, her breath tickling his beard and the hair over his ear. With limp hands she stroked his arms and down his ribs, sending tingles of contentment across his skin. He opened his eyes, breathing into her neck. Her skin was slick with sweat, and he kissed her, tasting her salt. Her aura glowed a healthy golden hue, the crimson subsiding to a lingering pink.

He lifted his head looking into her eyes. She grinned back at him, squeezing her arms around his middle. His world contracted to that one, single moment, and he realized he truly was free. Free to do anything and go anywhere. To make his own choices. Be his own man. And in spite of it all he only wanted one thing. "I choose you," he said, and lowered his head to kiss her.

In the two months since meeting Rubac, Madison had lost her apartment, quit her job, and passed up the scientific find of the century. And she'd never been happier. With Rubac's help, she'd filmed a smash-hit documentary about K'Kee'ei and dolphin society. She'd bought a boat and now lived a rogue life on the ocean. And she had a mate who loved the ocean even more than she did. She couldn't think of a better life.

She focused her binoculars on the last place she'd seen Rubac dive, worrying at a fingernail with her teeth. Today they were in pursuit of sharks—well, Rubac was. He'd assured her he could look out for himself, but he'd come back with bruises and lacerations more than a few times during his filming sessions. He could get close to creatures of the sea like no human diver ever could, and she'd already sold the rights to a second film.

Her career as a marine documentary film-maker had more than overcome the stigma of her university paper, but the opinions of the scientific community were the last things she cared about anymore. She'd never thought her greatest find would be this man—a being so special she would never, ever share him with the rest of the world. She now spent her days at sea filming or making love, sometimes on deck and sometimes in the water.

A dark head broke the water about a hundred yards away, and Rubac cleared the surface like a dolphin as he plunged back toward the boat.

"Hey, take it easy on the equipment!" she called, grimacing every time he hit the water. Waterproof didn't mean unbreakable, and if he damaged it, she'd have to spend time on shore to fix it.

He reached the side and held the camera up for her to retrieve before catapulting himself onto the deck. "They gave me a run for it today."

She set the camera aside and checked his muscular frame for cuts or bruises. "I don't like you taking chances."

He caught her hand and pressed the palm to his lips. "Taking chances is the only way to be free."

She leaned in, stroking his bearded cheek. Her nipples tingled at his nearness, and she lifted her knee over him to straddle his tail. He'd told her his brother had magically developed legs after bonding to a human, but Rubac never would. Legs were only possible with the magic of a mating bond, and Rubac's bonded mate was dead. But Madison didn't mind. Their love was real. He'd chosen her, not been forced by magic.

Besides, tail or legs, she'd never had a man as capable of pleasuring her as Rubac.

He grinned and rolled her to her back, pushing open the

folds of her water-soaked sarong. His gaze caressed her exposed belly and settled at the apex of her thighs. She opened her legs to expose more, and his eyes darkened. He slid his hands along her sides, covering her with his body. His hands slid beneath her buttocks, and in one, swift thrust, he plunged into her willing folds.

The sudden fullness made her gasp and buck, her inner walls pulsing deliciously around his cock. She locked her legs around his hips, drawing him deeper.

Rubac closed his eyes and bared his teeth in exquisitely restrained pleasure. "What you do to me, human."

He rolled his hips, sliding against her clit and making her vision waver. Lifting her head, she captured his mouth in a kiss. He returned it, plunging his tongue inside her with a matching rhythm to his slow, rolling thrusts.

She moaned, straining against him, on the verge of climax. He always managed to get her there so fast and could play her body with masterful intent. He continued kissing and pumping, in and out, intensifying the friction until the pressure inside Madison grew to impossible heights.

Her orgasm sparked like lightning and rolled through her like thunder, taking away everything except the here and now. He continued slamming into her, his muscles flexing and bunching as she came around him. A gush of heat filled her as he found his own release, sending another shock of pleasure to her middle that left her quivering.

He stilled, breathing hard and ragged as he supported himself on his elbows nose-to-nose with her. She opened eyes she hadn't realized she'd closed to find his emerald green ones staring into her soul.

"I love you forever, Madison."

She smiled in contentment. "I love you forever too, Rubac."

THE BOAT CAST A LONG, inky shadow over the water's surface in the moonlight. Rubac bobbed next to the gunwale, staring at his brother standing on deck. *Legs.* The sight still boggled Rubac.

A toddler's laugh bubbled from inside the boat's cabin, and soft, feminine laughter followed. Brianna and Madison were having something they called "girl time," cooing over Zantu's offspring. A *female* offspring. Unheard of among mer-children, who remained genderless until puberty.

Rubac was still in a bit of shock over the unexpected reunion. Madison'd tracked down Brianna and Zantu during her most recent trip to shore and returned with surprise guests. She'd proven over and over that human females were not like mermaids. Even now, the women laughed with an easy camaraderie in complete opposition to the vicious pecking order formed in mermaid covens.

Zantu stepped out of his shorts and tossed them on one of the cushioned seats next to the gunwale. "Ebby's been coming to see me." His deep voice sounded different in the air, rougher and less singsong than it did beneath the waves. "Since before she chose her gender."

"Depths! And you didn't think to tell me my child was sneaking out unprotected?" Rubac placed a palm flat against the hull to keep a swell from shoving him against it.

Zantu slanted a look at him, silver eyes gleaming in the moonlight. "You haven't exactly been available to chat since I took a mate."

A flush of regret washed over Rubac. Although he'd spied on

his brother since the mating, he'd never approached the shore, uncertain if human females were as benign as Zantu claimed. Now that he'd been with Madison, he had to acknowledge Zantu had been correct. Madison was loyal and kind and gave to him in ways he hadn't even realized he needed. He imagined Brianna was the same for Zantu.

The child's laughter exploded from the cabin and tiny feet pattered across the deck. Zantu caught the tiny figure before it reached the gunwale. "Camilla, you're supposed to be asleep."

"'Wim!" Camilla thrust a chubby hand toward the water where Rubac floated.

"It's too late for a swim. You can tomorrow." Although Zantu could shift between land and sea forms with apparent ease, he said the child had not yet exhibited any ability to form a tail.

Camilla wailed and buried her face against Zantu's shoulder.

Madison rushed from the cabin. "Sorry, she's faster than I expected."

Brianna followed right behind her. She reached for the child. "I've got her."

Mermaids had little maternal instinct and usually abandoned their babies to the father within days of giving birth, but Brianna comforted the child with graceful ease. Rubac's gaze flicked to Madison, and he wondered if she'd care for a child like that. Would he ever find out?

Madison glanced with obvious discomfort at Zantu's nakedness and moved to the gunwale to direct her gaze at Rubac. "I thought you two would be gone already, playing with the porpoises or whatever it is you plan to do."

It still felt strange to have a female who showed no interest in any man but him. But it pleased him. He said, "We were talking about Ebby."

Camilla's sleepy head shot up, and she looked around. "Ebby?"

"She's not here, little one," Zantu stroked her hair until she settled back against her mother's shoulder.

Madison's brows drew together. "Ebby? As in your daughter?"

Daughter. The word was strange to him, since mer-children were genderless until puberty, but he supposed that was what Ebby was. "It appears she has been stalking my brother's nest."

Brianna shook her head. "I wouldn't call it stalking. She's very polite."

"You raised her well, brother," Zantu added.

Madison speared Rubac with an incredulous look. "You said Ebby had turned into a monster. How can she be visiting Zantu?"

"Mermaids *are* monsters," Rubac replied and scowled at his brother. "You're being incautious. You should relocate your nest."

Zantu shrugged. "After my discussions with Ebby, I don't believe all mermaids have to turn into monsters. Ebby's shown remarkable restraint."

Madison shed the tee shirt she wore over her swimsuit and slipped into the water, pushing herself toward him. "Is it possible you're wrong? Surely she wouldn't harm her own father or the uncle who helped raise her."

"You don't understand," Rubac put his arm around Madison's waist and drew her close, supporting her in the water next to him. "Ebby's not human. Or a child. She's a mermaid. They can't resist their vicious female natures, even around their own sires or uncles."

His chest tightened as he recalled all the years he'd found joy in being Ebby's father. The child had been his only comfort each time his mate abandoned him to seek out other men. Ebby'd been strong through his weakness. It shouldn't have surprised him that she chose to be female.

Madison looped her arms around his neck. "Regardless of her chosen gender, she's still the child you raised. I'm sure she loves you."

Despite his sincere belief Ebby was lost to him, he felt a glimmer of hope; Madison had that effect on him. He smiled at her, brushing his lips against hers. "Perhaps. But it's impossible to know a mermaid's heart."

"All right, brother." Zantu dropped gracefully into the water, human legs shimmering and coalescing into a gleaming silver tail. "We'd better go on our adventure before the sun wakes the sharks. I've had enough encounters with those to last a lifetime."

Madison kissed his cheek and swam toward the boat. "Have fun. Come back to me soon."

"Always," Rubac replied, still thinking about Ebby. If he could break his curse and find love with a second mate, was it was possible for Ebby to overcome the inevitable, as well?

He shook his head, not ready to think on such things now. Zantu was here, and he was going to enjoy this time with his brother while he could. Jackknifing, he followed the trail of bubbles Zantu had left on his way into the kelp forest.

A Mermaid's Heart

Cruz watched his friend, Jake, run a finger down the bare arm of an over-tanned blonde and say something that made her giggle. The party boat's deck was loaded with inebriated targets, and apparently Jake was determined to bone every one of them. This vacation was supposed to be a diving expedition, and Jake had told him they'd be snorkeling today, but so far, no one had even dipped a toe in the water.

Cruz caught his friend's eye and signed, "You ready for a swim?"

Jake gave him a wicked grin that told him no and launched into one of his signature jokes.

Sighing, Cruz looked out over the glittering water, imagining the sound of the waves against the hull and the cry of gulls in the distance. Deaf since the age of seven, he vaguely remembered the sounds from TV shows he'd seen. He'd also learned that his voice tended to come off as less than charming, and as a rule remained silent.

The scent of coconut body oil wafted toward him and he returned his attention to the conversation, laughing a little too late—and possibly too loud—at Jake's punch line.

A redhead puckered her brows, her sangria-stained lips forming the words, "What's up with him?"

Knowing Jake was about to pull the deaf card—chicks dug a guy with a deaf friend almost as much as they dug a guy with a puppy—Cruz forced his mouth into a good-natured smile and signed, "Going lobster diving."

Jake lifted his chin in Cruz's direction in acknowledgment and kept talking to the blonde.

Cruz strode to the back of the boat and grabbed a snorkel mask. Diving into the blessedly cool water, he kicked toward a rock overhang in the reef. He'd always loved diving; deafness wasn't an issue underwater. Normally, he preferred full scuba gear, although he did equally well free diving. He had a keen eye for detecting spiny lobsters on the sandy floor and even made enough to pay his rent one summer selling them to a local market.

Within moments, he spotted a blue-green crustacean. He angled in to snatch it by its carapace and was ready to shoot back to the surface when he spotted one of the party girls peeking at him from behind a lacy green sea fan. At least one person had followed his lead and come in for a swim. Her long dark hair billowed around her face, and her bright red lipstick shone vividly even underwater.

Huh. He didn't think any of those women from the boat would actually want to get wet—at least, not with water. His chest was beginning to ache with the need to breathe, but he raised the lobster in greeting and made an eating motion. "Dinner?"

The woman opened her mouth as if to speak, beckoning him toward her with one hand.

She's interested? And she liked to swim, too. Maybe this party boat had been a good idea after all.

Grinning, Cruz pointed to the surface and kicked upward, keeping his eyes on the woman.

A flash of pale skin, black hair, and red… legs? shot toward him in a blur.

Startled, he stopped kicking. A woman with flowing purple hair swept up from behind him, close enough that her naked breasts brushed against his arm. She pulled his face to hers, clamping his lips in a kiss. *This is a bit fast, even for a drunken cruise.* Her hair enveloped him in a purple mist, blocking his vision. The lobster slipped from his fingers. He grabbed her hands, trying to pull them from his cheeks, but damn, the woman had a grip. His lungs burned for oxygen.

The woman not only continued forcing her tongue between his lips but now crushed her breasts and hips against him as if ready to do the nasty right then and there.

What the fuck? Unable to break free, he kicked for the surface for all he was worth, dragging her with him.

A second, distinctly feminine body pressed against his back. The snorkel mask was ripped from his head while two sets of hands slithered greedily over his skin.

He struggled against them, bubbles leaking from his mouth and nose. *How can they hold their breaths so long?*

A hand reached around him and dipped into his trunks, grabbing his dick.

The air left his lungs in a great rush. *Holy fuck!*

He resisted sucking in that fateful first inhalation of water. This couldn't be real, being mauled to death by beautiful women underwater. His head grew muzzy with the need to breathe. Closing his eyes, he felt like this had to be a bad dream.

A dream. He had to be dreaming. There was no other explanation—unless he was already dead...

He sucked in a draught of water.

And then another.

His eyes opened to the freckled cheeks of the purple-haired woman still enveloping him in a kiss. She rubbed her lithe body against him, her nipples teasing the fine hairs over his pecs.

If this is a dream, I may as well go with it.

Taking hold of the woman's hips, he noted the lack of a bikini bottom. This was the most vivid dream he'd ever had in his life. He swore he could even smell sex rising from her skin, filling the water. He wrapped both hands around the small of her back, pressing his erection hard into her flesh.

She wriggled in obvious pleasure and broke the kiss to nibble his jawline. While she worked her way down his throat and chest, the woman at his back slithered up over his head to take over the kiss from an upside-down position. Before her halo of hair once again blocked out his surroundings, he imagined he saw a huge, purple tail fin spread out in front of him...

His swim trunks were yanked down his hips.

Much as he loved the ocean, he'd never had a sex dream about it before. *This is awesome.* His entire bloodstream surged with need.

A firm tongue caressed the head of his cock. His hips jerked involuntarily, and a groan rose from deep in his chest. He didn't know where to put his hands—the woman at his crotch or the woman plunging her tongue into his mouth. He settled for one hand each, knotting his fingers in their hair and kissing back with deft strokes of his tongue. Immediately above his head bobbed his kissing partner's breasts, tipped by nipples as red as maraschino cherries.

Cherries on top, he thought, realizing he was feeling a bit drunk. *Why not?* It was his dream. He could do whatever he desired. He reached up to pull one within reach of his mouth when a third set of hands swept over the breasts. Delicate fingers and golden skin so dark it was closer to brown than gold pinched the nipples, coaxing them into sharp peaks.

Pulling his face from the kiss, he tried to get a better look at his partners, but long-nailed fingers pulled him roughly back into place. Somewhere in the back of his mind, he wondered about the forcefulness of this fantasy. He didn't mind a woman with an appetite but generally liked to do a bit of the steering himself. At the moment he felt like nothing more than a toy.

Three sets of hands and three mouths caressed his skin, his lips, his cock. He couldn't return their touches fast enough, slippery breasts and hard nipples under his palms, a slender neck, silky hair slipping between his fingers. Yet every time he reached for that sweet spot between their legs, they pulled out of reach.

Then one of them grabbed his hips, driving her pelvis against him. The familiar encasing warmth of her pussy nearly made him come. *Holy mother of God, no condom.* Good thing this was a dream. She pumped against him furiously. He reached around and grabbed her ass, only to have her ripped away without warning.

Dark hair filled his vision. Pointed teeth flashed between crimson lips. He blinked, realizing the dark-skinned woman with brilliant gold hair also seemed to have a bright gold tail instead of legs.

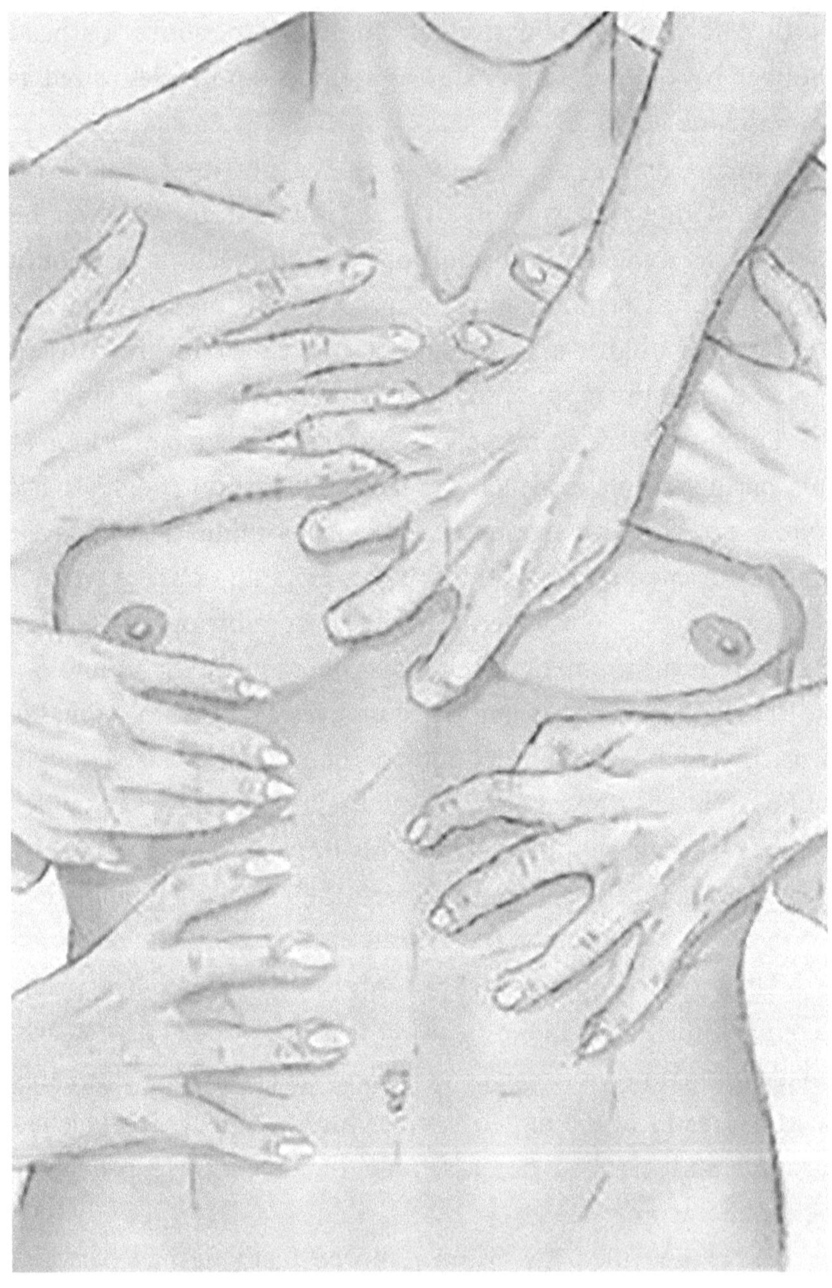

What the fuck? He knew mermaiding was a thing, with costume tails and all, but these women were so damn real.

He attempted to back away, pushing against the crimson-lipped woman's pale shoulders. A small white charm that looked like a turkey wishbone dangled from a cord between her naked breasts. Below her belly button, her flesh brightened to match her mouth. Brightened and coalesced into fins and a tail.

A fish's tail.

Realization exploded inside him like a breath of air after a long dive. He shoved harder, clearing more of his view. The rocks and reef were no longer in sight, nor was the shadow of the party boat at the surface. They'd drifted into a towering kelp forest, the filtered sunlight now hazy and green. Despite his flagging interest, his partners had lost none of their ardor, and continued to claw and thrust and grope, seeming to grow frustrated at his inattention.

Mechanically, he returned their caresses. Gave them what they wanted. If he didn't, he had no idea what might happen. This wasn't a dream, and these were no ordinary women.

He was underwater.

He was breathing.

And he was surrounded by mermaids.

CHAPTER TWO

*E*bby peered between the veins of a sea fan toward the orgy of mermaids in the kelp clearing. They passed a deeply tanned human between them, his muscular frame adjusting to their undulations with surprising agility for a land creature. His hands squeezed their breasts or pulled them into coital embraces with what seemed like an uncanny sense about how to prevent the orgy from becoming a violent, competitive frenzy. The current drifting toward Ebby reeked of sex, heightening the uncomfortable urgency low in her belly.

Finish already.

Two years ago, she'd chosen to be female. Not out of any biological urge, but because mermaids were obviously the stronger sex. Mermen like her da were destined to live out slow and miserable death-sentences, bound to the first female they mated with until their mate's unfaithfulness caused their hearts to literally break. Although Ebby was undeniably female now,

192

she refused to be like her mother, killing humans and subjecting mermen to inevitable misery.

With thoughts of her mother's behavior always on her mind, Ebby'd managed to remain a virgin—an unheard-of feat among the females of her kind—and merely watched these orgies from a safe distance, waiting until the unwitting human men were used up and abandoned. Then she swept in and towed them toward shore. Unfortunately, most were killed during the orgy. Those she found who weren't already dead always expired of their wounds during the journey toward land.

But that didn't stop Ebby from trying.

The man she was watching now had held up remarkably well, and she thought she saw signs of the mermaids tiring of him. If she could rescue at least one man from his demise, her abstinence would be worth it.

The mermaids' seductive song rose and fell, Urokotori's crimson claws stroking the twin prongs of the fish harp she wore around her neck. They rubbed their bodies along the human's, pulling at Ebby's instincts as surely as they pulled the male's. She slid one hand over her own pale breast and tweaked the sensitive coral nipple. A shockwave of pleasure rippled into her core.

Pinching her nipple harder, she let her other hand creep to the aching folds of her vulvar slit. Her tail twitched as she rubbed, her blood heating as she watched the man's length slide in and out of a mermaid. On the verge of climax, the orgy drifted close to her hiding spot and red-tailed Urokotori spotted her through the fronds.

"Come on, Ebby." The other mermaid clamped her bony fingers around Ebby's forearm, dragging her hand from her breast and pulling her free of her hiding spot.

Behind her, still half-buried in the sand, Ebby heard her pet mantis shrimp, Kato, shimmy himself deeper beneath the sand. The other mermaids laughed at her for keeping such a useless pet, but Kato had bonded to Ebby of his own accord, not because Ebby compelled him, and Ebby loved everything about him.

"We've all had our turn." Urokotori flung Ebby forward into the man's arms. "He can be your first."

The other two mermaids stopped their songs, pointed teeth gleaming between kiss-swollen lips. Lutana jack-knifed and stroked the man's backside with her gleaming golden tail fin. "Humans are so willing to play."

"He has inspiring stamina," Selachii agreed, her amethyst eyes hooded with satiation. Her triggerfish minion wriggled between the grotesquely scarred rip in her freckled tail fin.

The man's gaze met Ebby's, and she was struck by eyes that reminded her of pebbled tidepools. Was that a glint of alarm she saw? He'd been so willing and confident during the orgy, never hinting at fear or exhaustion.

The three mermaids encircled Ebby and pushed the nearly spent man against her. His long, lean thighs brushed her tail, the tip of his erection leaving a trail of fire along her skin. She'd never been this close to an aroused man before.

Urokotori commanded, "Sing, Ebby."

Her attention slid down his muscular chest to his perfectly rippled abs. A line of downy hair traced a path to his bobbing member. Only a few scratches marred his smooth bronze skin where the mermaids had grown careless or rough.

Ebby licked her lips, her nether regions pulsing despite her resolve. How could she escape this? Mermaids could be just as brutal toward their own gender as they were to any man. But she dare not risk getting pregnant. Mermaids were terrible mothers, and Ebby had sworn to never subject a little one to the abandonment and terror she'd endured as a child.

"He's ready," Lutana said. "You don't even need to sing. Just take him and get it over with."

Urokotori shoved between her shoulder blades, driving breasts against the man's hard chest. "Depths, you're boring."

The human's hands found her waist as if by instinct, neither pushing her away nor pulling her closer.

Boring. That was her way out. The only way to escape the attention of a mermaid was to bore them. That, or offer better entertainment elsewhere. She decided a long, slow kiss would be boring enough without inciting their wrath. She'd just have to reign in her own instincts and not take it farther.

To be fair, her only experience kissing had been with Lutana; the golden-tailed mermaid liked women as much as men. Ebby had found some pleasure in her touches, but not enough to keep coming back for more.

The man's hands, however, were different, padded by callouses, and broader than a mermaid's. The sensation of his palms on her skin made her ache with need. How would his thick fingers feel plunging between her folds?

No, Ebby, she chided herself. *A kiss is all you get.*

Placing her hands on the man's shoulders, she pressed her lips against his.

⋖⋖⋖

CRUZ HAD ATTEMPTED to get away from these voracious women only once—and paid the price. A set of bleeding lacerations down his hip still stung from the red-tailed one's claws as she'd pulled him back into an embrace. These females were strong, stronger than humans, and quick. They seemed to be out for more than just sex—they wanted blood.

To his relief, the frenzy seemed to be winding down. But his inner voice was already asking what happened next.

Then the red-tailed mermaid yanked a fourth mermaid from among the weeds surrounding the kelp clearing. Her apricot tail was flawless and her skin so pale she could have been a ghost. Atop her head, a fiery auburn halo of hair rippled in the current, and her coral nipples beckoned from the perfect peaks of small but luscious breasts. Although she had hips, her legs were fused into a single, supple appendage. Like the other mermaids, her feminine parts were exposed on the front, open to him, inviting his penetration.

But this woman's pulsing folds seemed different. More demure. As if she would've covered herself if she could.

The mermaids seemed to regain their flagging interest upon her introduction, and despite his exhaustion, his dick surged back to life. Yet where the other mermaids' gazes were feral and hungry, this pale beauty's eyes held... fear? Definitely hesitation. She didn't want to do this. Was being coerced by the others like a freshman girl at a frat party. He found himself wanting to protect her from these other man-eaters.

She was shoved into his arms. The other mermaids were obviously taunting her, threatening her. His hands met her waist, holding her at bay, her skin cool and silky to his touch.

To his surprise, she pressed her lips to his. Not an open, aggressive kiss like the other women. Tight-lipped.

Forced.

Oh, hell no. He was no rapist. These women had already all but forced themselves upon him. He would not be used as an instrument to hurt an innocent.

Her hands came up behind his neck, her breasts teasing the hairs on his chest. His dick surged again, arguing against his resolve and he dug his fingers harder into her waist, breathing through his nose in an effort to control himself.

He latched onto that sensation, breathing. This wasn't a dream, yet he was somehow breathing underwater. How long would this ability last? What would happen when the mermaids left? He glanced toward the surface, gauging how far it might be and if he could make it before drowning. Damn, he was in real trouble even if the mermaids didn't decide to have him as a post-coital snack.

Seeming to sense his drifting attention, sharp claws raked down his shoulders.

The apricot mermaid kissing him pulled him closer, crushing his dick between them, yet it felt as if she did it to protect him rather than pleasure herself. She didn't buck against him, and her grip on him trembled while the other mermaids continued circling. Although he could feel the pulsing folds of her sex against his hipbone, her mouth remained a rigid line beneath his lips.

Pulling her closer, he eyed the flashes of color from passing fins. His skin flinched at every brush of their clawed fingers. How was he going to get himself out of this, let alone the apricot mermaid?

As he was thinking, claws jerked his head backward. The red mermaid leered at him, hand still tangled in his hair, then turned and hauled him free of the apricot mermaid's grip. Like feeding sea lions, the brightly colored mermaids carried him away, leaving the apricot mermaid gaping in their wake.

CHAPTER THREE

It took a moment for Ebby to regain her composure. Then she darted after Urokotori's crimson tail fins, knowing exactly where the other mermaid was heading. While some mermaids cultivated schools of fish or vicious eels as pets, Urokotori kept a giant octopus in a cave not far from here. The mermaids delighted in feeding it, watching its arms and beak rip its meal to pieces—always while that meal was still alive.

"Wait!" Ebby cried as she pushed out of the kelp toward the rock face. Ahead, she spotted one of the octopus's giant red arms retreating back into the cave.

Floating near the entrance, Urokotori smoothed her long black locks away from her face in satisfaction. "That'll keep him."

There was no blood filling the water, yet the human had disappeared from sight. An angry-looking octopus eye filled the cave entrance. Surely the creature couldn't have eaten him that fast? "What did you do?"

Selachii stretched her arms languidly over her head and allowed her triggerfish to shimmy up her side, powerful mouth snapping the water. "Call for me when it's time to play. I'm going to take a beauty rest."

A stream of bubbles escaped Urokotori's lips, and she rolled her eyes. "For all the good *that* will do."

Lutana giggled. Selachii's freckled face darkened and her amethyst hair seemed to stand on end as she turned on her sister.

Ebby drifted backward, sure there was about to be bloodshed.

Urokotori emitted a soft trill and reached for her fish harp. A suckered red arm shot from the cave, tip curling with menace. "Watch it now, sister."

Selachii thrust out her jaw but backed into the kelp forest, disappearing from view.

Smirking, Urokotori turned to Ebby. "Timuri has permission to eat the human if he tries to escape. Don't even think about trying to take him out to play unless I'm here."

Ebby eyed the cave as the octopus resumed its camouflage among the rocks, then nodded. She knew better than to interfere with another mermaid's pet.

With a flick of her tail, Urokotori darted up and over the rock face, headed off to find mischief elsewhere.

Lutana regarded Ebby, her golden eyes not unkind. "How frustrating." Arching her back, she moved closer and ran a tender finger down the top of Ebby's breast and over the nipple. "I can help relieve your tension if you like."

Ebby took the other mermaid's hand to stop further advances. Of all the mermaids, Lutana was the most benign. "I'm fine."

On the ledge below the cave, Kato crept silently over the sand toward her from his hiding spot between some scattered boulders. Coming this close to the octopus's lair was dangerous, and she wished her tiny friend had stayed away. Releasing Lutana's hand, Ebby settled to the ledge and shielded him while he burrowed beneath the sand next to her. She wasn't ready to give up on freeing the man, but she wasn't sure what her next step should be.

"Once, Urokotori kept a man in that cave for over a month." Lutana curled her tail to one side and sat in the sand beside her. "Until she forgot to renew his breath."

"Oh." It was bad enough to use a man, but to imprison him and use him over and over only to let him drown? Despicable.

"Humans are wonderful in how they can love multiple women." Lutana's pretty coral lips pursed into a pout. "But tragically fragile."

Ebby stared at the dark cave opening. "We have to get him out of there."

"I'm not crossing Urokotori." Lutana spread her tail fin and stirred a flurry of debris from the ocean floor. "You saw what she did to Selachii's tail to get that fish harp."

A reflexive shudder passed through Ebby. That fight had been brutal. "Maybe I can offer her something in exchange?"

Ebby didn't spend a lot of time with the other mermaids, so she didn't know what kinds of things they might value, but her mother had liked Da's jewelry. She toyed with the conch-spiral bracelet on her wrist. Da had made it for her just before she entered puberty, telling her it would bring her luck once she chose her gender; he'd always assumed she'd choose to be male.

Her throat felt thick as she remembered the look of disappointment in his eyes when her breasts had emerged.

Lutana watched Ebby stroke the bracelet with avaricious attention. "What are you offering?"

Suddenly uncomfortable, Ebby shrugged. "There's all kinds of stuff buried around that shipwreck."

"Ew." Lutana withdrew her hand. "You expect me to dig in the muck with you? Forget it. And forget him. He's just a pitiful human." She rolled lazily onto her back and pushed off toward the kelp forest. "If you insist on having a male, at least find one of our own kind who can provide you a nest."

As the mermaid's gleaming tail winked out of sight between the fronds, Ebby rose from the sand. There was only one place she could go for advice on this; Uncle Zantu. He'd defeated mermaids before.

"C'mon, Kato." She settled his bony carapace against the crook of her neck and he promptly nestled into her hair, holding tight for the swim.

Giving one final glance at the cave, she darted toward the surface, praying Uncle Zantu could come up with a rescue plan before the poor human's breath-spell expired.

❖❖❖

CRUZ STARED at the mottled gray octopus blocking the opening. Its arms had to be longer than he was tall and its bulbous, pulsing head blotted out the dim light entering the cave. Was that the only exit? Why had the mermaids put him in here? Swimming with mermaids definitely hadn't been in the party-boat's brochure.

Keeping one eye on the octopus, he kicked upward, arms outstretched, searching for the ceiling. Hard rock met his fingertips, edges worn smooth by the water. Here and there his fingertips discovered pockets of air trapped between the water and the stone, none more than a few inches in height. How long would his ability to breathe underwater last? At least it hadn't gone away when the mermaids left. Hadn't he read a story about a mermaid's kiss granting water breathing? These mermaids fit the description he recalled, from their beauty to their voracious sexuality.

Using his hands to move along the dark cave ceiling, he reached a wall and followed it downward to the sandy bottom. The cave wasn't small, but it wasn't enormous, either, about the size of a large bedroom. Blinking, he realized he could see, at least a little. Was there a crevice somewhere letting light through? He lifted his gaze and was greeted by a trail of perfect teal-green handprints. Wherever he'd touched the wall now glowed.

Phytoplankton.

He purposefully rubbed his fingertips along the rocks, illuminating the cave's interior with dim green light. Spinning in a slow circle, he gauged his surroundings. The cave walls, though lumpy, had no visible exits except the one the octopus guarded. The sandy floor was littered with empty crustacean shells and a few bones from long-dead fish. He glanced at the creature guarding the entrance.

Someone on the boat must've noticed by now that he'd failed to come up for air. Surely, they'd send divers to look for him. Would they even think to look inside the cave? He needed to get a signal to them. Swallowing, he approached the cave entrance, praying the octopus was as frightened of him as he was of it.

One long gray arm shot out and struck him.

Bubbles burst from his lips and his chest felt like it was on fire as he slammed backward into the cave wall. Green light filled the cave—or was it the stars filling his vision? For a brief moment, he worried the blow had removed his ability to breathe water. Then he shuddered and breath returned to his lungs. *Fuck, that hurt.*

He ran his fingertips over the circular welts rising on his chest and glared at the octopus's pulsing head. The creature eyed him back with hungry intelligence. For all he knew, the thing was saving him for a midnight snack. Did octopuses sleep? Cruz wasn't sure, but he seemed to recall they were night hunters.

Backing up to the wall farthest from the entrance, Cruz kicked away the clutter of shells and settled to the floor. His exertion with the mermaids had tired him out, and he had no idea when they might return. *If* they would return.

He hoped he wasn't on the menu once darkness fell.

CHAPTER FOUR

*E*bby pulled herself onto a surf-washed boulder and looked up the cliff toward the human dwelling nestled there. Moonlight sparkled off the waves and painted the treetops and rocks silver. She'd never come to her uncle's home at night, and the blackness under the shrubbery surrounding the shoreline made her nervous. Several rectangles of light glowed on the hillside.

Keeping her tail in the lapping waves, she took a deep breath and sang out. The air coming off the shore smelled different in the dark, flowery and verdant yet also hinting at decay.

Her call wavered over the shush of the waves, a request, not a demand. Ebby never sang unless absolutely necessary; forcing other beings to do her will made her feel queasy. Not that she could force Uncle Zantu to do anything; he was immune to mermaid songs since he'd found his true mate.

Soon, a broad-shouldered figure appeared from the path up the hill, accompanied by a smaller figure who darted out ahead. "Ebby!"

Uncle Zantu shouted, "Camilla, stop!"

"It's Ebby, Daddy! I told you!"

Ebby smiled as her cousin splashed headlong into the water toward her. The girl wore a thin gown with a frill at the bottom that molded to her legs and looked vaguely like a tail. Ebby had trouble understanding how a child could have a predetermined sex, but Camilla was definitely female, which was the only reason her father allowed her anywhere near the water. Mermaids generally left female humans alone.

As the tiny figure clambered onto the rock next to her, Ebby patted her head. "Your da is right, you know. I could've been dangerous."

"Aw, I knew it was you. You have a pretty voice."

Uncle Zantu stopped with his toes barely in the froth and put his hands on his hips. "Is everything okay, Ebby?"

He wore a loose shirt, legs poking out below loose, knee-length shorts, but his broad shoulders and narrow waist were still evident, and his piercing silver eyes glittered in the moonlight. His mate, Brianna, seemed to appear out of nowhere, ducking beneath his arm to settle in against his side. Ebby still found it strange to see Uncle Zantu with legs, but she could see why Brianna had fallen in love with him.

"Did I wake you?" Ebby asked.

"We were putting Camilla to bed," Brianna answered, a wry smile twisting her mouth as she looked at her dripping daughter who now held Kato in her lap.

A jealous ache pulled at Ebby. Her own mother had never

looked at her that way. She slid back into the surf, keeping only her head above water. "I need your advice, Uncle Zantu."

Uncle Zantu moved to a nearby boulder and sat against it. "It must be pretty important to bring you here in the dark. Go on, then."

Gripping the slippery rock, Ebby told them about the human and the mermaids and the octopus cave. Zantu's fists balled at his side as he listened.

When Ebby finished, Brianna stepped into the water as if ready to go for a swim. "You have to save him!"

"I want to, but I'm not sure how," Ebby said, shifting her gaze to her uncle. "I was thinking of trading Urokotori some of Da's jewelry for him."

"I'd be careful of any deals." Zantu shook his head. "If you make him seem valuable, Urokotori won't let him go."

"What can I do, then?"

Zantu shrugged and rubbed his chin. "Wait until they get bored."

Brianna glowered at her husband. "She can't just skulk around and hope they let him go. What if his breath-spell runs out?"

"Or Urokotori kills him for sport?" Ebby added.

"I have an idea!" Camilla said. "Can you bring in a shark to get rid of the octopus? Like you and Mommy got rid of the mermaids!"

Ebby'd avoided sharks ever since that fateful encounter. "Mermaids can't actually control sharks very well."

Zantu straightened and paced the wet sand. "The idea has merit, though. Why don't you command a school of fish to swim in front of the cave? That might lure the octopus out long enough for you to free the human."

Ebby breathed deeply of the fragrant night air, trying to organize her thoughts. "I don't like to force others to do my bidding just because I'm female. I don't want to be like the rest of the mermaids."

"Believe me, you're not," Zantu and Brianna said at the same time.

"Jinx!" Camilla sang, clapping her hands. "You owe me a coke!"

Her parents laughed and Zantu put his arm around his wife, drawing her close.

Ducking underwater, Ebby rubbed her hands over her face. What would it have been like to grow up with a family like this? *I wish I could talk to Da.* But Da was gone, possibly even dead. Most mermen died of a broken heart after their mates died and children left. Her throat tightened. Surfacing once more, she said, "I don't think Timuri will leave his post. He's waiting to eat the captive." Kato squeaked and curled into a ball at her words. Then another thought occurred to Ebby. "And what about that poor man? *He* could starve to death before Urokotori grows bored."

"You'd better feed him, then," Zantu said.

What would the human do if Ebby brought him food? She couldn't control the octopus, but she could soothe it enough to slip herself in and out.

Camilla splashed off the rock, jarring Ebby back to attention and sending Kato tumbling into the waves. The little girl bobbed to the surface next to her, little legs kicking furiously. "Kato and I can pick some seaweed for you."

"Thank you, Camilla." Ebby guided the little girl back toward shore. "But I can handle it."

Zantu scooped his daughter from the water. "It's too dark for little nibblers like you to go swimming."

"Come on, Nibbler." Brianna took the girl, propping her on one hip. "It's way past your bedtime. Let's leave Daddy and cousin Ebby to talk."

"But I want to stay."

"Your cousin will come back and visit you soon." Zantu planted a kiss on Camilla's head then another on his wife's upturned mouth before turning back to Ebby. "When it's light out, right, Ebby?"

"Of course." Ebby had been coming to the cove to visit her uncle since before choosing her sex. She'd been sure her uncle would reject her just like Da had, terrified of her new violent nature. But Uncle Zantu hadn't shunned her upon discovering she was a mermaid. He *had* become subtly more cautious when it came to Camilla, however. She could sense him relaxing as his little family disappeared up the dark trail.

Leaning against the submerged boulder, Ebby let the gentle surf push her fins back and forth over the sandy bottom. She could feed the human and keep him alive, but what if his breath-spell expired? The duration of the spell could vary from a few hours to a few weeks, depending on everything from his activity levels to how deep he was beneath the waves. She'd have to remain nearby in case that happened. Then, she'd have to provide the kiss. "I'm scared about renewing his breath-spell."

"Why?" Still fully clothed, Zantu moved deeper into the water, allowing the wavelets to slosh over his shoulders. He said he didn't miss having a tail, but he still loved the water as if it was home.

"What if I... lose control?" Recalling the sight of him

pleasuring the other mermaids sent a tingle straight to her core. She thought back to how the human's touch had felt on her waist. The alluring heat of his erection against her hip.

"I don't think you have to be cruel or out of control just because you have breasts." Zantu gazed up at the moon. "The only thing we really have any control over is ourselves. I believe if you want to overcome your mermaid 'nature,' you can."

"But how can anyone defeat nature? Isn't that by definition undefeatable?"

Zantu lowered his chin into the water, silver eyes glinting in the moonlight as he turned his gaze toward her. Then he slowly rose, letting the water mold his thin clothing against his very masculine form. He was her uncle, but he was still a gorgeous man, impossible not to notice.

Flushing slightly, Ebby pointedly turned her gaze skyward.

He made a small, satisfied noise and sloshed back to shore. "You've been coming to see me for over two years now and never once has your 'nature' caused you to do anything inappropriate." Pausing on the bank, he looked over his shoulder at her. "I think most mermaids use 'nature' as an excuse to do whatever they want and not feel bad about their actions later. You're not like that. I have confidence in you." He resumed trekking up the path inland, speaking loud enough for her to still hear him over the waves. "Now, go do what you need to do to save that human. And yourself."

Ebby wanted to ask what he meant by that, but he was already gone.

CHAPTER FIVE

Cruz felt the bite of the seatbelt against his scrawny chest. The smothering punch of the airbags trapping him in place. The roar of tearing metal and breaking glass. The scream of his mother…

And jolted awake.

The familiar panic that had haunted his dreams since he was seven was replaced by disorientation of a different kind. His arms and legs churned, unable to find solid ground in the darkness. *Where the hell am I?* Heart racing, everything came back to him. The cave. The orgy. The mermaids… Had any of that really happened?

He took a cool breath of—water. Yep. He was still underwater. The mermaids must be real. Settling his bare feet back against the sandy floor, he located the patch of light at the cave entrance to orient himself, then floated upward, touching the ceiling. The phytoplankton ignited.

Hoping the octopus might have abandoned its station, he edged forward.

A knobby head and eight, suckered arms lurked at the opening, mottled skin blending against the stone. The thing's gills sucked in and out rhythmically as one bulbous eye swiveled in his direction.

This time Cruz halted shy of getting the stuffing knocked out of him. If he got out of this alive, his nightmares about the accident were going to have company.

A shadow blocked the light. Once. Twice. Cruz swallowed, wondering what could possibly happen next. He scoured the floor for a weapon. The scattered shells and bits of bone were too small to be useful.

The octopus curled in on itself, color shifting from mottled gray to deep red. Cruz tensed, sure an attack was coming. Instead of pouncing, the creature edged aside and the finned silhouette of a mermaid entered.

It felt as if the pressure of the water intensified, and Cruz forced himself to take a deep breath, acutely feeling his nakedness. What would be expected of him now?

The cave walls illuminated all at once, bathing everything in monochromatic green light. The apricot-tailed mermaid floated there holding a large, scalloped clamshell.

She moved forward, eyes wide as she studied him. He took the opportunity to examine her, too, now that he was no longer distracted by the need to fend off a violent orgy. Pert breasts topped by darker nipples accentuated her slender figure. She wore no clothing but did have a bracelet around one wrist and what looked like a bone needle dangling from one of her earlobes. Her delicate, fluttering tail fins reminded him of a woman wearing an evening gown in the wind. His gaze drifted lower, to where her sex should be, and saw no more than a discreet slit in her scaleless, apricot tail.

As if embarrassed by his attention, she thrust the clam toward him.

He'd never been a fan of raw shellfish, but refusing a gift might be interpreted as an insult. If he wanted to get out of here, he needed to play nice. He kicked toward her, hand extended.

She drew back, releasing the shell before he had a firm grip. It drifted to the floor, its two halves separating. An assortment of seaweed spilled out, drifting slowly to the sandy floor.

He blinked at it. Why had she brought him a shell full of seaweed?

She looked from the spilled contents to him and back. Features pinched, she sank to the cave floor and began gathering the bits together.

Okay, these were valuable for some reason. Moving slowly, he helped pick up the leaves, placing them back into the half-shell. She once again offered the shell to him, this time open like a platter.

He shook his head and signed, "What am I supposed to do with it?" He was used to signing whether people understood him or not. Most of the time his motions helped them get a sense of what he meant.

An uncertain smile lifted one corner of her lips. From between her fiery auburn tresses, two long antennae emerged, followed by the alien-looking face of a mantis shrimp. The antennae waggled, and Cruz could swear the creature was looking straight at him. The mermaid plucked out a green bit and placed it in her mouth, chewing and swallowing, then offered him the shell again.

Was he supposed to eat it? *Can't be any worse than raw clam.* Choosing a bit that looked a little less alien than the others, he put it into his mouth and chewed. He wasn't usually much of a salad eater, but the seaweed tasted okay—crunchy and salty, although weirdly rubbery.

The mermaid nodded in satisfaction and once more backed toward the exit.

He grabbed her wrist with his other hand and signed, "Stay. Please."

The mermaid stiffened, eyes going wide. She opened her mouth, the lines of her throat rippling with sound he couldn't hear. He could, however, feel a slight vibration through his hold on her wrist. Something about it made his insides flutter. Still, he held tight. She was his only hope to get past the octopus.

The green light filling the cave fluttered and rippled in response to her song. It reminded him of the first time Jake had dragged him to a rock concert and he'd discovered he could feel the beat even if he couldn't hear it. He'd been a fan of rock concerts ever since. She shut her mouth and stared at where he still held her wrist, then back to his face.

Cruz once again gestured to himself and then the door. "Can I go?"

The mermaid's delicate eyebrows drew together. Tilting her head, the mermaid moved her lips again.

He tapped a finger to his ear then lips, signing, "I'm deaf."

She blinked, gaze following his movement. Hopeful, he pointed at the door again.

Her features transformed into regret and she shook her head. She waggled her fingers in the direction of the octopus, then pointed to him and made a grabbing motion.

Well, that was obvious. The octopus would stop him if he

tried to leave. But she seemed to have some control over the animal, so why couldn't she tell it to let him go? He made the sign for octopus and then pointed at her and made the sign for swim. "Can't you get me past?"

She smiled, sharp teeth gleaming between her lips. His insides leapt in alarm, but the smile was without malice. She pointed to herself then the cave door, nodding. Then pointed at him and once again shook her head no.

So, she could pass, but he couldn't.

They seemed to be doing fairly well at the sign language thing, so he asked, "Why not?"

All she did was shake her head again. He wondered if the reason had anything to do with the other mermaids. Regardless, she couldn't or wouldn't help him leave, at least not yet. She tugged her wrist free of his grasp and backed away.

He'd heard what one should do if taken hostage was to make yourself human, but he wasn't sure if that would work when one had been captured by mythical creatures. *Hot mythical creatures.* Jake would advise him to get her name and number. What if he treated her like a woman instead of a jail-keeper?

Pointing to his chest, he followed it by his nickname in sign language, cupping his hands and bumping them forward like a boat. Calling himself Cruise was a lot easier than hand spelling Cruz to people, and he often got a laugh out of it.

She froze, watching his movement.

He repeated the motion a couple of times, then pointed at her. "Your name?"

Comprehension dawned on her features. She seemed to think a moment, then moved her hands like a falling tide. Cute. He liked that. Ebbing tide. One name was as good as another right now. He repeated the motion and smiled. "Good to meet you, Ebby."

He couldn't tell in the pale light, but it seemed like she flushed. His insides churned. He needed to convince her to get him out of here before any of her friends showed up. Those mermaids had been quick to heat up. Perhaps physical contact would help convince her to set him free.

Edging closer, he licked his lips, brushing her arm with his fingertips.

The mermaid's eyes widened. She spun and fled the cave, leaving nothing but churned up sand in her wake.

CHAPTER SIX

$\mathcal{E}$bby raced past Timuri and into the kelp forest as fast as her fins would carry her. Cruz had been immune to her song, but she was apparently not immune to her own desire. The way he'd licked his lips and moved forward had sent immediate heat flooding from her nipples to her belly... and lower.

On top of that, he was quite charming, speaking to her with his hands. Mermaid magic gave her accelerated understanding of all languages, but not instantaneous. She'd need a few more interactions to become fluent in this new form of speech and might actually enjoy getting to know this human.

She shook her head and swam faster, weaving between the swaying kelp fronds as if being chased by a killer whale. Remaining near him would be dangerous for both of them.

After a few laps across the current, she paused, blood pumping in her ears. Kato edged tentatively out of her hair and made a little ticking noise, stroking her cheek gently with an antenna. "Thanks, Kato. I'm okay."

What was it about this human that sent her into a panic when he touched her? She'd never been this affected by any of the other humans she'd tried to save. He moved with a grace she'd never seen before, more sensual. She remembered the way he'd pleasured the other mermaids and her insides tightened. For the first time, she truly understood why the other mermaids used men like they did. It was difficult to think of anything but relief when her core was crying to be filled.

She ran a flattened palm down her belly as if that act of will could banish the physical sensations threatening to consume her. If she didn't get control of herself, the human would die. Maybe not by her hand, but by any other number of things that could happen. Humans were not meant for the sea.

"If only we could get rid of Timuri," she said absently.

Kato reached out a claw and tugged on her earring, a gift from Lutana back when Ebby'd first introduced herself to the other mermaids. The jewelry was actually a needle-like dart infused with the deadly toxin of a sea snake. "Every mermaid needs an exit strategy," Lutana had said.

But killing another mermaid's pet was taboo and would unite the others against her, putting a death sentence on Ebby's head. She pulled the earring free of Kato's grasp. "You know we can't."

The mantis shrimp sighed in disappointment and slumped against her shoulder, curling his tail behind her shoulder blade.

A school of señorita fish flashed by, drawing her attention. She followed the sharply choreographed movement, listening to them chirp at each other and thinking of Uncle Zantu's suggestion.

Just because she directed fish past the cave didn't mean Timuri would catch any, right? The school might distract him from his duty long enough for her to extract the man, Cruz. "You think they can out-swim Timuri?"

Kato purred and scurried backward into her hair, readying himself for a swim.

Ebby sighed and nodded, out of ideas. Taking a loop around a rock spotted with palm-shaped corals, she drove the fish toward the cave.

At the edge of the kelp forest, the fish hesitated, unwilling to leave cover. On the other side of the swaying stalks, Timuri waited just inside the cave opening, his skin blending perfectly with the surrounding rock. Sea fans and coral spotted the cliff outside, but other sea life knew to stay far away from the giant octopus's grasp. Swallowing, she realized she was going to have to command these fish to move in that direction. *It's an emergency*, she told herself. But using her magic on these poor creatures was unfair.

A flash of crimson caught the corner of her eye and she pulled back into the forest just in time to see Urokotori somersault playfully over the edge of the cliff.

The crimson-tailed mermaid pirouetted at the entrance, shook out her hair, and let forth a song of command. Urokotori had no qualms about using her magic on other beings.

The giant octopus cleared the entrance, arms coiling and beak clacking. Kato withdrew further into Ebby's hair.

Urokotori continued singing, the notes shifting from command to seduction.

After a few moments, Cruz's tanned face appeared. Unmoving, he watched Urokotori undulate to her own song, her red fins flared in a full display of desire. Was he truly immune? The song was powerfully hypnotic. Almost strong enough to draw Ebby into its grip. She gripped a slippery kelp trunk in one hand and resisted.

The human remained in the entrance, regarding the dark-haired mermaid. Ebby still didn't understand how, but it was very obvious he was not compelled.

Urokotori's spine stiffened as she seemed to sense something wrong. Ebby's gut clenched. If the mermaid found out Cruz was immune to her, she'd likely kill him outright.

Darting forward, Ebby circled Urokotori, hoping to distract her. "I've been waiting for you."

The other mermaid's black eyebrows drew together and her red lips curled into a sneer. "You're still here? Go away. You had your chance."

"You said you'd share. That I should come back to play." Ebby paused, blocking the older mermaid's view of the cave entrance. Cruz wouldn't be able to swim fast enough to escape, but she could perhaps keep Urokotori from verifying he'd been unaffected by her song. Looking over her shoulder at the cave, she let out a trembling note of seduction and signaled for him to come out. She'd never sung that song before and a part of her rebelled its use now. *He's immune. He won't be affected*, she reminded herself.

His gaze flickered warily between her and Urokotori before he edged forward into the current.

Urokotori elbowed Ebby aside, shoving her hard against one of the nearby spiked coral. The abrasive edge cut into Ebby's hand and the hint of blood filled the water. *Great.* Now she'd be drawing every nearby predator to this location.

Timuri's arms flexed and his beak clacked.

Ebby backed away. "When did you last feed your pet?"

Urokotori shrugged and gestured to Cruz, who had drifted several meters away. "My pet will have a meal soon enough."

The octopus must've taken that as an invitation. One arm flashed out, grabbing Cruz around the ankle.

Instinctively, Ebby let out a sharp trill of command. To her surprise, the creature halted its attack. Taking control of another mermaid's pet was not only difficult but also highly taboo.

"How dare you!" Urokotori seemed to swell in size, her hair fanning out like a nest of sea snakes.

Ebby held her ground. "If you're going to kill the human, be merciful and do it quickly. He's at least earned that." She had no desire to see Cruz killed, but a quick death would be better than being eaten alive.

Urokotori sneered, her teeth sharper than Ebby remembered. "Why, Ebby, I think you like him. Have you been playing with my toys without me?"

Ebby licked her lips, heart beating painfully against her ribcage. Uncle Zantu'd warned her not to make Urokotori believe the man had value. Yet if Cruz had no value, he'd be octopus food. What other choice did she have? She pulled Da's bracelet from her wrist. "Let him live and I'll give you this."

Urokotori reached for the intricately carved shell.

Ebby yanked it out of reach. "Promise me."

The other mermaid's eyes narrowed to slits. Her crimson lips spread wide. "You may buy him one more day with that bauble. Tomorrow he belongs to Timuri. Unless you can bring me another gift?"

"Perhaps," Ebby answered, handing over the jewelry and reigning in her smile. If she'd known freeing the man would be this easy, she would've made this trade long ago, despite the hollow feeling in her stomach about losing her da's trinket. But Da would approve. Cruz would be safe on land by tomorrow. She waved a hand as if the bracelet was indeed no more than a bauble. "I'll bring you more if he pleases me."

Urokotori laughed, shoving the bracelet onto her wrist and crossing her arms. She eyed Cruz lasciviously. "Well, he did have me coming back for another round. I suppose he's worthy of a first time for you. Timuri, put him back."

Ebby stiffened. "You said he's mine."

Urokotori arched a brow. "I said he could live one more day. I didn't say where."

"That wasn't what I traded—"

Once again, the crimson mermaid seemed to swell, her obviously superior power radiating in waves that made the current seem to run in reverse. "That is exactly what you traded for. If you don't like it, don't come back."

All Ebby could do was watch helplessly as the octopus settled in to guard the entrance once again.

With Kato's clawed feet irritating the back of her neck, Ebby floated outside the cave, too flustered and angry to enter. Urokotori had tricked her out of her bracelet.

"You can go on in, darling," the mermaid sang. "There's not much room inside for acrobatics, but I'm sure you can manage."

As the red-tailed mermaid rounded up a nearby school of Garibaldi fish, Ebby fantasized about using her mother's fish harp to call every nearby predator to tear the other mermaid and her pet to shreds. Not that she'd ever learned to play the instrument; it lay securely inside Da's treasure chest along with the stash of jewelry he'd hoarded in the hope of impressing his mate.

At least Urokotori fed her pet, clapping gleefully as the

octopus grabbed the orange fish from the current with multiple arms and snapped them in two with its beak.

Ebby shuddered. Timuri, having been fed, would be impossible to lure away. And Urokotori would probably demand another payment at sunup. Until Ebby came up with another plan, she'd have to offer a second trade.

Turning, she sped into the kelp forest. The sunlight glancing off the surface overhead told her night would fall soon. She meandered around the towering kelp, looping back on herself a few times to be sure she wasn't being followed. Mermaids didn't build or keep nests, but she'd tried to maintain Da's, along with his jewelry box. In the vanishing light, she brushed aside sea fans and wriggled sideways between dense kelp stalks into the clearing.

Kato immediately clambered free of her hair and went to work snipping back the overgrown sea sponges that had once served as her father's bed. A gray layer of sediment covered everything, from the tall mirror Da had propped upright with a pile of stones to the waterlogged barrels they'd used as chairs. She'd need to come back here soon and do some maintenance or there wouldn't be any nest left.

Tugging the small jewelry chest free from the sand that had accumulated around it, she set it on the flat stone she and Da had used as a table and pried up the brass latch. The lid, however, refused to open. The light was fading quickly, but she examined the hinges. They seemed corroded, and barnacles had crusted over one corner.

Lying back on the sponges, Ebby stared up at the violet light illuminating the water above. "How am I going to select something to trade if I couldn't even open the box?"

Kato swept sand off the tabletop with short, fast brushes of his tail, seemingly content to have something to do.

Ebby sighed. Would Cruz know how to get the chest open? She didn't really want to take the entire chest with her; if Urokotori saw how much she had, she'd up her price for sure. Not to mention Mother's fish harp was inside. But how else was she going to come up with something to buy his freedom?

Knowing Urokotori might decide their deal broke at dawn, she tucked the jewelry box beneath one arm. "Kato, you coming?"

The mantis shrimp sighed, giving a last flourish of his tail that sent a cloud of sand drifting from the table before joining her. Ebby hurried back to the cave, dodging a school of night-feeding damselfish and humming a sonic warning to ward off any large predators who might be lurking nearby.

When she arrived at the cave entrance, full darkness enveloped the sea floor. Where was Urokotori? A quick, sonic query revealed only open water. A painful knot formed inside Ebby's stomach. The other mermaid had only promised he'd live another day, not that she wouldn't use him. Was she inside the cave with Cruz right now?

Ignoring Timuri's curious gaze, Ebby pushed inside, singing the phytoplankton on the wall to life. To her relief, Cruz was both alive and alone.

Then she realized what that meant.

She was alone with a lithe, naked man.

Uncle Zantu's words of confidence came back to her. *I have confidence in you.* She could do this.

Working in almost complete darkness, Cruz rubbed the broad edge of the clamshell bowl on the rock wall, pausing now and again to test the shell's sharpness. He hoped it might serve as a weapon of sorts. The way that red-tailed mermaid had smiled at him with those wickedly pointed teeth made him believe she had more than another orgy in mind. If he couldn't seduce his way out of this situation, he'd fight his way past the octopus and escape. However, if Ebby showed back up…

He wasn't entirely sure what to think of the apricot-tailed mermaid. His first instinct had been to protect her. Well, not really the first instinct. The memory of her lips against his caused a tightening low in his stomach. He shook it away.

She seemed to be protecting him. She'd fed him. Given him her name. Even done something to stop red-tail from… whatever she'd planned.

He halted his sharpening, staring at the glittering phytoplankton that had scraped free of the wall and now floated like tiny teal diamonds around him. He hardly knew Ebby, but the gushy sensation she created in his belly was unlike anything he'd experienced before. He needed to stay rational if he wanted to get out of here alive.

The cave filled with sudden light, and he twisted toward the entrance, clutching his shell in preparation for combat. Ebby floated in the doorway, a small box under one arm. Heart racing, he wasn't sure what to do. Part of him wanted to hide the weapon from her in embarrassment.

She didn't seem to notice his warring emotions, setting the box on the cave floor. The mantis shrimp hiding in her hair scurried down her arm and sat atop the box like a miniature guard dog. A smile twitched the corner of Cruz's mouth, despite his uncertainty. Why didn't it surprise him that Ebby had a shrimp for a pet?

She floated uncertainly in the doorway. Her pale arms were bare of the heavy bracelet. What had she traded it for? Obviously not his freedom or the octopus wouldn't have stuffed him back in here. Did he belong to Ebby now? For long moments, they exchanged silent stares. *Apparently, the first move is up to me.* But what that move was, he didn't know. Certainly not this silly shell weapon he was holding. He set the shell on the sand behind him.

When he looked back up, she pointed to the shell, then signed, "More?"

A flush rose up his neck, and he had to avoid glancing to the corner where he'd discarded the seaweed. She thought he was hiding the shell because he'd eaten it all. He shook his head. "What happened out there with Red-tail?"

She watched his hands carefully, a cute little pucker appearing between her eyebrows. "Food?"

Ah, hell. For a moment, she'd made him forget she didn't understand sign language. 'Food' and 'more' were just baby words even toddlers could master.

He sighed. Circling his wrist with his other hand to indicate "bracelet," he pointed to her now bare wrist. "You traded," he signed. "Why?"

Her face radiated uncertainty, then she nodded and repeated the wrist-circling motion. "My bracelet."

Most people didn't try to sign, expecting him to read lips. She was making attempts to talk to him with her hands. Warmth spread through his chest. He made the sign for trade again then pointed at himself. "Traded for me?"

She nodded and signed, "Traded my bracelet for you."

Damn, putting sentences together already. She was a fast learner. He pointed at the dark opening. "Can I go?"

Her eyes were sad as she shook her head. "I traded my bracelet," she signed, adding, "One day."

That gushy feeling rose inside him again. She obviously wanted more dialogue than simple pointing, which was better interaction than he'd had with a woman in a long time. He tamped down on his excitement. *Focus on the goal. Escape.*

The other mermaid was obviously the leader, but Ebby'd bought him a single day of reprieve from whatever was to be his fate. "What happens after one day?"

Ebby shook her head, eyes suddenly growing fierce. She pointed to the box she'd set on the floor earlier. "Open."

The box was covered in barnacles and the wood was swollen, but he now recognized it for what it was: a jewelry box. He reached for it.

The shrimp guarding the box took an aggressive stance, tail raised and pointed legs stiff. Cruz knew mantis shrimp could pack a wallop if threatened, delivering a blow that rivaled a small caliber bullet in force. He'd never heard of one attacking a human, but his world had been turned upside down by the impossible already today. He wasn't about to risk a misunderstanding. He paused and turned back to Ebby. "You want me to open it?"

She nodded and shooed the shrimp away. It scuttled to the back wall and quickly buried itself in the sand.

Cautiously, he knelt on the sandy bottom next to the small chest, watching Ebby from the corner of his eye. She wrung her hands, brow furrowed. The lid refused to budge. Looking up at her, he signed, "It's locked."

She bit her bottom lip. "You can't open it?"

He frowned. How did she suddenly know so many words? He gave her a hard look. It was one thing to put a few words together, but her vocabulary was growing by leaps and bounds. "Do you know sign language?"

She shrugged and pointed at him. "I learn fast."

He blinked, unsure he understood correctly. "You learned it from me? But how? We've hardly spoken."

She shrugged one shoulder. "Mermaid magic."

His eyes tracked the hand she fluttered below her waist to say mermaid and when he looked back at her face, she was flushed. *Damn*, she was intriguing. And the topic of magic wasn't even what had him most intrigued. He felt like he was on a first date, having a conversation over dinner. He had so many questions for her, he didn't know where to begin.

"Please, can you open it?" she asked again.

Feeling an unexplainable urge to please her, he examined the latch. Among his many jobs, he'd spent a brief time as a locksmith. But this wasn't a matter of popping a lock. Barnacles had glued the seam together along two edges and the hinges were corroded beyond use. Turning it on its side, he rubbed his fingers over the seam. "I could try to break it."

The sadness on her face made him reconsider. This chest obviously meant something to her. He glanced around the cave floor and his gaze lit on the big clam shell he'd been sharpening. It might be strong enough to pry open the lid with minimal damage.

He picked it up and dug it into the seam at one corner. The waterlogged wood indented, but when he applied pressure, the shell broke, leaving a nick in his honed edge. *Ah, hell.* So much for his weapon.

Using another section of the shell, he chipped off the barnacles and pried again, more carefully this time. After a few minutes, he managed to widen a crack large enough for his fingers, and from there, he forced the hinges to grate open.

Ebby beamed at him, a smile brighter than the gleaming contents of the box. The gushy feeling flooded from Cruz's stomach to his head. He grinned back before realizing what he was doing. *This has to be Stockholm Syndrome.* The funny thing was, at this moment, he didn't care.

Trying to get hold of himself, he focused down at the treasure. Loose shells, pearls, and bits of shiny glass were interspersed with man-made items. A teardrop diamond earring. A filigreed silver bracelet. A thick gold chain. "What is all this for?"

Her smile wavered. "I trade for you."

He had no idea what Ebby's motives were, but he was

grateful. There had to be thousands and thousands of dollars' worth of gold and jewels in here. In one corner of the box rested a silk-wrapped bundle not much larger than a cell phone. He picked it up and opened it to reveal a strange white shell with long, thin prongs tipped in gold. A tiara? He placed it on his head and gave her a playful wink, trying to make her smile. "Where did you get this?"

Her face looked stricken.

He sobered, gently folding the silk back around it. "Sorry. I didn't mean to be disrespectful."

She made an attempt at smiling and signed awkwardly, "My mother's."

Ah, hell. She was giving up family jewelry for him? Now he felt really guilty.

"I also find much on shipwrecks." She took the tiara from his hands and unwrapped it once more. Offering him the silk, she gestured toward his hips, her face pinkening. "Humans like to cover?"

He accepted the cloth gratefully, tying it around his hips like a kilt.

"Hand language is new to me," she signed. "Do many humans speak it?"

The comfort that had been developing between them crumbled. Why did it always come back to his disability? "Sign language is for deaf people."

"Deaf?" She repeated his motion, gaze curious. "This means you cannot hear?"

He nodded, steeling his spine. He received one of two reactions from women when they realized he was deaf: pity or disdain.

But Ebby seemed… excited. "You're very lucky to be deaf."

He laughed. *Lucky?* Why on Earth would she consider him lucky? "I don't think lucky is the word you mean."

Her lashes fluttered as she seemed to consider. "Favored?"

He shook his head. "Not that, either."

She pursed her mouth. "I try to say you have advantage."

Now it was his turn to purse his mouth. She did indeed mean lucky. "Why do you say I have an advantage?"

"You cannot be controlled by mermaid song." She glanced over her shoulder toward the dark cave exit. "But you must pretend to be if… I do not know how to say name… Red-tail? sings."

So, the mermaid myths were true. They could control a man by singing. What could they possibly have wanted him to do that he hadn't already done? Didn't mermaids want to drown sailors or something like that? "What does she want?"

Her fists knotted at her sides. "Songs force humans to play."

He widened his eyes. "Play?" All at once, he realized what she meant; the first orgy had been merely the beginning. "You mean sex?"

Cheeks flushed, she turned slightly toward the door. "Much, yes. But also, other sensation."

Her blush warmed his own blood. "Other sensation. What does that mean?"

She gestured to the octopus. "Swim chase. Torture harm. All is entertainment."

His veins went from hot to cold in an instant. After he'd been stuffed back into the cave, a school of fish had come near the entrance, pursued by the red-tailed mermaid. The octopus had snatched them up, churning up blood and debris while the red-tailed mermaid laughed and clapped at the carnage. "Red-tail wants to feed me to the octopus?"

Ebby slumped and nodded. "Probably."

He'd suspected as much, but the confirmation made his heart race. He had to get out of here. The sooner the better.

CHAPTER EIGHT

*E*bby watched the expressions drifting across Cruz's face with fascination. Learning a language was as much about connecting body language to words as it was about putting words together, and she found Cruz's rugged features mesmerizing. The firm line of his jaw had grown darker with a line of stubble, and his short dark hair had a tiny bit of curl to it. Hazel eyes seemed to speak to her even when his hands were still, and his mouth…

Heat rose in her cheeks, and she dropped her gaze. Their brief kiss seemed branded on her lips, making her yearn for another. Thank Neptune she'd salvaged that silk so he could at least cover his lower half. Just thinking about what lay beneath the thin fabric gave her flutters low in her belly.

His hand moved toward her and she backed away. "You must not touch me."

He dropped his arm and sifted his fingers through the

contents of the treasure box instead. After a moment, he signed, "Why are you helping me?"

She licked her lips. The question was more complex than he could imagine. How easy it would be to give in to her nature and take him. Use him up. But another part of her nature held onto the memory of her da and her resolve to never be like either of her parents. She rubbed her arm, feeling naked without the bracelet she'd used as a reminder of her vow. "I am not like other mermaids."

He smiled, teeth dazzling in the cave's bioluminescent glow. "I know."

The affirmation made her heart swell and her throat tighten. A happy note rose within her, causing the phytoplankton lights to flicker in joyful response.

Cruz glanced around, mouth slightly parted as he watched the ripples race along the walls. He seemed enthralled by the display, so she strengthened her notes and directed the tiny creatures to wink on and off in firework bursts and rolling waves and nautilus swirls.

When she'd finished, Cruz turned back to her, eyes alight. "You did that?"

She nodded.

One side of his mouth quirked up in a sly smile. "Much better than red-tail's entertainment."

Heat once again filled her face. *Depths*, how could he continually make her feel like this? She turned away and studied the wall as if it was the most interesting thing in the world. A noise inside the cave made her stiffen, and she spun, sure Urokotori had snuck up on her.

Only Cruz was here. He signed, "How am I breathing underwater?"

"Mermaid magic." She moved to the cave doorway and peered outside. No one. Turning back, she asked, "Did you hear a noise?"

Cruz's face reddened, and he pointed to himself, opening his mouth. "Hey." Then he signed, "I wanted to get your attention, and you said not to touch you."

Her jaw dropped. Had he lied to her? Why? "You said you're deaf!"

He shook his head. "Deaf means I can't hear. I can speak, just not well."

She moved closer. "How?"

His face hardened, making him difficult to read, but the lines of his throat moved in a swallow; whatever he had to tell her must be painful. "I lost my hearing when I was seven. Before that, I used my voice."

"Lost? Can you find it again?"

He cracked into a smile, but his sadness still made her heart ache. "No. Broken might be a better word. Destroyed. I will never hear again." His gestures were sharp. He pushed his shoulders back as if shaking off that line of questioning. "So, this spell makes me... what? A merman, now?"

She laughed and shook her head. "You won't grow a tail. That magic is beyond mermaids."

"But I'll always be able to breathe underwater?"

Oh. That's what he was asking. She pressed her lips together and shook her head. "The magic must be renewed."

He blanched. "What happens if it expires?"

"I'll get you out of here before that happens." She looked at the treasure chest, wondering how much she would have to give Urokotori to make that happen.

The items inside all had sentimental value, but none were as precious to her as the bracelet she'd already relinquished. None except the fish harp. That was the one item she could never let Urokotori lay hands on. Bending, she pulled the instrument from the chest, stomach churning with memories.

Da never knew she'd gone looking for it after her mother's death. Her mother had lured Da and countless other mermen into compliance with its melodies. Da always joked that the magic in the harp could convince a sea turtle to leave its shell. The delicate instrument was made from a rare sea sponge found in the deepest parts of the ocean. Although one tine had been broken when Ebby located it at the bottom of the Wild Deeps, the nine, remaining gold-tipped tines were exponentially more powerful than Urokotori's smaller harp.

Ebby'd never used a harp. She didn't dare. It embodied everything she despised about mermaids.

"The other mermaids must never lay hands on this harp."

"It's a harp! How do you play it? Like a juice harp?"

"No. This is a fish harp." She touched the tines, careful not to evoke a note. "It's very rare, even among mermaids. It increases the power of our song a hundredfold. The more tines, the more powerful. Mermaids don't need to be any stronger than we already are."

Looking around the cave, Ebby went to the corner where Kato had buried himself and dug a hole next to him. The shrimp's eyes were all that showed above the surface, following her every move. Settling the harp carefully in the depression, she pushed the sand back over the top. "Guard this with your life, Kato."

The shrimp would do just that, although if one of the mermaids discovered it was here, they wouldn't hesitate to kill him, despite his position as Ebby's pet. Kato bobbed his eye stalks in silent acknowledgment, cautious with the octopus so nearby.

Ebby returned to the chest and pulled out a few other pieces. Everything looked rather dull under the blue-green light. Her heart sank as she contemplated which items Urokotori might prefer.

She held up a thin chain which she remembered being rose-gold in the sunlight. Now it looked like nothing more than a fisherman's string.

Strong fingers brushed hers as Cruz caressed the length of the chain. Her stomach jumped into her throat and she released the chain.

With a deft twist, he had the clasp undone and held it toward her. "May I?"

The necklace seemed to have regained some of its brilliance in his hands and she found herself nodding.

He reached around her, within a hairsbreadth of touching her, and latched the chain. His shoulder hovered close enough to kiss if she bent her head. She resisted, her insides fluttering. This close, his refreshing herbal scent permeated the water and made her skin tingle with desire. How the depths was she going to carry him to the surface once she freed him if she couldn't even be near him without losing her mind?

Settling the thin strand so it barely dipped into the hollow between her breasts, he pulled back, his gaze caressing the path of the chain along her collarbone. Slowly, he signed, "Beautiful."

If she'd been flustered before, now she felt completely unstrung. Heat filled not only her face, but her entire body. She couldn't look away. Nothing in this ocean could be half as fascinating as this human. Backing away, unsure of what she was asking, she signed, "Please don't."

"Did I touch you?" He held both palms up. "I tried to be very careful."

She bit her lip and shook her head. He had been very careful. Recalling her uncle's confidence in her, she forced herself to relax. Before Urokotori returned, Ebby needed to acclimate herself to being around this human and practice keeping herself under control. But the thought of embracing him for the swim made her heart beat hard and fast.

Get it together, she thought, settling to the sand as far from him as she could. "Will you tell me about humans?"

They spent the rest of the night talking, and by daybreak, she'd grown quite proficient at sign language. Her eyes were bleary from lack of sleep, but her heart felt strangely giddy and alive at the same time. By midmorning, Urokotori had not arrived, and Ebby's middle was a pit of hunger. Cruz's stomach rumbled in agreement. For all she knew, the other mermaid might never return. She had to go out for food.

Selecting a silver bracelet from her chest, she scoured it shiny with sand and approached Timuri. The octopus was quite intelligent in a foreign way and could transmit a message to Urokotori. Ebby wished she could bribe him to allow the human to pass, but a pet could never break a mistress's command, even at the cost of his life. She held out the bracelet. "Tell Urokotori this is for the human. For another day."

Timuri uncoiled one arm and Ebby slipped the bracelet over the tip. He withdrew it, tucking the jewelry away beneath him.

Ebby looked back into the cave at Cruz. "I'll be back soon with food."

"Take me with you." He floated expectantly in the middle of the cave.

"I can't." She'd imagined all the ways she might subvert Urokotori's order, but the mermaid had been very clear in her command. *Prevent the human from leaving the cave.* "You will be safe until I get back."

She hurried away, hoping that last statement was true.

CRUZ DRIFTED BACK and forth at the back of the cave, leaving glowing imprints each time he pushed gently off the wall. If he didn't get out of here soon he'd go stir crazy before the mermaids even got around to torturing him to death. Ebby'd said she'd be back soon, but that could mean anything in mermaid terms.

He was just finishing his umpteenth circuit of the small cave when a curvaceous shadow blocked the light from the doorway. *Finally!*

He turned, expecting Ebby, and found himself face-to-face with a familiar, freckled face and purple hair. She was singing, making come-hither movements with her fingers.

Biting his bottom lip, Cruz recalled Ebby's warning that he mustn't let the mermaids know he was not compelled. But moving forward might be akin to sticking his head inside a hungry shark's mouth. He edged closer, playing the clumsy swimmer to buy him some time. Although she was smiling, her wicked teeth gleamed in the cavern's bioluminescent light.

The all-too-familiar genital slit on her front looked swollen and pulsing. His heart thundered as he tried to read her intent. Playful or hungry?

Either option was equally unappealing.

As soon as he was within range, the mermaid reached

beneath his kilt and grabbed his dick. None too gently, either.

She yanked him close and smashed her mouth against his, the sharp points of her teeth cutting into his lips. Attempting to accommodate her, he opened his mouth and kissed her back, swiping his tongue between her needle-like teeth. He reached up and pinched her nipple, working through his mind all the steps he might take to please a woman. His skin crawled everywhere it contacted hers, from her hungry lips to her hand on his cock demanding more than he wanted to give.

She thrust against him, hand firmly at the base of his shaft. Although he had a mild erection, he wasn't hard enough to enter her, and her thrashing grew more and more frenzied.

After a few fruitless minutes, she shoved him away, her face no longer remotely attractive. She bared her teeth in a snarl then opened her mouth wide. The cave's phytoplankton became blindingly bright, and the water seemed to shudder all around him.

He licked his lips, tasting blood, and moved forward, unsure what she might be commanding.

Obviously not sex, because she shoved him away again with a hard punch to his chest. He sailed backward, colliding with the wall hard enough to knock the breath from him.

The mermaid whirled and departed the cave in a flurry of sand.

Cruz pushed off the wall and choked on a mouthful of water. His lungs constricted in panic.

Remain calm. His years of diving experience kicked in. He opened his mouth to sip another breath like he would from a regulator when diving. Water rushed over his teeth, salting his tongue.

The breath-spell was gone.

$\mathcal{E}$bby had just placed the last succulent frond of seaweed in a shell bowl when a familiar, purple-tailed shadow swept overhead. Selachii circled back, her freckled face etched with disgust. "I can't believe you actually paid to keep that human alive. He's all used up. Ugh."

Imagining the other mermaid rubbing herself over him made nausea rise in Ebby's throat. How did Selachii know about the deal? *Depths!* Had Urokotori returned to the cave while she was gone? Was she still there? Clutching the seaweed shell tighter, she asked, "Is Urokotori there?"

"She wasn't when I left. But I can see why." Selachii flipped a lock of hair out of her face and smoothed her hand down her flank as if brushing off some invisible sand. Her triggerfish skittered up to clean the area. "He couldn't even get it up." The mermaid cackled. "Your boringness must've rubbed off on him."

Ebby turned away. "Like I care. Why don't you go find some sea lions to torture and leave me alone?"

"Good idea." Selachii clapped her hands. "You should come along."

Although her heart was skipping beats, Ebby didn't bother to answer, pretending to continue her harvesting.

"So boring," Selachii kicked pebbles toward Ebby as she darted away.

The moment the purple fins had faded into the murky depths, Ebby dropped her shell and raced to the cave. Was she already too late? Jetting past the startled Timuri, she burst into the cave to find Cruz floating belly-up against the cave's ceiling. She cried out, sending the phytoplankton into a frenzy of brilliance.

Cruz turned his head to look at her.

A wash of relief sank her to the sandy floor. He was alive. She didn't even care that he'd been with Selachii, as long as he wasn't hurt.

He signed, "I can't breathe."

Her gut clenched when she saw air bubbles leak from his nose. A glance at the ceiling told her he'd been hanging onto life by gasping pockets of air trapped against the cave's solid stone. He wouldn't survive long on those.

She had to renew the breath-spell.

Her insides quivered. The briefest touch of his hand made her nervous. How was she going to handle the intimacy of a breath kiss? Would her mermaid instincts overcome her?

It didn't matter. There was no time to lose.

Before she could second-guess herself, she tore him from the ceiling, pulled his face to hers, and planted a chaste kiss on his lips before darting away.

He convulsed and stuffed his face back against the ceiling.

She'd never given a breath-spell before and wasn't sure how it worked, but apparently merely touching their lips together didn't do it.

Depths.

Steeling herself, she moved forward again. This time she pulled him into a full embrace, locking her lips against his. His arms wrapped around her shoulders in desperation, as if he could suck air from her through the kiss. Maybe that was it. She parted her lips and released a stream of bubbles into his mouth.

His chest swelled beneath her embrace. He slipped one hand around to the small of her back, holding her close. The stubble above his lip tickled her mouth, and she became aware of the way their bodies seemed to align in all the right places. The hard plane of his abs against her softer belly. His bare chest against her breasts, the fine mist of hair tickling her nipples. He was breathing now, yet seemed reluctant to let go.

And then she felt his tongue touch hers. The contact shot straight through her as if he was kissing her in places other than just her mouth. The hand on her back roamed up her spine, and he threaded his fingers into the hair at the base of her neck, guiding her head to deepen the kiss, drawing her tongue forward to tangle with his.

Indescribable pleasure shot through her like a drug. She let out a moan and sucked on his tongue. He shuddered, arms crushing her against his hard frame.

She ran one hand across the stubble on his jaw and around his ear to the hard cords at the back of his neck. By Neptune, she'd never imagined a kiss could claim her so completely. Was this a side effect of the breath-spell? Her other hand traced the sleek muscles along his ribcage and up around a broad shoulder.

His lips moved against hers as if he could devour her, his arms holding her close. She hadn't seduced him with a song, and even if she'd tried, he was immune. Yet he wanted her.

He definitely wanted her.

His erection had grown between them. A gentle roll of her hips over the long, hard line caused him to moan into her mouth. The only thing blocking him from her slit was the thin silk kilt he wore around his hips. How easy it would be to lift it. To pull him free. To thrust herself forward and fill herself with his heat.

His hands swept down to cup her backside and grind against her, erection pulsing against her opening. Her core tensed with anticipation. What would he feel like inside her? Rubbing the deepest part of her. Filling her again and again. She wanted to open to him more than she'd ever wanted anything in her life. She wanted him to know her.

I need to stop this before things go any further.

She pulled away stiffly, reluctant to relinquish his touch.

His eyes were dilated, his fingertips slipping away from her skin with longing. Blinking once, he signed, "Thank you."

Ebby licked her kiss-swollen lips and nodded. "I'm sorry."

"For what?"

"I never considered Selachii a threat."

"Selachii is the purple mermaid?"

She nodded. Leaving him in here alone again wasn't an option unless she bought off all three mermaids, and she didn't have enough jewelry for that, not to mention it was only a temporary fix. She had to come up with a means to get him past Timuri and back on dry land.

Her hand went to the dart earring Lutana had given her. No, she'd already rejected that idea. Killing Timuri would be unforgivable. But what about commanding him? Mermaids were seldom able to exert control over a rival's pet, but Ebby had something Urokotori didn't—her mother's fish harp. Using the stronger harp, Ebby's command spell might overcome Urokotori's.

Sensing her agitation, Kato shook himself free of sand and crouched over the harp's hiding spot. She knelt next to him, lifting him in her palm to face level. "Don't worry, dear friend. I don't want a new pet."

His antennae waved in agitation.

She set him down and gently excavated the delicate harp. Commanding Timuri would require strong magic, and there was bound to be trial and error as she honed her skill. Despite its small size, the harp weighed heavy in her grip as she turned toward the cave exit.

Cruz's attention moved from her face to her hand and back. "I thought you said she could never have that."

"It's not for her." Ebby swallowed tightly. "I'm going to use it."

"Can I help?"

She realized then that she would need to stay close to Timuri to maintain control and move him far enough away for Cruz to escape. The human was going to have to swim for the surface on his own. Pulling her dart earring free, she held it out to him. Once he'd taken it, she clumsily signed one-handed, "This will kill a mermaid, but only use it as a last resort. The surface is far, and there are more mermaids than you have darts." She told him the rest of her plan. "I'll catch up to you once you're clear of the cave and make sure you reach land. Swim as fast as you can."

He set aside the dart and reached for the sea harp. She

jerked it out of reach. He signed, "Let me put it on your necklace so you don't drop it."

She'd forgotten she wore the chain. Relinquishing her hold, she allowed him to unfasten the chain's clasp. His fingers brushing her skin made her shiver. Within moments, he'd slipped the golden strand through one of the many small holes in the harp's spine and returned the necklace to her throat. The small instrument weighed almost nothing, yet felt like a lead weight around her neck.

"Ready?" she asked.

He nodded.

Squaring her shoulders, she moved toward the entrance just as a sleek red form blocked the light.

Urokotori put her hands on her hips and raked her gaze over Cruz. "Selachii, you said the human was dead."

Ebby covered the harp with one palm. Urokotori had nearly killed Selachii in a battle over the small fish harp the red mermaid now owned. What would she do to get her hands on a larger, more powerful harp?

Selachii's voice drifted through the water from somewhere behind Urokotori. "He's not dead?"

"Our little prawn has decided to save him." Urokotori's fingertips drummed against her hips. "What do you find so fascinating about him, Ebby, if you're not going to fuck him?"

"I don't understand." Selachii's face appeared over Urokotori's shoulder. Her purple eyebrows furrowed.

Ebby moved in front of Cruz. "I want to buy his freedom. For real this time—as in alive and returned to dry land."

Urokotori shook her head, her face masked with disappointment. "You should never have chosen to be female, Ebby. You're just not up to the task."

"What do you care if I am or not?"

Dropping her hands from her hips, Urokotori pointed a long, clawed finger into the cave, her hair writhing around her like seagrass. "I'm growing tired of this game, little sister. You will become a true mermaid today."

Ebby's heartbeat thrummed loudly in her ears. "You can't make me."

An evil grin thinned Urokotori's crimson lips. "Oh, really? That sounds like a fun challenge." She tilted her head to one side. "I'll make you a deal. Seduce him before nightfall and I will let him out of the cave."

"If he can be seduced," Selachii joined in. "When I was here earlier, he was useless."

Urokotori's laughter rebounded off the cave walls. "A challenge for our little sister, then. If she fails, we'll give the human to Timuri."

"No!" Ebby pressed the fish harp until the tines dug into her chest. If only mermaid song worked against other mermaids; she'd have no qualms about commanding these two to kill each other. But killing wasn't the answer. Was seduction? Would giving up her virginity be so bad if it saved Cruz's life? *What if you become like Urokotori? Like Mother?* Her insides trembled at the thought.

"Fuck him and get it out of your system," Urokotori crooned. "I'm doing this for your own good." She lifted her two-pronged fish harp from where it dangled between her breasts and plucked a tine. A single note quivered through the water. "Earn his freedom."

Both of the other mermaids sidled backward a couple of yards and began to sing.

CRUZ HAD no idea what was going on between Ebby and the other mermaids, but he knew it wasn't good. When the red mermaid lifted the turkey wishbone from the cord around her neck, he recognized it for what it was—a smaller version of Ebby's harp. He looked at Ebby, expecting her to use her larger harp to fend the mermaid off, but Ebby remained rigid, one hand clutching the harp pendant so tightly, he worried she'd crush the instrument.

Red-tail opened her mouth in what had to be a siren song, her clawed fingers plucking her harp.

Still, Ebby remained frozen.

Was red-tail using magic to paralyze her? The tiny dart was still in his hand, but there were two mermaids plus the lurking octopus. Reaching out with tentative fingers, he encircled Ebby's elbow and turned her to face him.

Her eyes were wide, her bottom lip caught between her teeth. She signed, "They're singing a seduction song."

Not paralyzed, then, at least not by magic. But she was afraid. Without turning his head, he glanced from the corner of his eye toward the entrance. "Can you counter their spell using your harp? It's bigger than Red-tail's."

"Harps don't work on other mermaids. Their song is supposed to work on you."

Her words settled over him like scuba-diving weights. All the admonishments not to touch her, and now she was supposed to have sex with him? Not that he didn't want her, but...

She took his free hand and placed it on one of her breasts. The nipple hardened beneath his palm, but he knew from experience that just because the body responded didn't mean someone was aroused. He pulled it away and signed, "Should we use the dart?"

A sad smile lifted one corner of her mouth and she shook her head. "It wouldn't be enough. They said that after I seduce you, they'll set you free."

Despite his hesitation, his dick hardened at her words. The kiss they'd shared when she restored his breath-spell had been amazing. The way her mouth had tasted of amber and musk, reminding him of an ocean at sunset. How warm she'd felt against his body.

She reached out and placed his palm on her breast again, sliding close until her lips were within inches of his. The hand cupping her breast was now trapped between them. His dick jumped to full attention. Perhaps he was immune to mermaid songs, but he was definitely still affected by her.

Taking the lead, he brushed his lips over hers. He wanted this. Wanted her—more than he'd ever wanted anyone, captivity be damned. At least if he died, he'd die happy.

She opened her mouth, back arching slightly as she accepted his kiss. Her tongue played over his lower lip and her nipple hardened beneath his palm.

Worried he might accidentally jab her with the dart, he let it slip from his fingers and stroked his hand over the smooth skin at the small of her back. She was so warm and pliable, the tiny dimples above what would be her ass making his dick harden even more. He wanted to explore every inch of her. Pulling her hips close to his, he claimed her mouth in a full, deep kiss.

She tangled her tongue with his while her fingers dug into his hair. If he'd thought the breath kiss had been magic, then this was nirvana. And Ebby was his goddess.

Ebby'd always assumed the mermaids did all the seducing, but Cruz was doing a pretty good job of it himself. His hands kneaded her backside, rubbing her against the heat of his erection, while his tongue plunged in and out of her mouth, a sex act all its own. One big palm slid up her back and gripped her hair, forcing her head back, and he left her mouth to trail his stubbled chin lightly down her neck, nipping and sucking her tender skin and giving her sparks of delight.

She ran her hands over his chest, intrigued by his hair. Humans had so much hair! His small nipples hardened to pinpoints under her fingertips, the defined curve of his pecs flexing as he adjusted his grip around her waist. Depths, he was a beautiful man. She suddenly wanted to see him. All of him. Close.

She gently walked her hands down his torso until she knelt on her tail fin, at eye level with the silk covering his throbbing erection. His hands remained tangled in her hair and his muscular legs spread wide, adjusting to keep him upright in the water. She ran her palms up his rock-hard thighs, enjoying the feel of his coarse hair as she pushed the silk aside. When she reached his balls, she cupped them, rolling them gently beneath her fingers. The fragile softness there contrasted completely with the hard shaft pulsing in response to her attention.

She gripped his base, squeezing and pulling until a milky bead appeared at the tip. A delighted shudder ran through her at his response. She'd never been this close to a man before, though she'd seen the way their bodies reacted during her many spying sessions. Experiencing his reaction was even better than she'd imagined.

His herbal scent filled the water as she swept her tongue across the head of his cock then plunged his thick length into her mouth. Under her tongue, his ridges and heat provided a whole new sensation, and she wanted more. Wrapping her lips over her teeth to protect him, she took as much of him inside her as she could, jaw aching as she sucked and pulled.

His hands caressed her scalp, urging her to meet the rhythm of his flexing hips. She wrapped her hands around his ass, sliding her fingers down to feel where his legs split. He seemed to like that, so she explored with her fingertips while her mouth conquered his length. Soon, he was quivering, ass flexed and thigh muscles hard as rocks. She sucked harder. But instead of exploding as she expected, he shuddered and pushed her away.

Was he done? Disappointment squeezed her chest. That wasn't at all what she'd expected.

She tilted her face up. His hazel eyes were dark with desire and his chest heaved. Smiling, he signed, "Slow down."

Thank Neptune he wasn't done. Remembering the other

mermaids watching, she glanced at them. They continued singing, sharp gazes possibly as hungry for climax as she was.

Cruz sank to his knees and dipped his head to her breast, once again surrounding her in the moment. The stubble on his chin seared a mark across her heart. When his tongue swirled around her nipple, her back arched as if lightning had hit her belly button. *Ah, Neptune, what delightful torture!*

Wrapping her fingers into his hair, she arched again, offering up her other breast. He nipped and sucked and teased until she wondered how she could stand one second more. A heat was building deep in her core. Her primal-self ached for one thing. One hard, thick thing.

Ebby stretched one hand downward, seeking his erection once more. But Cruz slid down her body, angling his cock farther away and trailing his mouth along her abdomen toward the sleek skin where her pulsing slit waited. She whimpered, frustrated yet delighted at the new sensation. His fingers massaged her backside, pulling her hips ever closer to his mouth until his tongue flicked out and entered the top of her opening. That brief contact sent a ripple through her and she flexed, desperate for more.

He obliged, tangling his tongue around the nub of her pleasure. *Depths.* She'd touched herself many times but never had it felt this good. Sucking and prodding, he penetrated her with his tongue, driving her wild. She bucked against him, ripple after ripple of pleasure running from her scalp to her fins.

Their activity had driven her backward into the cave wall, igniting a fury of teal-green light. The rough stone against her back only heightened her arousal, and she pulled him closer, wanting, wanting… His finger joined his tongue, finding her opening and pressing past her folds.

She exploded around him, the calloused pad of his finger deep within her. She'd experienced orgasm before, but under the control of another person, the sensation was mind-blowing.

He continued stroking until she'd finished shuddering. Withdrawing slowly, he pulled himself up the length of her body, his skin sliding along hers somehow raising her to new levels of desire. His mouth had been fabulous, his finger divine, but still, she wanted more. She wanted all of him.

Slipping a hand between them, she gripped the base of his shaft, guiding him to her entrance. He paused his kiss and pulled back just enough to meet her gaze. *I want you*, she thought, willing him with her eyes.

And he understood. He thrust forward, penetrating her. Opening her. Filling her.

Again and again he thrust, driving her against the cave wall, filling the water with tiny motes of bioluminescent light as phytoplankton dislodged and floated free. The heat of his body melding into hers seemed to be more than physical. More than primal. It was a spiritual thing, a thing above all others, and for the first time she thought she understood why the other mermaids were so driven to perform this act again and again.

It felt as if he *knew* her. As if he had access to every deep dark secret and lofty wish.

She never wanted it to end. Never wanted to be apart. She gripped him tightly, letting wave after wave break over her until her climax shattered her into a million pieces.

At nearly the same moment, he seated himself inside her with a final thrust, his hot seed shooting directly into her core and drawing from her one final shudder of ecstasy.

He kept a tight hold on her as she trembled, his warmth seeping into her, filling her, consuming her. Her head swam with thoughts and emotions as if she was unsure where she ended and Cruz began. Images flashed behind her eyes, lights, faces—things she didn't understand. And then out of the mist rose a coherent sentence. *That was some orgasm. How can a fish be so damned hot?*

Inside, she laughed. *I'm not a fish.* She would never think of herself as a fish. Then the satisfaction in her heart cooled as she realized what was happening. Sometimes a merman would bond to a mermaid so fiercely it allowed her to hear his thoughts. Such bonds were prized by mermaids because it gave them even greater control of their helpless mates. She had no idea humans were also susceptible.

His thoughts were content. Languid. His hands crept down to cup her backside. *Not a fish. A mythological creature. A woman.* He pulled her tightly against him. *My mythological woman.*

Despite her dismay that he was now under her power, a bubble of laughter filled her chest. He was as delightful in his head as he was with his hand language. More so, even. If only the connection wasn't one-way. She ran her fingertips over his stubbled cheek. *I wish you could hear me, Cruz.*

His lashes fluttered open to meet her gaze, his irises still dark with lust. *Get a grip on yourself, Cruz. You can't hear her thoughts.*

She frowned, her wish igniting into something closer to dread. Had he just said he could hear her?

His attention shifted to her mouth. *What's going on? I swear she's talking to me. Can mermaid magic restore hearing?*

Full-blown panic took hold of Ebby and she pushed him away. She could hear him—rare enough—but if he could hear her in return… *The mate bond.* No, it couldn't be. She was a mermaid. She should be immune to the mate-bond. Carefully, she crafted her next thought. *Cruz, can you hear me?*

He blinked slowly, his eyebrows pinching together, and nodded. *Is this more mermaid magic?*

The array of emotions passing through her threatened to make her pass out. She recalled the trips to the Deeps she'd taken with Da, where she'd heard the ancient blue whales sing of true mates and lost magic. *Something stronger. Only true mates can hear each other.*

True mates? He cocked his head again, raising his brows. He seemed to be taking this head-talking thing in stride.

Ebby wasn't. She'd become a mermaid to avoid the shackle of a mate bond. Mate bonds only caused heartache and a slow, living death. She'd watched it consume her father. This couldn't be happening. It just wasn't possible. She backed away in horror, arms raised to keep him away.

Cruz reached for her, eyebrows puckered with concern. *Ebby?*

She couldn't allow him to touch her again and incite her desire. Not when the unfathomable had just happened. The word *trapped* kept cycling through her mind. Spinning, Ebby shot from the cave and past the other mermaids, Cruz's voice calling her name in her head.

Laughter resonated through the water behind her, drowning out Cruz's words.

"We told you you'd see the light, sister!" Urokotori's voice twisted Ebby's confusion into fury.

Whipping around, Ebby found herself face to face with Selachii. Lightning quick, the purple-tailed mermaid snapped the chain from Ebby's neck, enveloping the attached fish harp in one clawed hand.

Ebby lunged for it, but Selachii's triggerfish snapped its powerful jaws, almost taking off her finger. New terror took root inside Ebby's chest. "Give that back."

Selachii strummed the tines, eliciting a mesmerizing note that sent Ebby flashing back to her mother. That harp had announced her mother's arrival every time she visited Da's nest, driving Ebby into hiding for the duration of her visit.

"Where did you get this, dear sister?" Selachii crooned in harmony with the harp.

The triggerfish circled Selachii's hips as if doing a victory dance.

"It's my mother's," Ebby grit through her teeth. How foolish she'd been, bringing the harp into the open.

Urokotori drifted to a halt beside her purple-tailed sister, eyes narrowed. "Let me see it."

Selachii bared her teeth at the red-tailed mermaid. "Don't think for one second you can force me to hand it over like you did last time." She eyed the one hanging around Urokotori's neck before brandishing the one she held. "This one's got nine tines."

"It's not the size of the instrument." Urokotori flicked a lock of hair over her shoulder and tossed her chin. Her gaze never wavered from the tines poking like grotesque fingers from Selachii's grip. "It's how you play it that counts. You're going to need a lot of practice."

Selachii let out an offended screech, her purple hair fanning out around her head like a puffer fish. She hesitated a heartbeat, as if considering a frontal attack, then jerked around and darted through the kelp, her triggerfish close on her fins.

"Wait!" Ebby cried, flexing her tail muscles to follow.

Strong, clawed hands trapped her wrist, jerking her to Urokotori's side. "Oh, no you don't. It's time to put an end to your childish resistance once and for all."

The larger mermaid took off in the opposite direction, grip tight enough to make Ebby's arm feel as though it might rip from its socket.

Balling her other hand into a fist, Ebby slammed it into Urokotori's kidney. The other mermaid grunted, her hold loosening. Ebby ripped herself free, swimming back toward the cave.

Urokotori plucked a tine on her harp, and a cluster of yellow-bellied sea snakes darted upward from the rocks, intercepting Ebby's course. They coiled their tails tightly around Ebby's throat and arms. One venomous beast stared her in the eye with fangs bared.

Ebby froze, letting the current carry her stiffly back toward Urokotori. Sea snakes were generally not aggressive, but under a mermaid's command, they became the deadliest creature in the entire ocean.

Urokotori laced her fingers through Ebby's as if they were the best of friends and led her onward. "You're pathetic. You could've been the most powerful mermaid in the sea with that harp. It's completely wasted on that idiot Selachii."

Ebby hooked her tail fin on rocks and coral, hoping to create some drag. "You're not going to let her keep it, are you?"

"Of course not," Urokotori yanked on her arm. "Once you're secure, I'll take care of her."

"Secure? What are you talking about?"

"You'll see."

Ahead, the jutting mast of the slave ship pierced the faint blades of sunlight bisecting the current. The pit of Ebby's stomach grew ice cold. Years ago, she'd been horrified by the bones in the human ship, arms and legs still attached to heavy chains within the hold. Her father had bypassed the gory spaces, sifting through the upper levels where the crew had stayed. But the memory of all those helpless humans had remained with Ebby.

Urokotori dragged her over the bow of the ship toward the hatch.

"Let me go. We have more important things to do. Like get that harp back before Selachii figures out how to use it." Ebby didn't like the idea of Urokotori getting her hands on the instrument, either, but at this point, any distraction would be useful. "You don't want her to be stronger than you are, do you?"

Seemingly deaf to Ebby's words, Urokotori shoved her into a hallway, following it lower into the dark recesses of the ship. No light penetrated the underbelly, but Ebby's mermaid gaze could see enough to know the skeletons were just as she remembered. A fine filter of sediment covered the remains, but the outlines of human bodies were clear. Row upon row of the dead, chained to the floor of the hold as the water flooded in, unable to escape, unable to break the bonds that held them down.

The sea snakes were growing agitated, tails tightening around Ebby's throat. Any sudden move could get her killed. A hum built low in her throat, instinct telling her to at least attempt to countermand Urokotori's hold on the creatures. Without a harp, she stood little chance, but her proximity to the snakes might give her a small advantage.

She'd just opened her mouth to utter her directive when a cold weight settled around her wrist.

"There," Urokotori said. "I've always wanted to do that."

A heavy iron cuff chafed Ebby's skin, connected to the grisly floorboards by a thick chain.

Urokotori clicked her tongue, freeing the snakes from her charm. They let go and wriggled away. Ebby jerked ineffectually against the chain, the metal links grating and clunking against each other. "What are you doing?" The rusty manacle was securely locked around her wrist. "Do you even have a key for this?"

Urokotori waved an unconcerned hand. "I'm sure there's one around here somewhere. Once you've learned your lesson, I'll track it down."

"What lesson?" Ebby recalled the trips with her father and the detritus scattered around the ship's cabins. Finding a key would be next to impossible.

"Don't worry. I'll be back with your pathetic human." Urokotori pushed herself toward the hatch.

Ebby jerked her wrist again, rough iron biting into her skin. "No! You said you'd set him free!"

Urokotori turned, a dark silhouette within the hold's deep shadows. "I said I'd let him out of the cave. What do you find so appealing about that male, anyway?" Without giving Ebby a chance to respond, the mermaid spun and exited the hold. Her voice floated back through the corridor. "Not that it matters. You'll see how fragile humans are once I've finished with him."

"Come back! Don't leave me here!"

Only the thrum of the ever-pressing current against the ship's hull responded.

Cruz paced the cave a safe distance away from the octopus guarding the exit. Confusion was tearing him apart. Ebby's voice inside his mind had been the most intimate thing he'd ever experienced, even more gratifying than sex in a way, and her sudden departure had cut him to the quick. Did he sound as stupid in her head as he did when he spoke aloud? People had been rude to him lots of times, making fun of his impairment, but he didn't think he'd ever put off anyone badly enough to drive them away.

This entire situation was fucked as hell. Why had Ebby run away? She seemed to think he was her true mate, but he didn't know enough about mermaids to know what that meant or even make a guess about her true motives.

For all he knew, she'd been able to hear his thoughts all along. Maybe that's how she'd figured out sign language so quickly. *Shit.* Had she lied to him this whole time? It hadn't felt like she was lying to him. Maybe she'd been right and losing her virginity really did change her into a man-eating monster like the others. Yet obviously Ebby would rather flee than hurt him.

So maybe she wasn't a monster?

He shook his head and ran his fingertips over the dart, careful not to prick himself on the sharp point. Ebby's mantis shrimp had helped him locate the ivory sliver. If the poison was strong enough to kill a mermaid, would it kill an octopus? He glanced at the entrance again. He'd need to get close enough to do it.

Edging forward with the dart in one hand, he watched the octopus watching him and remembered the searing blow it had delivered last time he'd come too close. What if it killed him this time? *Fuck.* No way he could dart the animal before it knocked him senseless. He threaded the dart into the hem of his makeshift kilt. What a useless weapon. All he could do was wait for Ebby—or one of the others—to return.

When a female figure finally blocked the light at the entrance, Cruz forced himself to keep his hand away from the dart. If it was Ebby, he didn't want to hurt her accidentally, and if it was one of the others, he needed to somehow get out of the cave before he struck, or he'd only succeed in becoming trapped with a dead mermaid.

Blue filtered sunlight illuminated the mermaid's tail fin as if it was purple tissue paper. The mermaid who'd stolen his breath. His heartbeat increased as she slithered into the cave followed by a huge triggerfish. Was she singing to control him? He had to assume she was.

Pretending to be under her spell, he floundered toward her until he was close enough to see her face. Her amethyst eyes assessed him, lips parted provocatively. Then she lifted her hands, and he saw the gold-tipped prongs of a harp with one missing tine. *That's Ebby's.* Dread tightened his chest. She'd been very clear the others mustn't get their hands on the instrument. If this mermaid now carried it, then Ebby must be in trouble.

Or dead. He shook the idea out of his head, refusing to believe it. He didn't want to think of her as gone.

The purple-tailed mermaid ran her fingers over the tines, and the cavern lights flared in response. He could only imagine the sound reverberating off the walls. Although he couldn't hear, the vibrations were strong enough to cause an uncomfortable stirring in his groin. Ebby'd said it would amplify a mermaid's power, and it seemed to be working even despite his deafness.

He swallowed thickly and moved within range of her arms. The triggerfish zipped back and forth at her shoulder, toothed mouth snapping. Now wasn't the time to worry about the song or the harp. He was trapped in here unless he could convince her to take him outside. Hating to expose himself, he reached down and lifted the fabric, stroking his shaft into forced readiness. With his other hand, he pointed outside.

She grinned and reached for him.

He pointed toward the exit once more and tried to pull off a seductive smolder with his gaze.

She seemed to consider, eyes taking in the cave with distaste. Then her smile widened as if she'd realized something. Looking over her shoulder, she fluttered her fingertips over the harp.

The octopus swelled, then shuddered before withdrawing from sight. The triggerfish spun in frenzied circles around the mermaid as if performing a victory dance.

The mermaid turned her attention once more toward Cruz,

her eyes feverishly alight. She held out a clawed hand as if in invitation.

Cruz's heart threatened to stampede out of the cave ahead of him. *Patience.* He couldn't be sure the octopus was gone. Keeping up his pretended desire, he took her hand. He'd have to be close to use the dart, anyway. Once they were clear of the cave, he'd stab her and make his escape.

In a sudden, snake-like move, she pulled him against her and swept them both into the filtered light. Coral and stones swept by with dizzying speed.

After a few moments, her grip loosened enough for him to get his bearings. Her clawed hands cupped his face, her lips pursed for a kiss, and pulled him toward her expectantly.

Cruz fumbled with the hem of his kilt, feeling carefully for the splinter of the dart woven into it. Where was that damned thing? The mermaid shoved her mouth against his, tongue forcing itself between his lips. Her claws dug painfully into his cheeks, but he forced himself to remain compliant, using one hand to pinch her nipple while his other continued to search the edge of the silk.

There. Her tail thrashed the water, hips thrusting against his as the violent kiss threatened to shred his lips. If he wasn't careful, he'd drop the dart. Or worse, poke himself. Did he actually have to jab it into her or would a scratch be enough? He couldn't risk failure. Yanking the dart free, he jabbed the sharp point into her waist.

The mermaid's body stiffened. She twisted to look at her waist, claws fumbling at the protruding dart. Yanking it free in a cloud of blood, she turned her furious gaze back to him and tightened her grip on his forearm.

His stomach dropped to the sea floor. *It didn't work.* All he'd done was make her angry. He braced himself to receive her killing blow.

Suddenly, her back arched and her grip clamped down like a shark's bite. She opened her mouth wide, exposing razor-sharp teeth. He threw up an arm to shield himself. But instead of teeth, her tail slammed into his ribs with a force that knocked the breath from his body. Still caught in her grip, Cruz was thrown into a wild downward spin. He lost all sense of up or down as they plummeted past a wall of rocks and coral. Stones scraped his shoulder. Bruised his knee. He pried at her grip on his arm until they hit the bottom with numbing force.

The impact broke her hold, and he gulped grateful breaths of water while the mermaid continued convulsing, stirring up a cloud of debris. With a final arch of her back, she settled to the sea floor, eyes staring sightlessly toward the shifting pattern of sunlit ripples high above. Around her neck, the gold tines of the harp caught the light, sparkling through the settling haze.

Was she really dead? Much as he needed to kick toward the surface, he forced himself to approach her body. Her tail quivered, but her slack face gave him courage. Broken tines lay scattered on the sea floor around her, but on the chain around her neck, the harp's spine still bore two golden prongs. He reached for the instrument. Was it still as powerful as Ebby claimed? The chain's clasp was broken, and the mermaid had tied the gold links into a knot behind her neck. Her purple hair had tangled in the chain, but he broke it free.

Nervous she might revive, he backed away. She remained lifeless, sand settling over her skin.

Rising from the carnage on the sea floor, he looked around. The purple mermaid's fall had dropped him into a gulley between coral-studded rock walls. He was reminded of another time he'd climbed from a ravine, leaving behind a crushed vehicle with his mother inside. He clutched the harp tighter in one fist. If Ebby'd lost this, it meant she was in trouble.

He wouldn't leave until he knew she was safe. She'd stood up for him when the other mermaids wanted to rip him apart. She'd fed him, taken the time to learn sign language, and even given him her virginity. Her parting words about being true mates had him kicking upward, surveying the wall to get his bearings. Part of him seemed to think the purple mermaid had swum up the current with him, but he couldn't be sure.

He gazed down current. Going back might be dangerous, but Ebby's pet shrimp was still there and might know how to find her.

He struck out across the current toward the kelp a short distance away, planning to use it as cover while he paralleled the wall. His arm ached where the mermaid's claws had drawn blood, but there wasn't enough spilling into the water to concern him about sharks. Half swimming and half pushing against the slippery kelp stalks, he wove through the forest, keeping sight of the wall through the gaps between the fronds. Small fish darted away at his approach, flashing silver and teal and orange in the shafts of sunlight. How far was he below the surface? It felt odd to be swimming this deep without any gear to weigh him down. He pulled in a breath, marveling again at how easy it was. How long would the spell last?

A darker spot on the wall caught his attention, and he paused, treading water and peeking through the swaying leaves. It looked like the cave he'd been imprisoned in. Was the octopus still guarding it? Gripping a thick, slippery stalk, he looked closer. A flash of movement caught his eye on the sandy floor.

His pulse thrummed loudly in his ears as eight boneless legs twisted and furled, propelling the beast toward the kelp.

For a brief moment, he wondered if it had spotted him, but then he noticed a small plume of sand that seemed to be leading the creature forward. Some sort of prey. The smaller plume settled without warning and the octopus paused. As the sand settled, Cruz realized it was a mantis shrimp. Ebby's pet must be trying to make his escape.

The octopus coiled itself, poised to pounce. The shrimp faced it on its hind legs like a boxer daring a bully to come closer, raptorial claws pulled tight against its chest. He'd read that those claws could deliver a bullet-like punch strong enough to break glass, but would it be a match for a creature the size of an octopus? In short lunges, the octopus tested its prey. The shrimp stood its ground, back legs scurrying to keep it facing its enemy.

Cruz held tight to the kelp, unsure what to do. The shrimp hardly stood a chance, yet Cruz was no match for the octopus, either. His chest still felt bruised from being slammed back in the cave. But leaving Ebby's pet to be devoured seemed cruel. He glanced down at the sea floor, looking for something to throw before remembering how ineffective that would be under water. He still held the harp in his other hand; too bad he couldn't sing like a mermaid, or he'd just tell the octopus to back off.

He looked back up in time to see the shrimp jet toward the octopus in a motion almost too fast to see. All eight of the octopus's legs shot out straight and stiff. The shrimp appeared to ricochet off the larger creature's head, changing trajectory like a billiard ball and zooming straight toward the kelp. Behind it, the octopus sank stiffly to the floor.

Holy hell! Had that tiny shrimp just killed the octopus or only stunned it? He held aside a swaying frond, watching the octopus. A brief moment later, its legs curled back in and it woozily crawled back toward its cave.

Dropping toward the forest's knobby floor, Cruz moved down current searching for signs of Ebby's pet.

He found the little guy cowering in the midst of a group of spiny black sea urchins. Would it recognize him as a friend? He held out a hand like he'd seen Ebby do.

The creature waved its long antennae at him but stayed firmly entrenched between the poisonous spines.

He couldn't blame the guy. The only other times he'd hunted for crustaceans had been for an entirely different purpose. Maybe if he made it clear he meant no harm? He opened the hand holding the harp and held it out for the creature to see. Maybe a familiar object would convince it to come closer.

The shrimp shot forward, and Cruz flinched, expecting to end up like the octopus. The harp was wrenched from his fingertips. Pointed legs prickled along his arm toward his face, then settled on his shoulder. Cruz opened his eyes, shoulders relaxing as he realized the creature had settled in for a ride, harp clasped protectively between its claws.

Cruz smiled in relief and signed, "Any idea where to find Ebby, my friend?"

Tiny legs tickled his shoulder, and the creature adjusted itself to face down current.

Okay. Down current it was.

He pushed through the kelp, trying not to shrug off the tickle of the shrimp's feet against his shoulder. How did Ebby stand it? The current had already pushed him past the cave, and a short while later, the kelp forest ended. The sea floor dropped away at an abrupt edge.

Below, three masts of a shipwreck jutted upward like pointed teeth. On his shoulder, the shrimp jacked itself up and down on its hind legs, as if signaling him to go on.

Cruz tread water, looking at the open expanse before him. He was a strong swimmer, but without scuba gear, he'd be helpless against the currents and large predators found in open water, not to mention he'd no longer be hidden from potential mermaid eyes.

"She's in there? You sure?" he signed, looking at the shrimp.

The creature responded by launching off his shoulder, carrying the harp with it as it drifted down the rocky drop-off.

Sighing, Cruz followed, skimming the wall behind the shrimp. He hoped he wasn't reading too much into the shrimp's actions. For all he knew, this wasn't even Ebby's pet, and he was following some random creature to some random place. At least the current was assisting in pushing him toward the wreck. What if Ebby wasn't here? He didn't want to think of how he was going to overcome it to get back.

As he moved deeper toward the ship, the water got colder, and the light dimmed until all he could see was shadows of blue and green. His heart thundered against his ribs, and his muscles trembled with exertion and chill. What he wouldn't do for a few of the phytoplankton from the cave to light his way.

Below him, the shrimp disappeared between a small outcropping of rocks. Cruz swam past, taking a moment to realize it hadn't emerged again. Turning to see if the shrimp had changed direction, he froze, gaze lifting toward a sinuous shadow outlined in the light coming from the surface.

A mermaid floated a few arms lengths above him, her tail gyrating lazily, long hair fanned out like a halo. *Ebby?*

She dipped toward him.

In the dim light, her features resolved into crimson lips and a slow, predatory grin.

Ebby pulled against the chain, the links rattling and clanking as she tried to jerk free again and again. Her wrist was throbbing and raw and blood scented the stale water inside the ship's hold, but sharks were the last thing on her mind.

She'd been calling Cruz, hoping to warn him for what felt like hours, but apparently, the mate bond connection was limited by distance. Why had she fled the cave? She'd not only lost the harp, she'd abandoned Cruz to the mercies of the other mermaids. Everything she'd done, everything she'd sacrificed, had been for nothing. She thought of his voice in her head, a connection she'd never dreamed of experiencing. She should have savored it, not run away. A mate bond was so rare it was almost impossible. And she'd squandered it.

A familiar song outside the ship grew stronger, the dulcet notes of Urokotori's seduction magic approaching.

The other mermaid must be returning with Cruz already. Ebby's stomach roiled as she called yet again. *Cruz, can you hear me?*

His voice entered her mind, frantic and gasping. *Ebby? Ebby, where are you?*

He was alive! *Cruz! Do you have the dart? Use it now! Get away!*

I already used it on the purple mermaid. Cruz's voice was tight, as though he spoke through gritted teeth.

Nausea filled her. Was he hurt? She should've realized Selachii would want a test subject for her new harp. Then another horror struck her. If the purple mermaid was dead, that meant Urokotori had the harp. She would be unstoppable. Ebby twisted her hand, trying to unscrew it from the manacle until her bones ached.

From the hatch, a tentacled leg appeared, then another and another. Ebby drew back as Timuri boiled into the hold. He pulsed with angry color, but instead of attacking her, he pulled himself against the ceiling in the far corner to await his mistress's arrival. Urokotori wasn't far behind, towing Cruz along by one wrist. His other hand grappled uselessly against her grip. *Ebby, are you in here? I can barely see.*

I'm here. Ebby sang a wavering note that ignited the few sickly phytoplankton drifting inside the hold. The pale green bioluminescence made the fresh bruises and cuts marring his skin look terrible. *You're hurt!*

I'm okay. His tone belied his words.

"Your human somehow convinced Selachii to set him free." Urokotori shoved him toward her pet, who sullenly wrapped several legs around Cruz's limbs. "And he appears to be immune to my song."

Oh, no. If Urokotori knew he was deaf, there was no telling

what she might do to torture him. *Why didn't you pretend to hear her?*

She came up behind me while I was looking for you.

The octopus jerked the flailing man toward its beak. Urokotori issued a command at the creature to halt. Beak clacking, the octopus quivered, obviously chafing against her control.

A diversion came to Ebby's mind. "You seem to be struggling with your pet, Urokotori. Maybe your song isn't as strong as you think."

The other mermaid rounded on her, jabbing a long, clawed finger her direction. "He's agitated because your pet attacked him!"

Ebby's throat tightened. She'd abandoned Kato in the cave along with Cruz. Although the little shrimp packed a big punch, she doubted he could hold his own against Timuri for long. Poor Kato had become a meal because of her. Grief blurred her vision with briny tears. It seemed everyone she loved was falling prey to Urokotori's whim. *Oh, Kato!*

Don't worry, Cruz soothed. *Your little shrimp clobbered the octopus and got away.*

A weak smile tugged at Ebby's mouth. Her mate was facing a horrible death, yet here he was comforting her. She raised her chin and glared at Urokotori. "It's not the size of the pet, but how you use it that counts."

Urokotori's upper lip curled into a snarl. "You want me to use my pet? Fine." She commanded Timuri to spread Cruz's limbs like a sacrifice.

Muscles bunching, Cruz released a growl that could rival a sea lion, jerked one hand free of the octopus's tentacle, and reached for Urokotori's throat.

She slipped backward with a delighted chuckle, sending the glowing phytoplankton swirling around her. "He's ready to play!"

"Leave him alone!" Ebby stretched at the end of her chain, her free hand inches from Urokotori's back. "I'll do whatever you want!"

Urokotori remained focused on Cruz's grimacing face while he flailed against the octopus's grip. "This is going to be fun."

He bared his blunt teeth at Urokotori, limbs quivering as she slid her tail fin upward between his legs. Urokotori trailed her claws down his chest to his navel. His six-pack bulged as he attempted to curl away from her touch.

Ebby's blood surged in her ears, every heartbeat a countdown to certain death. She had to protect her mate.

Her fingers brushed the ends of Urokotori's black hair. Straining against the manacle, she gained another centimeter. More hair threaded between her fingers. She curled her hand into a fist and yanked, snapping the other mermaid's head back.

Lightning quick, Ebby swept her tail up and smashed into Urokotori's back.

The other mermaid jackknifed, taking the hit against her tail, instead. She spun, leaving Ebby with a handful of hair, and raked her claws down Ebby's cheek. Blood misted the water.

Ebby curled her own claws and swiped at her opponent, catching the mermaid on the forearm.

Urokotori's crimson lips were slashes of fury against her pale face. "Finally found your spine, little sister?"

"Let me go and we'll battle this out fair and square." Ebby pulled on the chain, wondering how she could lure the other mermaid close enough to wrap it around her throat.

"You know I don't fight fair. I'll deal with you once I've

finished my fun with your lover. I'm curious how pliable I can make him without the effect of a mer-song." With a swish of her red fins, she spun and slithered her body up Cruz's, her hands lifting his kilt.

Cruz's thoughts churned with helpless anger, fear, and indignation.

Ebby felt the same way. She scoured the floor around her for a weapon, a distraction, anything that might give Cruz a chance to escape. To her left, something moved beneath the broken floorboards. Kato pulled himself between a gap and scuttled toward her, little gills fluttering with effort. Two gold-tipped prongs jutted from his front claws like a moray eel's bottom teeth. *My harp?*

Bending quickly, she took the instrument. All but two tines had been snapped off, leaving jagged nubs along its base. She glanced at Urokotori, whose tail undulated as sinuously as a sea snake while she rubbed herself over Cruz's body, crooning a lurid description of her plans to milk his seed dry.

Was there enough power in the broken harp to negate Urokotori's magic? Timuri was already agitated, and Urokotori was occupied tormenting Cruz. If Ebby could break Urokotori's hold on the octopus and command him to release Cruz, the human might stand a chance. On the other hand, breaking the mermaid's control might free the monster to rip Cruz to pieces.

What other choice was there?

Swallowing hard, she brought the harp in front of her and gently stroked the tines, sending a quivering chord through the ship's hold. The phytoplankton seemed to brighten. She steadied her grasp on the instrument, adding her voice. She sang of peace and gentleness. Sunlight and sweet water.

Timuri's limbs rippled, coiled tips loosening. Cruz pulled his limbs free.

Urokotori twisted, gaping at Ebby. "How dare you!"

The tip of one suction-cupped arm curled over Urokotori's shoulder. She spun, strumming her smaller harp. Her practiced voice clamped down on the creature, forcing him to recoil in cringing submission.

What's happening? Cruz kicked through the water toward Ebby.

Ebby couldn't spare a thread of concentration to answer.

"Your human will suffer for this!" Urokotori poured anger into her song, commanding the octopus to rend and tear.

Timuri shuddered, beak opening and closing as the command songs overlapped.

Ebby pulled notes from deep in her chest, stroking the tines more firmly and countermanding the violence, trying to calm the beast. But years of conditioning had made the creature hostile. It's long arm snagged Cruz's ankle.

Urokotori laughed, alternating her dual notes in a chaotic melody that caused the surrounding phytoplankton to flicker. Timuri's skin rippled with frustrated colors, slitted gaze on his mistress even as he pulled Cruz toward his gaping beak. Ebby couldn't overcome the creature's nature. An octopus was designed to hunt and eat. Urokotori only had to encourage his instincts.

The answer came to Ebby like mid-morning light into a kelp clearing. It was time to stop fighting Urokotori's song.

Shifting her key, she sang of vengeance, complementing Urokotori's command for violence. Enhancing it.

And redirected it toward Urokotori.

The beast must've been waiting for the opportunity for

years. In a flash, Timuri released Cruz and swelled in size, looming over the mistress who'd held him captive to her will for so long.

Urokotori's song went sour with panic.

In a flash of motion, all eight of the octopus's legs engulfed her, pulling her body inward. His hungry beak pierced her chest in an explosion of blood. Urokotori's screech cut short as the creature ripped her heart from her ribcage.

Fighting the urge to retch, Ebby gentled her command, asking the octopus to find a more secluded place to consume his meal.

Timuri shifted his grip on the mermaid's limp corpse, furled his other legs beneath him, and disappeared through the hatch.

CHAPTER THIRTEEN

After the cloudy water ceased churning, Cruz pulled himself from the clutter of broken barrels and crates. The red-tailed mermaid was no longer in sight. Only Ebby remained, her apricot tail and billowing auburn hair a beacon in the dim bioluminescent glow. Through their mental connection, her mind flowed like a riptide, her internal song both ferocious and melodic.

Cruz glanced toward the dark corners, checking for the red-tailed mermaid before darting forward and taking Ebby into his arms. *Ebby, you can stop. They've gone.*

Her song went silent, her eyes staring through him with blown pupils. *Oh, Neptune. I killed her.*

Ebby, it's okay. Crushing her against him, he felt her pain as if it was his own, yet he was relieved as hell they were both alive. *You had to. We're okay.*

She stiffened in his embrace. Her emerald eyes met his. *You mustn't touch me.*

Stop saying that. He pulled her closer. The chill clawing through his bloodstream seemed stronger now that his adrenaline was fading, and her warmth was a welcome respite. *I'm never letting you go again.* The prongs of the harp trapped between them dug into his chest. Keeping one arm firmly around her waist, he used his free hand to gently pluck the instrument from her fingertips. *How did you get this?*

From beneath her hair, a large mantis shrimp emerged on her shoulder and pumped himself up and down on his hind legs in a happy dance.

Cruz grinned. *You're one bad-ass shrimp. I owe you.*

The shrimp scurried forward and snatched the harp from his hand, then ducked back beneath Ebby's hair once more. Cruz shook his head. *You weren't kidding when you told me that harp was powerful. I'm glad you used it.*

I swore I'd never command another creature against its will. Ebby closed her eyes and laid her forehead against Cruz's shoulder, her body going limp. *Now Urokotori is dead.*

Lifting one gentle hand to her chin, Cruz tilted her face to look at him. *I hardly think killing her was against the octopus's will. I bet he's wanted to do that for ages. And he's gone, now. You freed him, didn't you? We weren't the only prisoners in this mess.*

Her trembling arms slid tentatively around his waist, the chain attaching her to the floor sliding coldly against his legs. *I suppose, yes.* She sighed, tiny bubbles escaping her lips. *I'm sorry I ran away and left you in the cave after...*

The rest of the sentence hung between them, and he felt a stirring in his groin. Her mouth was so close. So kissable. He feathered his mouth across hers, wanting her. But his chest felt tight with cold, and he could feel his fingers going numb. His dive training told him to stay on task, conserve his energy. He took her manacled hand. *Let's get you free so we can get out of here. You don't have a song to open this, do you?*

She shook her head and pulled her hand away. *Our song only works on living things. You need to swim for the surface right now before anything else happens.*

Not without you. I assume that mermaid had the key? He looked toward the corridor. *Ah, hell. Where did the octopus take her?*

There is no key. Ebby squirmed free of his embrace, pushing him toward the hatch. *You need to go back to your kind where you're safe.*

No key? He grabbed her arm again, scowling at the manacle. *She locked you up and didn't have a key?* Flipping it over, he ran his fingers along the chain. The heavy links were corroded, but still too thick and sturdy to break. What he wouldn't give for a pair of bolt cutters right now.

There may be a key somewhere on the ship. I'll send Kato to look. She lifted the shrimp off her shoulder, setting him swimming through the hatch. Then she tugged on the chain, trying to take it from him.

Anger burned inside Cruz's chest. She'd sacrificed everything for him. Now she wanted him to just abandon her? He tightened his grip. *Hell, no. You said we're mates. That means we're in this together.* He squinted around the ship's interior. *I need to search for a tool. Can you make it lighter in here?*

No. There are very few phytoplankton down here.

He stared at the minuscule drifting lights, trying to stay calm and think straight. They were like little bugs, which gave him an idea. *I used to collect fireflies in bottles as a kid.*

Releasing her hand, he swam toward the broken crates. Among the debris, several bottles remained intact. He turned to

Ebby and held one up. *If we can concentrate some phytoplankton in this, we can use it like a lantern.*

He pushed at the cork, trying to dislodge it, but his hands were shaking. The chill running through his veins was infecting him with panic, despite his dive training. Turning to a crate, he swept the sediment covering the other bottles aside, hoping for one that was open. Instead, he spotted a familiar twist of metal. A corkscrew! His panic subsided. For once, luck was with him.

He began to work at the cork and then realized he was an idiot. He was holding the very tool he'd been looking for. Calf muscles threatening to cramp, he returned to Ebby's side. As he reached for her bound wrist, a bone-deep shiver rocked him. The corkscrew slid from his fingers.

Cruz? Are you all right? Ebby grabbed his shoulders. *Depths, you're freezing!*

Without warning, she put both hands to his cheeks and pressed her mouth over his. Small bubbles rose between them while her tongue played over his lips and her nipples grazed his chest. *What are you doing?* He pulled away, torn between wanting her and knowing he needed to stay on task. He ducked down to retrieve the corkscrew. *This isn't the time!*

I just refreshed your breath-spell. She pointed toward the hatch. *You need to get out of here. Now.*

Leaving you isn't an option. The breath-spell had revived him somewhat, but his heart still slammed against his ribs, trying to keep his blood flowing to his extremities. *No way in hell. Give me your hand.*

Jamming the end of the corkscrew into the lock, he began to twist.

CHAPTER FOURTEEN

The corkscrew slipped, scraping painfully into Ebby's wrist. She flinched, and he eased his grip. *Sorry. It's so dark down here.*

He rubbed his thumb over the scratch, then placed the corkscrew back into the lock. She could feel the cold taking a toll on his mind. Sapping his strength. *Cruz, go find land before you become too cold to swim. You can come back later and free me.*

He kept working. *Finding this location again would be impossible. I don't have mermaid magic to traipse around the ocean like it was my backyard. I'm lucky to have found you as it is.*

She had the feeling he meant more than simply finding the shipwreck. The determined set of his shoulders as he returned to his work made her tail fin grow weak.

Besides, I left someone once before. Turmoil filled his thoughts. *I won't do it again.*

Who did you leave?

Cruz's memories coalesced around a human contraption,

and Ebby understood immediately it was something land dwellers used much like the boats they used atop the water. *My mother rolled our car into a ravine when I was seven. It was raining out, and dark. I couldn't get her seatbelt loose. Blood was everywhere. I didn't realize I'd lost my hearing, and she kept pointing out the smashed-in window. So I climbed out of the ravine to find help.* His heartbeat thudded like sonar through the dim water. For a few moments, he said nothing, continuing his work on the manacle. *Rescuers didn't locate her for two more days. She died waiting for me.*

Ebby's heart ached. Although her own mother had been cold and heartless, her father would've done anything to keep her safe. He'd even sent her away that fateful day in the Deeps when the mermaids found them. If it hadn't been for Uncle Zantu and Aunt Brianna, both she and Da would've died.

She reached up to place a palm against Cruz's cold, stubbled cheek. *You were a child. What else could you have done? Stay there and die with her? She wouldn't have wanted that.*

His throat bobbed, and he pressed one hand over hers, sandwiching her palm against him. *I won't lose another person I care about.*

Her insides fluttered. Care. That's what true mates did. She'd never thought of the bond as anything but a shackle, but it wasn't a shackle. It was a strength. The bond didn't divide her; having a devoted partner doubled her. Cruz was her mate. A loyal, caring, smart, and stupidly determined forever-mate. The other mermaids, in their quest for sexual conquest, had no idea what they were missing.

She slid closer to him, circling her hand behind his neck, and kissed him. *I love you, Cruz.*

His heartbeat quickened. Angling his head, he kissed her back, lips solid against hers. She opened her mouth, and his tongue plunged inside, his chest and thighs aligned against her body. *I love you, too.* His hand left her manacled wrist to cup her jaw, fingertips threading into her hair. His other hand feathered up her arm to her shoulder blade, pulling her tighter against his chest, kiss becoming hungrier. *You're so warm. Is it strange that I want you? Now?*

No. I want you, too. Ebby walled off her thought that this might be the last time they could be together. Arching into him, heat pooled in her middle at the feel of his erection throbbing between them. She wanted him more than she'd ever wanted anything in her entire life. All of him. No more hesitation or fear. She slid her manacled hand between them and gripped his thick shaft at the base and stroked upward slowly before angling it toward the mouth of her entrance.

He moaned into her mouth. *God, you feel so good.*

She slid forward an inch, reveling in the feel of her mate teasing her opening. His mouth left hers to trail over her collarbone then down to pull one of her nipples into his mouth. He sucked hard, drawing a cry from her that made the weak phytoplankton flicker. *Neptune*, she'd never known her body could feel this way. His tongue stroked her sensitized breast rhythmically, causing her breathing to become shallower until she was panting. Trailing biting kisses, he moved to her other nipple, gripping the back of her neck.

She wriggled against him, wanting it all. Wanting to be filled. He sucked hard at her nipple then thrust forward, burying himself inside her. She gasped, her hands on his ribcage as the chain clinked along the floorboards. His big hands pulled her hard against him, bodies meeting at every point with a heat that seemed to raise the water temperature ten degrees.

Once more his lips returned to hers, his tongue plunging into her mouth. His cock was thick and hard and she took all of him. He pulled out of her, then thrust in again. In and out, faster and faster. He was no longer cold, but searing hot. His length burned her with pleasure, with lust, his own desire matching hers as they pounded together, sending the phytoplankton into swirling patterns of brightness through the ship.

But her awareness of their surroundings barely registered as Cruz slammed into her, pounding her clit in a rhythm that wound her tighter and tighter until she was sure she couldn't take anymore. The pressure in her middle intensified, and she moaned, swept helplessly into a current of passion. She threw back her head. *Cruz, oh, depths, Cruz!*

Sensing her imminent climax, he gripped her hips and buried himself deeper, grinding hard.

Pressure changed to tingling, spreading upward from deep inside her until she exploded. Stars filled her vision, and she clutched his shoulders like a drowning woman as her warmth pulsed around him.

Cruz shuddered, a feral sound in his throat. His hips jerked, shooting throbbing jets of heat deep into her core. Moving slower, smoother, he slid in and out as his release pulsed in rhythm with hers.

Ebby relaxed, sated like she'd never been before. His lips grazed her shoulder, the base of her neck, her jawline, her lips. He tucked an errant strand of her hair behind her ear. *Well, that warmed me up.*

She smiled, her eyes fighting to stay open. *Me, too.*

Wrapping both hands around his waist to pull him close caused the chain to tangle around his leg. Reality crashed down around her. She was chained to a ship at the bottom of the ocean with a mate who was going to freeze to death or starve.

He seemed brought back to reality by the sensation, as well, reaching down to disengage himself from the links. *Much as I'd love to curl up and nap with you, I think we should get you free now.*

The deep pools of his eyes were filled with such devotion, she wanted to cry. He was as stubborn as a sea otter determined to open an oyster, and no matter what she said to him, he'd stick by her until they died.

He ducked down to retrieve the corkscrew that had fallen loose during their lovemaking, and she ruefully admired his broad back, muscles rippling as he moved through the water toward the bottle that had rolled away. She would never see him at her da's nest, tidying the sponge bed, tending the seaweed garden, sunlight dancing over his skin.

Then she realized the phytoplankton surrounding him were brighter than they had been earlier, glowing like a halo. Not only around Cruz but also herself.

Holding her free hand near the lock, she illuminated the mechanism. Cruz returned to hand her the dimly glowing bottle and his mouth dropped open. *I thought you said they couldn't get any brighter.*

She shrugged, as confused as he was. *Our lovemaking must've rejuvenated them, somehow.*

He shook his head and began working on the lock. *I'll never understand mermaid magic.*

She laughed, holding still as his long deft fingers gently inserted the coiled metal into the small opening. *I think we just warmed them up is all.*

Whatever did it, I'm grateful. Face close to the metal, he rocked the corkscrew, twisting the tool back and forth.

She watched, bottom lip caught between her teeth. Having light was all well and good, but she could already feel the water cooling. Eventually, they'd be back to where they'd started. Cruz smacked the butt of his hand against the base of the corkscrew and the lock popped open. The manacle fell away, each link of the chain clunking to the floor.

You did it! Elated, Ebby put both hands on his cheeks and planted a sound kiss on his lips.

He grinned against her mouth and grabbed her hips, sweeping her into a celebratory spin. *Let's get out of here.*

She didn't need any urging. Taking his hand, she led them out of the ship's hold and toward the distant, glowing light of the sun.

CHAPTER FIFTEEN

Cruz kicked alongside Ebby, trying to keep up with
the effortless swish of her tail. Now that he was free
of the cave, the ship, and the other mermaids, he looked
around the ocean with a new appreciation. To their left, a vast
school of big-eyed scad darkened the water, creating cloud
shapes as they evaded a smaller school of boxy-shaped
jackfish. Below, a pair of gray-green dragon wrasse flipped
pebbles among swaying eelgrass, taking turns eating any
dislodged prey. As Ebby led him out of the deep water to the
warmer currents among the coral and kelp, several orange
striped butterfly fish peeked from beneath plate-shaped coral
on the lower reef.

Where're we going? he asked

Ebby pulled him around the antler-like prongs of a coral
and began weaving between the golden kelp fronds. *I'm taking
you to my da's nest.*

He hadn't thought of mermaids having parents, and the

thought of meeting her father felt strange. *I'm going to meet your dad?*

A surge of sorrow and regret filled their connection, strong enough to make him wince. *No,* she said. *He's gone.*

Cruz longed to pause and take her into his arms, but she only swam faster. *What happened to him?*

He's probably dead now. She used her free hand to push aside a thick stand of kelp and pulled them into a clearing. The oval-shaped area had a ceiling of thatched kelp fronds and the floor had been set up like a small cottage under the sea.

Dead? Cruz sized-up an antique brass headboard abutting an overflow of sea sponges arranged into a multicolored mattress. Sediment covered most surfaces, but a spot on the bed appeared to have been recently disturbed. *You don't know?*

He left when I became a mermaid. Ebby released his hand and moved to a flat stone in the center surrounded by waterlogged barrels. Taking a seat on one, she curled her tail gracefully at the barrel's base.

Her pet shrimp, Kato, had joined them as they left the ship, and now launched off her shoulder, carrying the harp to a small alcove. He promptly excavated a hole and buried the instrument. Then he began sweeping clouds of sediment from the floor with rapid movements of his tail, exposing a mosaic of shells and multi-colored stones.

Cruz moved to the barrel next to Ebby, glad to be resting after everything that had happened. *Became a mermaid?* A mirror at her back reflected her smooth back and gently rounded hips, hair floating wild and sexy about her head. He could almost imagine her with legs. *Were you human before?*

Ebby chuckled. *I forget you humans don't get to choose. Merchildren are genderless until they reach puberty.*

His gaze slid down to her breasts. *It's a little difficult to imagine you as anything other than female.* To his satisfaction, her nipples visibly tightened. Hunger for her drove heat to his groin. But her mind was full of sadness, and he wanted their next lovemaking to be full of joy, not sorrow or regret. *Why did your choice of gender make your dad leave?*

She chewed her lip, gaze sliding down to the tabletop. *He didn't trust being around me. Mermaids are dangerous.*

Indignation burned in his heart. *But he was your father.*

Doesn't matter. She reached out and swept sediment off the surface in front of her, exposing the pitted stone beneath. *Mermaids are violent, possessive, and can't be trusted, not even with their family.*

She'd mentioned before that mermaids were bad. That all they wanted to do was play, and most of their entertainment was some form of torture. But Ebby was a mermaid, and that wasn't her at all. *If they're so bad, why did you choose to be female?*

A wistful smile swept over her features. *As a child, I always assumed I'd choose male. I used to play nest building, and I helped with the baby before...* She swallowed visibly. *The baby died. But when the time came, the choice was clear. I didn't want to end up like my da.*

What do you mean? There was so much about Ebby he didn't understand, and the more he learned, the more he wanted to know.

Her free hand clenched into a fist on the table. *I never wanted to be a slave to the mate bond.*

His throat tightened. Strange as it was, he was delighted with this bond that allowed him to share himself with another person. On land, he could never have something like this, not even with a wife. A mate who could hear him was so much better, and he could easily envision himself living beneath the waves with Ebby for eternity. He'd never considered that perhaps Ebby didn't want to be attached to him. He released her and folded his hands in his lap.

If you don't want to be attached to me, you can take me back to land. I'll be all right. That was a complete lie, but he'd find no joy in a life with someone who didn't want him.

No! She reached toward him, then hesitated, her delicate brows furrowed. *Unless you don't want to stay with me? I won't force you.*

Cruz melted, relief flooding him. He lifted her, carrying her toward the bed. *I'd like nothing better than to spend the rest of my life with you.*

She closed her eyes and leaned against his chest. He settled her against the soft sponge mattress and lay down next to her, cocooning her in his arms. The next thing he knew, darkness had fallen. Ebby lay slumbering in his arms, warm and soft. He'd never felt so at home, like he'd finally found where he belonged, right here in her embrace.

She must've sensed he'd woken because she turned to face him. *I promise I will never do to you what my mother did to Da.*

Have you been awake thinking this whole time? He pulled her closer against his chest.

I dozed. I just want you to know you are safe with me.

What did your mother do? Were your she and father mated like us?

Oh, no. A harsh laugh shook Ebby's chest. *My father adored my mother. He couldn't help it. But she didn't return his love. Every time she left us, she took a little piece of him with her until he was a mere husk of a man. I was glad when she finally died because it meant Da was free.* She sighed heavily. *Only, he wasn't. Not really.*

Humans call it depression.

She seemed to shrink in his arms. *When I became female, it broke him for good.*

He put a hand on the soft skin of her cheek. *You cannot blame yourself for the way someone else feels.*

One of her fingers traced over his lips, sending a shiver through him. *Not even you?*

He gently bit her fingertip, holding it between his teeth. *Depends on what kind of feel we're talking about.*

She wriggled slightly, and his cock surged to attention. *How about that kind of feel?*

Splaying his hand on the small of her back, he ran it up her spine until it tangled in her hair. Gently, he tugged her head back and to the side, leaning forward to brush his lips against her throat. Her breasts were soft against his chest, her skin silky on his mouth.

He dragged his free hand up her ribs and cupped her breast. Her chest heaved in an excited breath and her nipple tightened. Lifting himself on one arm, he rolled her back against the sponges. He couldn't see her in the dark, but he could feel her desire meeting his through their mental connection, urging him on.

He rubbed the smooth skin over her hips and up to the transition of her belly, over her breasts, stroking her cheek. With gentle, feathering kisses, he worshipped her, adored her, covering every inch of her skin before he slid one hand down her taut belly to her sex. Her folds were slick and waiting, and she arched upward into his touch. Without hesitation, he buried his middle finger inside her.

You're so perfect, he said as he slowly fingered her.

She rolled her hips against his touch. He inserted a second

finger, his thighs straddling her. Her inner walls pulsed around him, quivering with every stroke against her innermost ridges. She bucked and writhed, reaching for him with both hands and pulling him down atop her. Her mouth met his, soft and yielding, one hand cupping the back of his head. The tips of their tongues met, sending a blaze of desire up his spine.

Never breaking the kiss, he reached down between them, positioning himself at her entrance. She rocked against his dick and he groaned mindlessly. In one swift thrust, he buried himself inside her. She rolled against him again and he kissed her harder, one hand cupping her cheek as he rode her. She felt so good wrapped around him, so tight and hot. A perfect fit. A perfect mate.

She bucked up to match his rhythm, their bodies moving together, and he buried his face against her neck, crushing her body to his, rolling his hips faster. Her skin tasted dewy and musky, driving him wild as he slid in and out of her. The pressure inside him built with every stroke, and he could feel within her mind that she was also on the edge of ecstasy, panting his name with every thrust.

One hand bracing her hips, he ground into her, gritting his teeth against his orgasm. He pulled back, hovering at the edge of her entrance. *Come for me*, he growled and slammed back inside her.

She let out a cry and arched upward, rocking with the first pulse of her orgasm. He clutched her tighter as the water buoyed them upward, continuing his thrusting until he was sure he'd pulled every last response from her body. With a shudder and a groan of his own, he allowed her aftershocks to milk him into oblivion.

CHAPTER SIXTEEN

The morning song of a batfish outside the nest woke Ebby. She stretched and opened her eyes. Cruz slept soundly beside her on the sponge bed, one arm pillowing her head, the other wrapped loosely over her hip. Quietly, she tried to sit. His arm around her hip tightened and pulled her backward against him.

Not so fast. His voice in her head was adorably groggy. *Where's my morning kiss?*

She smiled and turned in the circle of his arms to place her palm on his stubbled cheek. Nibbling kisses against his lips, she said, *I'm hungry.*

Me, too. Cruz kissed her firmly and sat up. *I would offer to cook you breakfast, but I'm not sure what you have to eat around here. Or how to cook it.*

Ebby'd heard of this 'cooking' thing, but the purpose was a mystery to her. She rose from the bed, looking around for the knife Da used to keep for harvests. *I'll show you the gardens.*

Sediment had all but smothered the patch of seaweed just outside the nest, but Da had kept several plots of seaweed farther out along the reef. Handing Cruz a knife, she led him through the thatched kelp and out of the clearing to a leeward stretch of stone where the seaweed had once grown thick and lush. Her infrequent visits weren't enough to maintain the gardens, and several parrotfish had moved in, shearing the bulk of the succulent fronds.

Sending a sonic warning to chase the fish away, she escorted Cruz among the patchy growth, teaching him how to harvest, how to remove the invading sea slugs, and how to avoid the anemones hiding among the fronds. *Tending the gardens is part of keeping a nest,* she explained, then realized with giddy joy that she had a nest. A nest she wouldn't only visit occasionally, but one she would help maintain, with Cruz at her side.

Cruz sampled various bites as they filled the bowl. *I could really go for a cheeseburger right now.*

What's a cheeseburger?

Meat with melted cheese between two soft buns. He held up a frond, eyeing it critically before stuffing it into his mouth. *Kind of hard to explain, but I'm making myself hungrier thinking about it. This is like only getting the lettuce.*

You'll be too full to eat when we get back, she teased.

He wrapped an arm around her waist and held a piece to her lips. *You'd better eat, too. I have other plans than eating when we get back.*

Giggling, she accepted the bite, sucking his finger playfully.

Naughty mermaid. He grinned at her.

She wrapped both hands around his backside and gripped his hips, grinding herself against his growing erection. *Insatiable human.*

Something gold caught the light on the rise above them, and a pair of citrine-colored eyes met hers above a red sea fan. Ebby shoved Cruz behind her.

Rising from the ridge, Lutana's coral lips spread into a grin.

Fuck! Where's my knife? Cruz scrambled toward the bowl of seaweed resting between the rocks several meters away.

Ebby rose into the current, hands on her hips, and glared at the other mermaid. Lutana by herself Ebby could handle. But if she'd brought friends… "What do you want?"

Lutana cocked her head. "The currents are singing that Selachii and Urokotori are dead."

Ebby glared at Lutana in silent challenge. "I can't imagine you have a problem with that, Lutana. You'll no longer be forced to play their games."

Cruz floated up beside Ebby, knife brandished in one hand. *Found it.*

Tinkling laughter rippled the water. "Oh, he's a fierce one, isn't he?" The golden mermaid's gaze swept over Cruz. "How long do you plan on keeping him?"

Throat tight, Ebby considered her next words. There was no rule protecting a mermaid's mates, likely because mermaids had no affection for any given merman. But Cruz was human. Didn't that make him special? Kato peeked cautiously from beneath a palm coral, giving Ebby an idea. "He's my new pet."

Lutana narrowed her eyes, lips curling into a scowl. "You are the strangest mermaid I know. The others are going to find this quite interesting."

"Others?"

"Like I said, the currents are already whispering about the open territory." Lutana shrugged and turned to go.

"What if I told you he's my mate?" Ebby blurted.

Lutana halted, then moved back to the edge of the ridge, her shrewd gaze once more raking Cruz from head to toe. "I think you're confused, sister. You're a mermaid. Not some love-sick merman."

A part of Ebby felt sorry for Lutana. The other mermaid didn't revel in cruelty like Selachii and Urokotori had, but she was still influenced by their expectations. Ebby moved forward. "We don't have to be defined by our gender or our sexuality. Only our actions."

Lutana blew out a sharp string of bubbles and crossed her arms.

Ebby moved forward a few centimeters. "It's not too late for you, Lutana. If I can find love, then so can you."

Lutana made a non-committal sound in the back of her throat, then without another word, spun and disappeared over the rise.

There will be other mermaids, won't there? Cruz's voice entered softly into her head. *Someday, one of us will get hurt.*

Briny tears stung Ebby's eyes. Her dream of having a nest with a mate and partner, a dream that had seemed so real only moments ago, had been ripped from its roots like kelp during a storm. She turned to Cruz, taking in his muscular handsomeness, from his rippled chest and strong arms to the legs he kicked gently to keep himself afloat. It would have been difficult enough to protect a merman as a mate, but a human was all but helpless beneath the waves. If only he could grow a tail like Uncle Zantu had grown legs…

A dam inside her chest opened. Was there another way? How had Uncle Zantu grown legs? There was only one way to find out. She took Cruz's hands in hers. *I have someone I want to introduce you to.*

$\mathcal{E}$bby cautiously approached the small cove where her uncle lived. A storm was coming, and the waves crashed strongly against the shore. She struggled to resist the undertow that wanted to toss her and Cruz against the rocky bottom.

A small yacht bobbed in the surf near the point, making her pause. The beach wasn't private, but unless one had a boat, it could only be accessed by climbing over the sharp, surf-washed boulders on either side of the crescent-shaped beach. *Depths*, of course she'd choose the day someone decided to drop in for a picnic.

What is it? Cruz asked as she sent a sonic query to the nearby fish, asking how long the vessel had been here.

She pointed toward the shadow of the boat above them. *I don't know who that belongs to.*

He tilted his head and his grip on her hand tightened. *That might be my friends, looking for me.*

Gesturing to her billowing tail fin, she said, *I can't let humans see me like this.*

The current drove them toward a submerged boulder, forcing her to pull Cruz crosswise to avoid it. She backed them farther from shore and wrapped her arms around his neck, burying her head against the crook of his shoulder. She couldn't imagine life without him. But if she was bound to the sea, and he to the land, how could they make a life together?

He cupped the back of her head and pressed a kiss against her ear. *We could go find another beach.*

There're no other beaches without humans. She thought of the coastline, miles of noisy boats, people swimming, homes overlooking the water. *And I need to talk to my Uncle.* She'd told him about her uncle while they swam to the cove, and how he'd grown legs to be with his mate on land. But she was a mermaid, and that might not be possible for her.

Ebby. He craned his neck to look into her eyes. *We'll just wait until the boat leaves, okay?*

A ragged clump of feathers drifted by, the remnants of some bird fallen prey to the dangers of the ocean. Cruz wasn't safe here. He had to go back right away, whether she could join him or not. *You should go and tell your friends you're all right. I'll come in once the coast is clear.*

He gripped her tighter. *We've been through this. I won't leave you.*

She grimaced. *There's a storm coming. Staying this close to shore is dangerous. You need to go to land.*

His mouth thinned into a dissatisfied line. After a moment, he said, *Promise me you'll come to shore as soon as you can?*

She nodded. *I promise.*

Keeping them below the surface until she was certain he

could power through the waves on his own, she released him to strike out in long, powerful strokes toward shore. When he reached shallower water, she bobbed in the waves with only her eyes above the surface, watching him rise out of the surf. His muscular form was even more magnificent on land, water gleaming from his golden tanned skin in the sunlight. Oh, how she loved the broad muscles of his shoulders and the defined cords of his legs.

Propelling herself back out of the cove and away from the surging waves, she rolled onto her back and stared at her tail. Could she grow legs like Uncle Zantu had? He'd told her it had something to do with the mate-bond. Without Cruz here, fear struck her that mermaids really might impervious to the mate bond. What if she'd only imagined the connection all along? Now that Cruz was on land, maybe the magic was broken.

The crashing waves could be dangerous, even for a mermaid, but she couldn't resist moving into the maze of submerged boulders along the south edge of the cove, just to be closer to Cruz. Holding herself vertically, like a razorfish in the spines of a sea urchin, she poked the top of her head above the waves. On the beach, two men conversed, but there could be other humans farther back among the trees. She dared not show herself until she was sure it was safe. How close did she have to be to talk to Cruz? *Cruz, can you hear me?*

No response.

Her fin grated along the rocky bottom and she gritted her teeth. She couldn't get much closer without ending up bruised and bloodied. Over the roar of the waves, a child's laughter sprinkled the air.

Ebby lifted her head and shoulders above the water for a better look, praying no one saw her among the rocks.

A small figure that could only be Camilla jumped up and down on top of Ebby's favorite boulder, talking to someone in the water. Brianna? The human liked to swim, but Ebby was surprised to see her braving this kind of surf. Most likely she was trying to get Camilla to come off that rock and back to shore.

Uncle Zantu's voice echoed from the beach, barely audible over the crashing waves. "Come on, Ebby! It's fine!"

Relief so great it took her breath away swept through Ebby's chest. Cruz had done it! He'd met her uncle and now everything was going to be okay. Keeping her head above water, she pulled herself from among the boulders and allowed a curling wave to carry her forward. Her heart swelled as she recognized her uncle's silver-blue hair and Cruz's broad shoulders, both men facing the water.

Ebby! Cruz called, his faint voice infused with excitement.

Then a flash of emerald behind Camilla's rock made Ebby's heart falter. Was that a mermaid? Where was Brianna? Dread took root in Ebby's stomach. Was everyone on shore under a mermaid's spell?

A deep, familiar song pulsed through the water, a lullaby she hadn't heard in over two years. She froze, confused, as another wave broke over her, driving her against the sand.

She surfaced again as an emerald-tailed merman pulled himself onto the rock near Camilla.

"Da?" She couldn't breathe, couldn't move. Da was alive! Alive and here! "I thought you'd died!"

Her father's wary eyes met hers before glancing over his shoulder toward the beach. "You're sure she's no danger?"

Camilla threw her arms around the merman's neck. "Stop worrying, Uncle Rubac. Ebby would never hurt anyone."

The elation in Ebby's heart soured. He was still terrified. Still believed she would rip him apart just for fun.

Cruz's soothing voice came to her. *He doesn't know any better. Not yet.*

Ebby pulled herself onto another boulder several meters away from him, hands gripping its barnacled surface as another wave tried to push her over. Cruz was right. She needed to move slowly, even though she yearned to race to her father, to hug him like Camilla was now. But she understood his fear.

He remained silent, gaze drifting over her apricot tail. He looked the same as she remembered, emerald tail just as bright, jewelry gleaming from every limb and piercing. What should she say to him? Her voice wobbled in her throat as she fought back tears. "Hi, Da."

Camilla let go of Rubac's neck and stood to face Ebby again, her pudgy belly pink from the cold water. She wore a frilly two-piece bathing suit that made her hips look like a jellyfish. "He has a new mate named Madison! She brought me candy. Come on! I bet she'll give you some, too!"

A second mate? Ebby hadn't thought that was possible. "You have another mate?"

Da rubbed a hand through his hair, brow furrowed. "I don't know what to call her, but I love her."

Ebby looked toward shore. Cruz had moved into the waves, wobbling with each shove of water against his legs. If Da had a mate, he should have legs, right? Maybe the magic was special only for Uncle Zantu...

Shaking her head, she shoved the thought away. By Neptune, she was going to grow legs if she had to cut herself in half to do it. She pushed herself off the rock toward shore. "I have a mate, too."

Cruz raised both arms toward her. *Come to me, Eb—ah, hell!* A wave swept his feet out from under him.

Ebby plunged forward, grabbing him before the wave could roll him into the undertow. Next thing she knew, rocks were digging into her back and Cruz lay on top of her as the wave departed, leaving them exposed on land.

He looked into her eyes, gaze reflecting love as surely as moonlight reflected off a calm sea. Pushing up onto his hands, he rocked back on his heels. His eyes moved down her torso and came to rest somewhere below her belly, and a slow grin spread across his lips.

She followed his gaze to a flattened triangle of hair just below her belly button and bolted upright. Her apricot tail had been replaced by long, pale thighs, knees and shins, and feet with ten perfect pink toes covered in sand. "I did it!" She looked up into his eyes. "I really did it!"

Camilla raced up, holding up a pink and purple towel. "Want to use my towel?"

Ebby took it, knowing humans had an aversion to nakedness, and wrapped it around herself. She'd never been self-conscious as a mermaid, but this new body was too fresh, too new for her to feel comfortable in it yet, anyway. "Thank you, Camilla."

Another wave came crashing toward them, and Cruz slipped his arms beneath her shoulders and knees, carrying her as easily as she'd transported him through the water.

"C'mon Ebby." The little girl grabbed her hand. "Let's ask Madison for more candy!"

"Hold on, little nibbler." Uncle Zantu swept in and lifted his daughter to his shoulders. "Ebby needs some time to adjust and maybe talk to her da before we make her race up the hill."

The little girl started to complain, but Ebby smiled at her cousin and promised, "I'll be up soon, okay?"

"Hurry, please." Then Camilla squealed in glee as Zantu started jogging up the path.

Cruz carried her across the sand toward her father. He stopped at the edge of the crashing surf and lowered Ebby's feet to the sand. *You want me to leave you alone?*

No! She took his hand, glancing up into his face. *Depths, you're tall!*

He chuckled out loud. *No more fins to make you seem big.*

Or scary, she thought as she turned back to the surf where Da waited, head and shoulders above water. Signing and speaking at the same time, she said, "Da, I'd like you to meet my mate, Cruz. Cruz, this is my father, Rubac."

Da couldn't seem to drag his gaze from her legs.

Cruz signed, "Happy to meet you, sir."

"He says happy to meet you," Ebby translated.

Da blinked, finally seeming to notice Cruz. A slow smile spread over his face. "Your mate. He has a good aura. Strong." His eyes met hers. "As do you, my daughter."

Ebby's heart developed a pang she wasn't sure how to interpret. "Da, are… are you still afraid of me?"

Da shook his head and moved toward shore until his tail was fully exposed and gleaming in the frothing water. "Come give me a hug."

Stumbling forward in the wet sand, Ebby dropped to her knees and threw her arms around his neck, a sob sticking in her throat. "I missed you so much."

His arms wrapped around her shoulders, one hand patting her gently. "When you decided to become female, I thought you'd never be the same. I thought you'd turn into a monster. I was wrong. I'm sorry." He squeezed her tighter. "And I'm proud of you."

"I love you, Da," Ebby choked out, squeezing her father hard.

"I love you, too, Ebby." A wave surged over them, nearly pulling the towel free, and she released her hug to keep it in place.

Da drifted back into the water, but he didn't stray far.

As she rose to her feet, Cruz stepped forward and put an arm around her to steady her. *Everything good now?*

Leaning against him, she wiggled her toes in the damp sand, watching her father's emerald tail. *Everything's amazing.*

From the water, Da called out, "Now go up and introduce yourself to Madison. Then tell her to come down here. I think it's time we had a proper family reunion."

Ebby straddled Cruz where he lay on the beach blanket, still amazed by the feel of him between her thighs, and looked out over the waves. The wind coming off the water had picked up, kicking sand over the rocks, while the sunset painted the sky vanilla yellow. Music drifted down from the cottage up the hill, partygoers having abandoned the beach in favor of pizza and party games.

Ebby took in a long, slow breath of salty air, thinking of the cake she'd baked for Camilla's birthday. Since coming on shore, Ebby'd developed quite a taste for human foods, especially chocolate, and spent much of her time in the kitchen experimenting with different flavors. Her butterscotch seaweed hadn't been much of a hit, but her chocolate dulse-cake was good enough that Camilla'd requested it for her party.

"What are you thinking?" Cruz signed.

They'd developed some basic rules about delving into each

other's minds in the months they'd been on land, not to mention the courtesy of allowing the people around them to participate in their conversations. Zantu and Brianna still needed Ebby to translate most things, but Camilla was already fluent. She might not have a tail, but it seemed she'd inherited a mermaid's ability to pick up languages as easily as she collected seashells.

Since they were alone, Ebby opened her thoughts to her mate. She wasn't exactly sure how to approach the subject she really wanted to talk about. *I could sure go for some chocolate right now.*

He laughed and ran a light finger down her spine. *Shall we go see if Camilla has left us any cake?* His hand slipped into the waistband of her swimsuit to cup her ass. *Or do you want to stay here?*

She giggled, clenching her buttocks, still unused to the new sensations of being human. Or at least, of having a human shape. She would always be a mermaid. *I'm not a fan of sand in my crevices. But I'd really like some cake.*

He wiggled his fingers, sand already grating her skin, and she squealed, trying to squirm away. He held her firmly, flipping her onto her back. A giggle drew her attention and Ebby tapped Cruz's chest. *We have company.*

Cruz rolled away while Ebby straightened her swim top. At the bottom of the path, Camilla's pixie face grinned at them from behind a tree.

Ebby rose, hands on her hips. "Camilla, spying is rude."

Camilla waited until Cruz faced her, then signed, "Mommy says to bring you up before we light the candles."

"All right, little nibbler." Cruz used the family's name for the child, and Ebby's heart felt like it might burst. He'd make a great father. "We're right behind you."

As he shook out the blanket, Ebby decided to approach her issue in a more straightforward manner. She'd never discussed children with Cruz and was still uncertain about her abilities as a mother, but she'd already thrown aside her misconception about a mermaid's heart being incapable of loving a mate. Why not a child? *Ever think you might want one of those?*

One of what? He rolled the blanket around their water bottles and tucked it under one arm.

Ebby donned her flip flops, her heart in her throat. *A little nibbler.*

Cruz raised an eyebrow at her. *I'd love nothing more. Is there something you want to tell me?*

Ebby'd been waiting for the right moment for two days now, ever since Brianna had helped her use the home pregnancy test. She'd cried over the little plus sign on the stick, fearful of the future, of her skills and responsibilities. Brianna had held her, promising to be there every step of the way, and at that moment, Ebby'd decided to go ahead and try. Perhaps she'd have a little boy like Cruz, with dark hair and hazel eyes and a smile that melted her heart.

She bit her lip and looked at her mate through her lashes. *I hear if it's a girl, I'll crave chocolate and pickles.*

Cruz's eyes widened then he dropped the blanket and put both hands on her shoulders. *I'm going to be a father?*

She nodded.

He let out a yell and swept her into his arms. *Have I told you I love you today?*

Ebby wrapped both legs around his waist, letting his joy

sweep over her. She could do this. With the love of her mate, she could do anything. *Better tell me again just to be sure.*

I love you. He kissed her slowly, lingering over her mouth with soft, slow strokes of his tongue.

She pulled him more tightly against her. *I love you, too.*

BONUS EPILOGUE

Keeping a sharp eye out for Lutana or other mermaids, Ebby pushed through the kelp toward Da's nest. In addition to discovering she could swap back and forth between tail and legs, she'd also found that her breath spell still worked, allowing Cruz to swim alongside her free of heavy scuba equipment. She glanced over her shoulder toward where he sliced through the water now, clad only in trunks and long fins on his feet. If he'd had a tail, he'd look every ounce like a merman born to the sea. He met her gaze, face creased with a smile so deep it reached his eyes.

Ebby smiled back and scanned the water around them, unable to shake the anxious feeling in her stomach every time they ventured out. She'd feel better once she retrieved the harp from Da's nest. They needed extra protection now that they were helping Da and Madison with underwater films full-time.

Today wasn't a filming day, however, and Cruz carried a small harpoon gun instead of a camera. Two knives were in easy reach strapped to his thighs. He'd wanted to arm Ebby, as well, but she'd've only felt bogged down. Now that she was willing to use her mermaid song, she didn't need anything else to protect them—well, anything except the harp.

The kelp parted before her, revealing Da's nest, and a nostalgic sense of sadness swept over her. After experiencing life on land and the nests humans called houses, the refuge below the kelp felt so small. The familiar shell-and-stone floor and the pocked surface of the table were cleanly swept, the kelp ceiling well-trimmed. Kato was keeping the place tidy as if he expected her to return any time.

She glanced around but didn't see the little mantis shrimp anywhere. He'd visited her at her uncle's cove several times since she'd moved to land, but hadn't come by for a few weeks, and worry gnawed the back of her mind. Without her around to protect him, she wouldn't put it past the other mermaids to torture or even kill her friend.

Knife in hand, Cruz slid past her into the kelp clearing toward the spot where they'd buried the harp. *I'll grab the harp while you check around for anything else you might want.*

She swam toward the cracked mirror in the corner and adjusted it to better reflect the light coming through gaps in the kelp overhead. There weren't many things left in the nest. Da's jewelry box was still in the cave where Cruz had been held prisoner. Timuri might still claim the cave as home, and they'd decided to wait to retrieve the jewelry until after they had the harp.

She drifted to the corner where the large chest with her childhood toys still rested—dolls with flowing yellow hair, small blocks that clicked together, various human dishes and utensils she hadn't known the use of until living on land. An oblong lump of brown plastic Da had called her creature rested bottom-side up in one corner. She lifted it, grinning at its interchangeable red lips and bulbous eyes. At the moment, a white hand protruded from the place its nose should be.

She'd loved rearranging the parts to create monstrous, malformed playmates. Perhaps her child would enjoy playing with it as much as she had.

After placing it into the mesh bag they'd brought, she began plucking silver and gold utensils from the clutter. Humans valued the metal more than she or Da had imagined, and hopefully there was enough here for her and Cruz to secure a home of their own once the baby was born.

Behind her, Cruz's thoughts radiated concern. *The harp isn't here.*

She turned and drifted to the center of the clearing, fins barely brushing the floor. *Are you in the right spot?*

Several depressions Cruz had excavated were slowly smoothing themselves as the sand resettled. He dug furiously at yet another location. *I'm pretty sure.*

Her stomach twisted, but she refused to entertain the idea that the harp was missing. There was no way someone could've found it with Kato on guard. She ducked toward the alcove where Da used to keep his treasure chest. *Maybe Kato moved it to keep it safe.*

Inside the nook, a pair of long antennae poked up from beneath a stone, followed by a red and blue carapace.

"Kato, you're here!" She reached toward him but he emitted a warning hiss. Alarmed, she drew back her arm.

The little shrimp readied itself to strike.

Cruz swam to a stop beside her. *What's wrong with him? Is he sick?*

Ebby held onto Cruz's arm to keep him from moving any closer. The shrimp's curved tail was shorter than Kato's and its colors slightly less brilliant. *That's not Kato.*

Her stomach churned as she glanced around the nest again, noting tiny changes that had escaped her earlier. A pile of small shells on the table. A new hole in the kelp ceiling to let in light. The newly-trimmed sponges that made up the bed. Had someone else taken over the nest? How had they found the harp? And where was Kato?

The unfamiliar crustacean stood on its hind legs, rocking side to side like a boxer. Although the creatures couldn't talk, they could understand simple questions and communicate through small gestures.

Wishing she had a bit of fish to use as a bribe, Ebby smoothed her fins and tried to appear non-threatening as she addressed the strange shrimp. "Do you know my friend, Kato?"

The small crustacean continued rocking, eyestalks swiveling to keep both Ebby and Cruz in view. Most animals didn't like mermaids and with good reason. Why wasn't it fleeing? It acted like it was protecting something. Ebby scrutinized its shape and coloring again and realization washed over her in a gentle wave. The shrimp was female. It was protecting its eggs.

Ebby spun to face Cruz. *Kato has a girlfriend!*

Cruz lowered the harpoon gun he'd held half-poised. His eyes twitched, then his mouth split into a grin. *Kato's been busy!*

She chuckled. *I guess so. He'll be busy for a long time. Kato's species mates for life.*

Joyful clicking to her left drew her attention and she turned her head just as Kato bowled into her. He dove beneath her hair, small feet prickling along the back of her neck until he emerged on the other side with a happy wiggle. She reached up and ran her fingertips over his carapace. "There you are!"

He stroked her cheek with one antenna and then once more launched into the water, retrieving a small snail from where he must've dropped it on the floor. He scurried toward his mate with the meal.

Cruz held a thumbs-up in Kato's direction. *Tell him congratulations! She's a real beauty!*

Ebby watched the female strike the snail to break its shell. She pulled out a morsel and offered it to Kato before taking another bit for herself. "Congratulations from both of us, Kato."

Kato pumped up and down on his legs. If a mantis shrimp could blush, Kato would be solid red.

Ebby pointed over her shoulder toward where Cruz had been digging. "Kato, did you move the harp?"

The shrimp spun in a circle and disappeared into a nearby crevice. Moments later, he emerged with the two-pronged instrument. Ebby breathed a sigh of relief. "I knew you'd keep it safe. Thank you."

Kato's mate disappeared back into the den as Ebby accepted the harp. The instrument felt so light. Whether it was the missing tines or the fact that she no longer feared its power, she wasn't sure. All that mattered was that she could use it to keep her family safe.

While Cruz sifted through the other items in the toy box, she looked around the place she'd called home for most of her life. She swallowed, vision filmed by briny tears. She'd been more emotional since getting pregnant, but right now she felt stupid silly. It wasn't like she'd ever dreamed of raising a family of her own here. Yet all she wanted to do was cry at the thought of leaving. "I guess this is your nest now, Kato."

Cruz pulled her into his arms and tilted her chin up to face him. *Hey, now. It's not like we'll never be back. Kato's going to have a family we'll need to visit. And I doubt he's been keeping the furniture dusted for his mate.*

Kato wriggled his tail in agreement, then disappeared into his burrow at the edge of the alcove, as if relinquishing any claim.

Ebby pressed one palm against Cruz's cheek and stretched forward to kiss him. *You always know just what to say.*

Cruz stroked the soft swell of her belly before pulling her tightly against him, sprinkling kisses against her brow and down her cheek.

Sighing in contentment, she scanned the sunlight illuminating the kelp ceiling, the way the fronds moved as if caressing one another. Once upon a time, she'd thought she'd roam the seas forever alone. She'd thought she couldn't be trusted to love and be loved, that her nature wouldn't allow her to have a mate and a family.

Cruz had helped her discover that the woman inside her was stronger than she'd ever imagined possible. Human, female, mermaid—no matter her physical form, she could choose who she wanted to be, how she wanted to be. He'd given her the impossible, and she couldn't imagine a future without Cruz at her side.

His kisses reached her mouth, and she closed her eyes, enjoying the way he teased her lips until electricity raced through her veins. How could his kisses always make her crave more? Cupping her backside, he drew her hips against his. His erection made it very clear he, too, was thinking about more than a kiss.

Pulling slightly away, she met Cruz's eyes, eyes filled with love and trust and desire. She glanced toward the bed before looking through her lashes at him once more. *Want to play house?*

A wicked grin spread over his face. *You naughty little mermaid. All you think about is play.*

With a returning grin and a flick of her tail, she pulled him down onto the inviting sponges. Her playmate. Her lover. Her everything.

Thank you for reading. I hope you liked my take on mermaid mythology. More yummy mythological heroes await you in the Mates for Monsters series with THE CENTAUR'S BRIDE, *where sexy shifter secrets await. Riding a cowboy never sounded so good! Keep reading for an excerpt or use the link below to jump right in and read it now.*

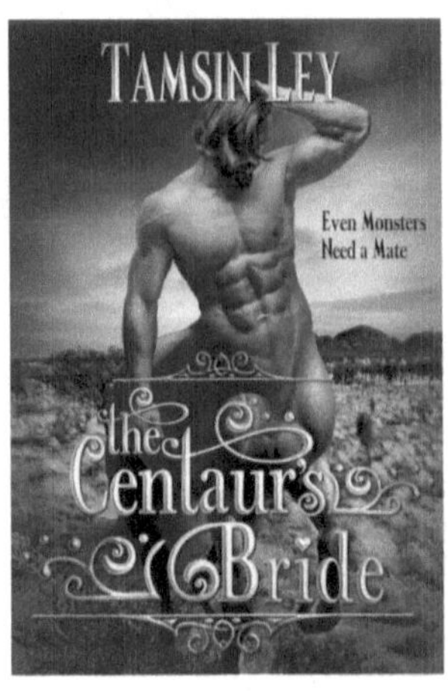

< START READING
THE CENTAUR'S BRIDE NOW >

EXCERPT FROM THE CENTAUR'S BRIDE

Sunlight danced through motes of dust as Renee pulled to a stop in front of the wide covered porch. Almost expecting Grandfather to emerge from the house to greet them, she cut the engine.

Her friend, Steph, flung open her door and glanced at Renee with her nose wrinkled. "Whew, what's that smell?"

"Horses," Renee replied, recalling a younger self who'd also wrinkled her nose. Today the smell stirred something in her, as if a trembling bud was about to bloom in her chest. She squashed it down, reminding herself she was only here to hand everything over to the real estate agent. Hopping out, she gazed at the fancy log-frame house with its high windows and country décor. An old rusty wagon wheel hung from the wood shake siding, and the front door fixtures were made of black wrought iron, right down to the old-fashioned knocker shaped like a horse shoe. Two square planter boxes on either edge of the porch steps held nothing but wisps of dry brown grass.

Behind her, the metallic rattle of the barn's bay door opening made her turn. A very tall blonde woman emerged, pointed toes of her cowboy boots impossibly shiny for a ranch worker. The woman raised her chin, as if smelling them as she approached. "Which one of you is Renee?"

Renee stuck out a hand to the giant of a woman, at least giant compared to Renee's five-foot-one frame. "I am."

The woman gripped Renee's knuckles with uncomfortable firmness. "Name's Lori. I've been running the place since your grandfather's death. Sorry for your loss, by the way."

Steph pushed forward, her hand out. "Good to meet you, Lori."

Lori took her hand, eyebrows high. "And you are?"

A look of irritation passed over Steph's features. "Oh, sorry. I'm just so used to being recognized. Steph Bilmore." She cocked her head coyly. "You might have seen one of my music videos?"

"Ah. That would explain the fellow at the gate taking pictures. Hope he knows people in Montana carry guns." The woman turned back to Renee. "How long you planning on staying?"

"Uh," Renee automatically glanced at Steph for validation. "A few days, probably? I've got a realtor coming out tomorrow."

"We're on a treasure hunt," Steph added. "Plus I want to ride a cowboy. I mean a horse." She held up her camera for a selfie next to the wagon wheel on the siding.

Lori's nose flared. "A realtor? I see. Well. The housekeeper's inside. He'll show you your rooms. I'll be in the barn." She spun and strode off without looking back.

Steph sniffed as if unimpressed. "Amazon woman there acts

like she owns the place. I suppose we have to get our own luggage, huh?"

"You were a little bold with that cowboy thing," Renee said, feeling strengthened by the Montana air. "We don't even know her."

"This is your property. You can do what you want. She needs to get over herself."

Self-assurance dwindling, Renee nodded and wandered to the fence near the barn, allowing Steph time to sort through her usual mountain of luggage. Leaning against the rough wood rail, Renee surveyed the pasture. Beyond the green, irrigated section within the fence, the rolling hills were calico-spotted with patches of yellow broom and silver-green sagebrush. A shirtless man in a cowboy hat knelt next to one of the sprinkler boxes inside the fence. She admired his broad, tanned back as he picked up and discarded tools and parts. A baby horse with zebra-striped legs pranced around him while its mother grazed placidly nearby.

The man reached a hand behind him while he continued working, wiggling his fingers until the baby nosed them and darted away in delight. The pit of Renee's stomach danced with butterflies watching his obvious affection. The man's throaty laughter floated across the field as he rose and dusted his hands against the front of his jeans. He crouched and did a playful football shuffle, taunting the tiny horse who kicked up its heels and ran back to its mother.

Momma horse flicked her black tail and continued grazing without concern.

Gathering up his toolbox, the man glanced in Renee's direction, sending the butterflies in her stomach into overdrive.

He adjusted his hat off his forehead, letting the sun hit a fine, straight jaw with a haze of stubble. She fluttered her fingers at him, a little thrill chasing down her spine when he lifted a well-muscled arm in a reciprocal greeting. *God, he's hot.* Looking over her shoulder, she realized Steph hadn't yet spotted him. Renee never got the jump on her, often due to her own hesitancy. Well, not today. This was her ranch, and she was going to own it for as long as she could. Heart beating in her throat at her own boldness, she called, "Dibs."

"What?" Steph abandoned the luggage and crunched across the gravel to stand beside her. "Aw, not fair! There'd better be more delicious cowboys around."

Renee grinned. Wow, that felt good. Most of the time, Steph picked the targets and left Renee to play wingman, which meant spending the night fending off the target's wingman. Not this time.

Setting her chin atop her forearms, Renee leaned into the fence, watching the rancher stroll toward the barn. His jeans hugged his lean hips and muscular thighs in exactly the right places, and his muscled abdomen flexed with his gait. He didn't look at her directly, but she could feel his attention igniting her core.

Face heating, she looked away.

Steph turned back to the car. "If you don't seal the deal before tomorrow, all dibs are off."

Her previous thrill of confidence crumbled. "Hey! I called dibs!"

"Dibs are first shot, not exclusive. So don't screw it up. Just screw." Steph smirked and rattled her wheeled suitcase across the gravel into the house.

Yanking her own suitcase from the jumbled pile of Steph's castoffs, Renee scurried after her.

CLICK HERE TO BUY THE CENTAUR'S BRIDE NOW

ACKNOWLEDGMENTS

To all my readers out there who email me, message me on Facebook, like and share my posts, and leave reviews on my books, I couldn't keep writing without you. You mean the world to me. Thank you!

ABOUT THE AUTHOR

Once upon a time I thought I wanted to be a biomedical engineer, but experimenting on lab rats doesn't always lead to happy endings. Now I blend my nerdy infatuation of science with character-driven romance and guaranteed happily-ever-afters. My monsters always find their mates, with feisty heroines, tortured heroes, and all the steamy trouble they can handle. I promise my stories will never leave you hanging (although you may still crave more!)

When I'm not writing, I'll be in the garden or the kitchen, exploring Alaska with my husband, or preparing for the zombie apocalypse. I also love wine and hard apple cider, am mediocre at crochet, and have the cutest 12-pound bunny named Abigail.

Interested in more about me? Join my VIP Club and get free books, notices, and other cool stuff!

www.mates4monsters.com

facebook.com/TamsinLey

bookbub.com/authors/tamsin-ley

amazon.com/author/tamsin

Galactic Pirate Brides series

Rescued by Qaiyaan

Ransomed by Kashatok

Claimed by Noatak

Mates for Monsters

The Merman's Kiss

The Merman's Quest

A Mermaid's Heart

The Centaur's Bride

The Djinn's Desire

Khargals of Duras

Sticks and Stones

Bite Club

First Instinct